THE
CHRIST
OF THE
BUTTERFLIES

THE
CHRIST
OF THE
BUTTERFLIES

a novel by

ARDYTHE ASHLEY

AVAILABLE
PRESS

BALLANTINE BOOKS
New York

An Available Press Book
Published by Ballantine Books

Library of Congress Catalog Card Number: 90-93514
ISBN: 0-345-37045-7

Cover design by Don Munson
Cover photograph © 1975 The Image Bank
Text design by Beth Tondreau Design/Mary A. Wirth

Manufactured in the United States of America
First Edition: July 1991
10 9 8 7 6 5 4 3 2 1

TO THE MEMORY AND

IMAGINATION

OF

MAURICE

THE
NAME
OF THE
FATHER

by Bess Arden

IN REMEMBRANCE OF

AIDAN

It is a wise father
that knows his own child.
—

WILLIAM SHAKESPEARE
The Merchant of Venice

ONE

The Arrival

Mara followed the sound of the doorbell up out of Gwendolyn's world, across her darkened living room and out into the foyer where she pushed open the heavy front door, expecting only a brief distraction. In the hot, white glare of the early morning sun, Aidan stood before her. Aidan had been dead for seven years.

"Aidan," she whispered. He looked so young, so strong, so sure. "Aidan."

"His son," said the apparition. "You wrote a novel about

my father, and I've come to revenge him." Then he extended his hand.

Stunned, compulsively polite, Mara took the outstretched hand into her own, unprepared for the shock of the touch. Same skin. She pulled her hand away, feeling faint.

"May I come in?" he asked, stepping with authority into the darkened room. "Oh! You look quite pale. I've frightened you. I'm so sorry." She heard genuine apology in his voice. His familiar voice. "It was a terrible thing for me to say . . . about the revenge, I mean . . . I meant it as a joke to cover my nervousness. Stupid of me."

"Yes."

"Are you all right?"

"Yes." She sat down abruptly on the small table next to the door. Sat, looking up at him as he swiftly took possession of the room with his eyes. He was tall, a little taller than his father. He stood with his feet slightly apart. Tense. Alert. The resemblance to Aidan was more striking in the dimness than in the light. He turned and looked at her.

She was suddenly self-conscious, aware of her nearnakedness. She was wearing a thick, white bathrobe and nothing else. Her hair was still damp from her morning shower. She had not put on any makeup. His eyes were approving. They made another circuit of the room, taking in the heavy, overly carved furniture, the tiled floor, the half-closed wooden shutters.

"The apartment is exactly as you described it."

"Yes."

He looked at her again, concern informing his expression. "Can I get you something? Water? Sit here." And he took her arm gently, bringing her into the room as if she were the guest. She sat again, where he indicated, sinking into the worn, velvet couch.

"I would like some coffee," she replied. "It's just made, on the stove."

He turned without hesitation in the direction of the kitchen. In a moment she heard him moving about . . . a rattling of dishes. An old sound. Comforting. From childhood? No. She concentrated on her breathing. He returned with two cups of coffee, black and sweet and strong.

"I should have liked to bring cappuccino," he said, "but there was no milk."

He sat down on the tapestried footstool. Near her knee. Now it was he who looked up to her—and she could see the shyness in him.

"Why are you . . . why were you nervous?" she asked.

"I was afraid you wouldn't see me."

"How did you know where to find me?"

"I tried all the usual routes: your publisher, your agent, phone books. Your pen name hid you well. There was no way I could trace you through a family name. Then, when every attempt had failed and I had given up, the idea, the answer, arrived, came to me, as in a dream, although I was wide awake at the time. I suddenly knew you could only be here."

"And how did you know where *here* was?"

"I followed your descriptions in the novel. The gargoyle on the corner house all but winked at me. The letter box—"

"So you are here."

"Yes."

"Why did you come?"

"To know you. And through you, to know him."

"Impossible."

"Which?"

"Both."

He put his cup down on the Turkish carpet. She put hers on the Chinese table with the carved sea monsters curling up the legs.

"What may I call you?" he asked.

"You may call me by my pen name, Bess, if it feels natural to you," she said. "Or you may call me by my given name, which is Marina. Or you may call me Mara." As your father did, she thought.

"So many names . . . I will call you Mara. It's a beautiful name, and it's the most like Mira, your name in the novel."

"The novel is fiction. I am not in the novel."

"Aren't you? Then how did I find you?"

She chose not to reply. Instead she rose and went to the window. With a strong, practiced gesture she pushed open the shutters, enjoying the familiar shock of the sun as it bounced off the canal and shot across the room, bringing the movement of shimmering light into every corner.

She turned to face him where he sat, squinting in the sudden glare.

"What is your name?"

It was his turn to be shocked. Now we're even, she thought.

"You don't know it?"

"He never said it."

"I can't believe that."

"Why not?"

"I have a name in the novel."

"You are not in the novel. The novel is a fabrication."

"But why did he never mention me? Was I so unimportant?"

8

"On the contrary. He would not speak your name to me. You were sacred." She was watching him closely as he absorbed the import of her words. "And I was profane."

He looked stricken. "What a terrible thing for him to think! How wrong of him to say it."

"Don't. You cannot speak for him."

"You did."

"Did I?"

"Didn't you?"

"I didn't." What she didn't know was why they were sparring.

"But you used his real name. You called him Aidan."

"I liked his name. He was dead. What did it matter?"

"It mattered to me!"

There was a painful silence. Both were aware of the sudden, hot intimacy that had arisen between them in the few short minutes since their meeting. Both were bewildered.

He changed his tone. "Look . . . Mira . . . Mara . . . someone sent your novel to me five years ago when I was still reeling with the loss of him. It made a tremendous impression on me, as I'm sure you can understand. I don't know who sent it. I always thought, given the content, that it must have been you. Maybe I was wrong."

She looked as if she might interrupt him, but he raised a gentle hand. He had come a long way to say this. "I have always believed that the story was real—thinly disguised, as they say, but true. After all, he did leave us—mother and me—and he did come here, and he did die here. According to the belated and woefully incomplete reports that we received from the Italian authorities, he died in the garden of this apartment." A solemn expression crossed his face

9

like a shadow. "Anyhow, when I read your book I felt that I had been given a gift—shocking, perhaps, but a gift of a glimmer of a glimpse of his last months—however distorted."

"You are mistaken—"

"I felt as if I began to understand him a little . . . why he left . . . why he never came back . . . the story *must* be real."

"It's fiction."

"It *feels* real . . ."

"It's good fiction."

"And you're *here*. In the very apartment."

"And he is not!"

As if slapped by her words, he bent his head and hunched his shoulders. He looked small and defeated, there on the footstool. Bruised.

From where she stood, Mara watched the reflected light as it played on the nape of his neck. She felt a horrible surge of pleasurable feeling deep inside herself. She looked away abruptly, out of the window, across the canal now brimming with the early tide. She needed to look anywhere but at the neat line of black, curly hair that cut across the dark, smooth skin of his curving neck. She wanted to kiss him exactly there. She knew how his skin would feel, warm against her lips, how he would taste of soap and salty sweat, how he would respond to her touch and, smiling, take her into his arms, there, on the velvet couch.

"Please," he implored her, "please, help me to know him. I loved him. He left so suddenly and so completely." And she felt the grief come straight up through her body like the winds of San Michele—fast and cold and full of force.

"No . . . no, Aidan, no." And a black fissure of sorrow

opened beneath her, where there had been floor a moment before.

"My name is James," he said, as his arms went around her, catching her as she began to fall, supporting her, lifting her, carrying her to the couch.

He held her closely while she cried, her body shaken by seven years of grief that had suddenly welled up within, surfacing in spasms of lung-deep sobs that threatened to tear apart her chest and throat. Time dissolved.

She didn't know how long she wept, how long they were locked together in sadness—his, as well as hers, she knew—for his face, too, was tearstained when at last he relaxed his protective embrace. They were quiet together for a while.

As he drew slightly away, a grimace of pain crossed his face, and she realized he had been kneeling next to the couch throughout the ordeal. Feeling embarrassed, and grateful, she reached over and touched his face. The face of James, not Aidan.

"Perhaps you were right to be nervous," she said.

A stripy-gray, one-eyed tomcat catapulted from a ceiling beam and thudded onto her chest.

"Wally!" exclaimed James. "Wally?"

"Yes."

"I thought he was a literary device."

"No. He's a cat." She smiled.

"His aim is excellent."

"Also, his appetite." Mara struggled to rise from the depths of the sofa, holding the cat close and warm against her breasts. "You should leave me now," she said to the boy who had held her like a man.

"Will you be all right?"

"I'll be fine. I need to rest and to write. That's all."

"The work."

"Yes. The work." The cat began to squirm and purr in anticipation of its breakfast.

James stood shaking his head slowly from side to side. "It's hard to take it all in," he said, "meeting you and fighting with you . . . why were we fighting? And then the sadness . . ."

"Will *you* be all right?"

"I'll be . . . fine . . . too." She could tell *fine* was a word he seldom used. "If you tell me that you will see me again?"

She heard the anxiety in his voice. She had not been important to anyone for a long time. It was disquieting.

"I will see you again. Tomorrow. At two? After I've written and had my lunch."

"Here?"

"Not here."

"Where, then? The Piazza San Marco? Florian's?"

It was a startling idea. She had not been to San Marco in months, to Florian's in years. But Florian's . . .

"All right. It will be quiet at two. They all sleep."

"Who?"

"The Venetians."

"Will the waiters be awake?"

"Barely—and the sun will be full on us. You don't mind the sun?"

"I'm on my vacation. It will be wonderful to sit in the sun." She wondered if she should ask him about himself—what work he did, how long he planned to be in Venice—but she was too exhausted from the sudden excavation of her emotions to dig in unknown places. There would be time enough tomorrow to unearth what was worthwhile in this man.

She walked him to the door. He turned once more to look at her, then reached out tentatively to stroke the cat.

"It's all right. He's quite tame." James smiled a little as he gently made friends with the animal.

"Until tomorrow."

"Tomorrow." And he was gone. Back into the glare.

Mara stood staring at the closed front door as she often stared at the closed front cover of a book. What new world was there to be discovered?

She held the cat away from her body for a moment, at arm's length, and looked into his one, hungry eye. He made a slight twist of objection and she put him down.

"I can tell I'm in a very precarious state right now, Wally," she said, as he, unconcerned, jauntily led her off into the kitchen. "Everything has been shaken loose in the shock of . . . him . . . and in the earthquake of grief he let loose. Have you ever seen me cry, Wally? Maybe not. I don't think you would understand it anyway. Crying is a human experience. Not for tomcats. Not for me, either, for years. I think I was drying up inside. No wonder the work hasn't been good lately. Dry. Until this boy—this man, James . . . his son—arrives . . . James—a saint's name . . . I got *that* right. He's about the age I had put him . . . young . . . twenty-five or -six . . ."

She put down the dish for the cat, and he immediately lost what little interest he had been taking in their conversation. She stood looking at him for a while, letting her emotions catch up with her. When they did, she went down: her knees on the cold tiles next to the cat. She was doubled up, as if in physical pain—but it was not physical. She felt a deep, sick revulsion that had not overtaken her in years, and she had almost forgotten its existence—but, of course, it was what lay behind her solitude: this horrible reaction to other people, to the communion of souls, hers and another's. What had she done? *You let him touch you . . .* only to hold me . . . *you're disgusting . . .*

She let the wrenching self-loathing take her, run its course through her psyche, and, already on her knees, leave her body beaten, as if from the inside out. Then she very slowly stood up again, steadying herself on the kitchen table, breathing evenly as Aidan had taught her. Aidan had known about pain. There, she thought, it's passed. I will be all right now. I will be allowed to live in this world for yet a while.

She wrapped the robe more tightly around herself and stepped out into the small back garden to rest. It was still cool here, still fresh where the garden walls made morning shadows. She sat in the bright corner, legs apart, letting the sun warm the inside of her thighs.

"Aidan," she said. She waited a long time—until she felt the deepness of the shadows, the richness of the light. "Aidan, we have to talk." A slight breeze disturbed the flowers. "Aidan, I never thought I could feel . . . well . . . *those* feelings for any other man. I thought they belonged to you and to you alone. I've never even looked for anyone else. You know I've been lonely. Did you send him to me? Your son? With your look and your manner all about him? I don't know what you want me to do." But the breeze had died. There was no answer in the air.

What an unexpected woman, thought James, as the heavy front door swung shut behind him. He, too, felt stunned.

He looked up and down the empty *fondamenta,* seeking direction. He found himself smoldering in the full sun of a mid-August morning with no idea where to go. He wandered back the way he had come, thinking he could get a map and some hotel information at the train station. He had, on arrival, come directly to her.

She was so different from what he had imagined. In the book she had made herself Botticelli beautiful, but she was not. There was no translucent skin or red-gold hair. She was tall and dark like himself. Her hair was cut just above her shoulders, feminine, but not flowing. He felt familiar with her body, having held it so close to himself while she cried. She was not thin. Not overweight, but full and soft. Titian. She had intelligent eyes, set into an even-featured face. Enigmatic. Self-possessed. He had the impression of an inner strength in spite of her faintness at the sight of him, and the bout of uncontrolled weeping. Allowance had to be made for the shock, of course. He had surprised himself when, after carefully trimming his newly grown beard, he had stepped back from the mirror to gather the effect. It was uncanny the way he had come to resemble his father. He had always copied his father's walk and stance, first as a small boy consciously imitating his dad, then, as he grew into his own ways, unconsciously, and then again consciously, after his last analysis had brought these habits to his attention. For this adventure he had chosen to dress as his father had—excellent fabrics wrought by Aidan's tailor. The effect was daunting. Had he accomplished this transformation because he wanted to shock her? Perhaps.

And she looked much younger than he had anticipated. In the novel she was thirty-two. If he were to add the seven intervening years—but even now she seemed no older than thirty, or at the most thirty-five. Was that possible? Was she so much younger than his mother? It was disquieting.

A small, yellowish flower on a rubbery stalk caught his attention where it pushed up between the paving stones of the *fondamenta*. He smiled in recognition and bent to pick it, then stopped, deciding to let it live . . . the grandson of the grandson of the flower that grew here in his father's time. His father's time. His father's place. His father's woman.

Suddenly exhausted, he decided to hurry back to the station and collect his bags and find a place of his own. He had never been in Venice before. It was a place that had haunted his imagination since adolescence. To him it had been a magical place, a fictional place . . . created by this woman . . . Bess . . . Mira . . . Marina . . . Mara . . . her.

How had he known what to do? It seemed to James that when he had first stepped across her threshold, a foreign power had taken possession of him. Words had been given to him. He felt that he had uttered profound truths. He felt he had done great deeds. He had caught her up and held her in her sorrow with a maturity beyond his experience. He could still feel the wetness of her tears on his rumpled shirtfront. Or were they his own tears, or his own sweat? In reality it had all been mundane, he knew. In the unfamiliar kitchen he had simply poured the coffee and added the crumbly brown sugar. He had said what had to be said, done what had to be done—but it had felt heroic.

And he had felt, just for a moment, a flash of desire such as his father might have felt. Not when he held her, as might be expected—her body warm beneath the robe of soft, white toweling—but when she had opened the shutters and stood with the sun behind her. Then. He had wanted her then. In the darkness . . . with the light . . .

The world surrounding him now, though busy and bright in appearance, felt paltry . . . unsubstantial. The beads worn by a passing woman were red, but not red enough. The sky was unclouded blue, but not blue enough. Richness seemed confined in the apartment with Mara. Would she bring it with her tomorrow to San Marco? Would she come at all? Or, perhaps, once she recovered from the confusion of his unexpected arrival, might she not change her mind? Retreat? Refuse to see him? Leave Venice? No. She would not leave Venice. He had hunted her down and trapped her, here, in her burrow. Did she know she had been captured? He would see her again. He *must* see her again.

He looked around now, actually seeing the city for the first time. The buildings were standing in the water. How absurd, he thought.

But the most absurd thing of all was that she was real.

TWO

Piazza San Marco

James awoke abruptly. He had heard a thud close by, but in the darkness of the night he could not see who or what had made the sound. Frightened, he strained to make out familiar shapes in the unfamiliar room. Thin shards of light slipped through the cracks in the wooden shutters, and he realized that it might no longer be the night at all. He relaxed a little, then heard another unidentifiable thump. He tensed again and began to climb slowly out of the bed. Just before his feet touched the floor he saw the stranger standing at the foot of his bed. His heart dropped.

"Who are you? What do you want?" he challenged in a frightened voice.

The intruder did not respond or move. It was, after a terrorized moment, the figure's inhuman stillness that caused James to realize he was staring at a lifeless, life-sized male portrait on a museum poster. He had much admired the poster on the previous evening when he had first entered this otherwise unadorned hotel room. It represented a detail, much enlarged, from *La Sacra Conversazione* by Piero della Francesca. Perhaps it had been pinned up by a previous guest. Feeling a little foolish, he breathed a sigh of relief. He heard another thump and a muffled voice, but he thought now that the sound was somewhere outside and below the window.

Where was he? In Venice. In Venice to find Mira . . . Mara. And he had. And he would see her again today at two. James leapt out of bed at the thought. He had no idea how long he had slept or what time it might be now. What if he had missed the appointment? On his dash to the window he slammed his hip into the corner of the massive dresser, causing himself a considerable amount of pain. He then managed to pinch his finger on the unfamiliar hardware of the shutters. James was always at war with the material world—dropping wineglasses, burning himself on teapots, tripping over steps. His chronic awkwardness was an eccentricity he had accepted about himself long ago, deciding he was not really meant to be in this world at all—that he had been dropped down, unsuspecting and unprepared, onto the wrong planet. He was supposed to be in a world that was more ethereal, where spirit and mind prevailed, not lumpy, unimaginative, ungiving, hard-edged matter. He particularly suffered when traveling—when objects about him were unknown, and pathways untried. Yet he marveled at the adventures available to him in this bruising world, and was determined to make the most of his stay, however long, however hurtful, in the haunts of mankind.

The clumsy shutters, once successfully maneuvered, admitted a day as sun-sodden as the one before it. He leaned out and, rather tentatively, looked down. In so doing he discovered the source of the thumping noises. A colorfully cursing boatman was working his vegetable barge around a tight corner of the narrow canal directly outside the window. James reached for his watch and was relieved to see that it was still early morning. He took another breath and went back to bed. There he closed his eyes, composed himself, and decided to begin the day again.

First, he listened to the sound of the boat. Yes. It did sound as though it was inside the hotel room. He listened to the other sounds of the morning—a child's shout, a bird's call—then he slowly opened his eyes to the morning, admiring the poster at the end of the bed. The young man in the picture was beautiful. Was he an angel? There was a curve of wing over his left shoulder. With close-set, intelligent eyes he looked boldly back at James. He seemed to be saying, "Welcome to Venice."

His own eyes took in the rest of the room. It was a comfortable, if somewhat cramped space: wooden furniture, uncarved; straight-beamed ceilings; a terrazzo floor rolling and buckling across the room. He noticed the extra blocks of wood placed under the legs of the furniture to level out their surfaces, and the angled planing of the doors to adapt them to the out-of-kilter doorjambs. This was an amusing city. He knew that it was slowly sinking into the lagoon, but it hadn't occurred to him that it would be sinking unevenly, twisting rooms into funhouse shapes and turning floors into roller-coaster surfaces. He would have to be especially careful. He took the time to note the placement of the dresser, chairs, and table, hoping thereby to minimize the possibility of future collisions.

He lay reviewing the recent events of his life.

Who are you? What do you want? Those had been the questions his father had asked of himself upon his arrival in Venice seven years before—according to Mara. Now James had inherited the questions, and his arrival marked the culmination of a long journey in his father's footsteps. First, the unfruitful trip to Beirut; then Texas with its mixed messages; then New York, to the office, where his father's name was still carried on the letterhead, but not in the minds of the current staff—except Helga, who had run the place in his father's time, but wouldn't talk to James about anything personal. After New York, the flight to Milan, the train to Venice, and the walk to Mara's apartment. Her doorway marked the end of one phase of his quest and the beginning of another, one that would take him chapter by chapter through Venice: first the apartment, then San Marco, Santa Margherita, the Rialto, a walk along the Zattere, Torcello, San Michele, San Rocco, the old museum in the Fondaco dei Turchi, and, finally—if they both survived—back to the apartment and garden. He was sure by the end of the itinerary he would know his father, Mara, and, with luck, himself in new and unimaginable ways. Somewhere under her confusion and annoyance he hoped that she would be flattered to have her novel treated as a holy pilgrimage.

So far he had been fortunate. Before arriving he had

entertained a number of fantasies about what his first encounter with his father's last and, by all accounts, loveliest,
mistress would be like. He had imagined her outraged at
the invasion of her privacy, slamming the door in his face.
He had pictured her properly married to a brawny gondolier. One who would beat him up on sight, while their pack
of surly half-Venetian children looked on in delight. He
had feared that she might be dead. Or crazy. Well, she
wasn't raging, married, crazy, or dead. What was she? Who
was she? He wondered. He had wondered about her for
years. He had loved her from a great distance. He had been
drawn to her across the waters. James had hopes for Mara
and himself that depended on an initial acceptance, one of
the other. Having had the good luck to step into her good
graces, he wanted to remain there.

He got up then, stretched, and went to the window. The
boat was gone. He could hear the water lapping against the
side of the building. It was time to shower and dress and
explore the city for a while before meeting Mara.

When he was ready to go, he looked briefly at the map
which the clerk at the tourist office had given him. James
had an uncanny sense of direction. Once having visited a
city, however briefly, he could return to it years later and
still make his way around it, occasionally bumping into it,
perhaps, but never getting lost. Friends who knew of this
strange talent had predicted that Venice would defeat him,
but one glance at the map reassured him. The two major
sections of the small city fit together like lovers, the Grand
Canal marking the curve of their cuddled bodies. The third,
La Giudecca, lay unhappily off to the side, and James knew
it was unlikely he would stray so far on the short, intense
mission he had planned for himself.

He quickly memorized the major points along the Grand Canal and the position of the Piazza San Marco to all the rest. Piece of cake. He left the map on the dresser and went out to add dimension to this newfound terrain.

Mara awoke determined to put an end to the startling, new, unsought relationship with the man, James. Yesterday had turned into an unproductive day after the emotionally depleting morning. And it had been followed by a restless night.

She wished she hadn't set an appointment to meet him. She wasn't ready. She hadn't had time to sift through her reactions, the assortment of thoughts and feelings that his sudden appearance had aroused and revived. She shuddered at the remembrance of the self-hating episode on the kitchen floor. Her knees still ached. Perhaps she should let James do the hating. He must hate me, she thought, though he doesn't show it.

Still, agreeing to meet him was the civilized choice. He was, after all, Aidan's son. And he had come a long way to find her. Mara admitted to a mild degree of curiosity. Curiosity befit a writer, she assured herself. But there was more to it than that—dangerously more, she knew. She had felt desire. Or *desire*, as the more romantic novelists would put it. It had marred the self-image that she had held up for herself and followed for so many years. The image of a woman destined to love only one man in a lifetime—waiting for him to arrive, caring for him when he did, mourning him when he died, remembering him in the art of the day and the dreams of the night until she rejoined him in death.

23

There was no place for another, for James, in her life.

Wrenched as she was, she would go to the meeting with James and, once there, she would bring matters to a close. First she would answer a few appropriate questions about his father. She had been uncommonly abrupt with him in that regard. She was chilled by the ice of her own defensiveness, but he had arrived so shockingly, and with such grandiose expectations, that abruptness on her part was, in the light of a new day, forgivable, she felt. Maybe.

Before all else, she must write. She must make something valuable of her morning. Yesterday her mind had wandered far from her current story, and she had, instead, retrod on weary thought-feet the memories of the time with Aidan . . . returned again to the novel that had been produced in its wake. *The Name of the Son,* it was called. A good title, she thought, though the novel itself she judged with less charity. She considered it unsuccessful in spite of the good reviews and respectable sales. Publishing the novel had been an attempt to heal the wounds of that brief, intense love affair. She had gathered up her memories, spun them out into threads of meaning and woven them into a novel bandage. The healing, too, had been incomplete. Every time she thought about him, she hurt.

After the final edit, she had never read the book again.

And now, the son. With a name. James. What did it mean? she wondered, and she climbed out of bed to go and look it up. *James: the supplanter.* How like Aidan to have so named his child.

And then, quite suddenly, with the book of names still held open in her hands, she felt a small, internal quake. She was unblocked. She had been at a virtual standstill in her current work for weeks—to be honest with herself, for months—and now, as if a curtain had been torn asunder, she could see the characters come to life again in the stage set of her mind. She knew what they feared and how they would fare. Perhaps this James-son-of-Aidan would have some small acceptable place in her life after all.

Oh, but what would she do with another dying man?

James had never felt better in his life. Venice, he was discovering, was entrancing—everywhere a delight to the eye, a prod to the imagination. He had meandered the morning away amid the ancient architecture, thinking of Tintoretto and Othello and Shylock and Casanova and his father. He had, in his mind's eye, restored the city as he walked, bolstering sagging foundations and repairing crumbling balconies; he had applied plasters and caulked cracks in the peeling facades of ancient palazzos; and he had replaced tiny bits of glass to glittering mosaics. Deciding to rest from his labors, he stopped for lunch in a canalside restaurant, arcaded with ripening grape vines, where, in the mottled sunlight, he had watched people walk by and float by and chug by throughout the meal. This was a place worth coming back to, for an extended stay—perhaps on his honeymoon. If Mara was the woman he thought she might be, if she could accomplish what he hoped she might accomplish, a honeymoon might someday even be possible.

As he made his crooked way through Cannaregio, he was surprised by the crowds. The place was full-bodied, rich in activity. People pushed through the alleyways and crammed the campos. The idyll that Mara had written had given him the impression that she and his father wandered here virtually alone, with an occasional assist from a picturesque gondolier. By her account there had been tourists in the Piazza San Marco and at the Rialto Bridge, but even in those places the people were only a backdrop, and they seldom amassed anywhere else. For the lovers in *The Name of the Son,* Venice had been a secluded haunt. The unexpected glimpse into the private parts of his father's world had, in the discomfort of late adolescence, made him sick. Now, with a collection of romantic, if failed, adventures behind him, James found himself more forgiving.

James stepped in and out of the countless old churches along his way. The ones situated near the canals offered him a vision of living stained glass as the sunlight reflected from the gently rippling water through the beautiful windows colored with biblical tales. Saints are people the light shines through, he had once heard a minister say, aware of his own opacity.

His plan was to get to Florian's a few minutes before the scheduled meeting so that he could watch Mara as she approached across the piazza. He wanted to know if she walked now as she had written she walked then. From his cursory glance at the map he had determined which was the most predictable direction for her entry. At one-thirty he emerged from the dark, narrow lanes of the Mercerie, out from under the great arch of the clock tower, into the sun-washed piazza, where he was caught off guard by magnificence.

Mara's description of the square had been a good one. She had caught the grandeur: marble, mosaic, towers, and domes. But architecture had outdone literature—for this place, this gesture of man to walk across the waters in stone, was astounding.

He dropped appreciatively into a chair at the café and gawked.

At a quarter to two by the clock in the tower, Mara entered the piazza from the far colonnade. She had decided to come early, so that she could watch James as he approached the café. She wondered if he would today remind her, in such a poignant way, of his father. She remembered the first time she had seen Aidan. She had been sitting, sketching, at one of Florian's tilting tables. He had caught her attention, out of the corner of her eye, because of the unusualness of his appearance: American clothes and American walk, but a foreign countenance . . . not Jewish . . . Was he Turkish? Armenian? As it turned out, he was an advanced state of Arab—brilliant, gentle, but with a rough, sandy surface to him. After circling Florian's indecisively for several minutes, he had finally positioned himself at a nearby table and ordered a Coke (for which, she had decided, he could be forgiven because of the oppressive heat). She had drawn him unawares while he took in the facade of the Basilica. While he had gazed at the great church, his face responsive to the splendor, his expression awed, curious, intense, Mara had gazed at him. And she had fallen in love with him. And fallen. And fallen. Until he, himself, had been felled. He had not been right for her, not with his sophistication, his experience. He had not been especially good to her, though they had had their good times, especially in bed. She sighed. You can't choose who you love. She still had that

27

first sketch of him somewhere. She should have dug it out and given it to James. It was an artifact that she would not mind turning over to him. She was prepared to offer him so little else.

But James was already in place, looking very much like the sketch himself: lost. She decided there was nothing to be lost by beginning with a pleasantry.

"*Buon giorno,* James."

She had startled him. Inwardly, she flinched. She could almost never do anything gracefully with men. Would their meeting, however brief, be another battle of nerves? She hoped not. The experience of yesterday's encounter had convinced her that her nerves were not sturdy enough for skirmishing.

"I'm so glad you came." His expression shuttled like an airport callboard from awe (at the architecture) to surprise (at her sudden salutation) to genuine pleasure (as he recognized her). She knew her own features were not so easily read, partly because she didn't show her feelings, partly because she often didn't know what her feelings were—not until she had gotten off alone with herself for a while to run the tongue of her mind around the teeth of the experience. This delay in the knowledge and expression of her feelings had been a problem for all of her adult life. Normal human relationships seemed to require an alacrity of spirit that she simply didn't possess.

"How would you like to begin?" she asked. Her thoughts, unlike her feelings, were usually sudden and direct.

"Maybe with you sitting down next to me?" he suggested.

"Of course." She sat, awkwardly, with an uncertainty

unlike her solitary self. I *hate* this, she thought.

"I'll order us some cappuccino. Will that be all right? It seems right. A remembrance."

She nodded. At a loss for words. Where was this boy's angry edge? Was he all syrup and sentimentality?

"Look," he said, "perhaps I should be the one to lead this conversation."

Again, she nodded. Why not? she thought; let's see where he takes us.

"I didn't know my father very well . . . I guess he told you that we were not very close. He and my mother lived apart throughout most of my childhood. But I loved him. In the novel, you wrote that he thought I despised him. Did he really imagine such a terrible thing? Did he die trying to write his way into my affection when he already had it?"

"I don't know, James. As I told you yesterday, he didn't discuss you."

"Then why did you write that he wrote . . . that he wrote for me?"

"I had to write something."

"Why did you send me the novel?"

"I didn't."

"You didn't?"

"No. It's an enormous assumption, isn't it? Given the circumstances. And I have no idea who might have done such a deed."

The coffee arrived.

So did a long silence.

So much for his ability to lead, she thought.

"James, we will do a lot better, get a lot further, if you understand something about the book. I made it up. You, more than anyone, must know that it's fictional. Stop and think. Did your father work in the theatre? Did he live in a creepy hotel? Was he organized?" She waited.

"No. No one could ever leave his affairs in more of a tangle at the time of his death than my father did."

"Well, if those things are fabricated, what makes you think any of the rest of it is true? Trying to understand me *or* your father *or* our relationship from that novel is a hopeless idea. I think if you need to know something—something specific—you should ask, because if we keep sparring about the book—what was real, what was fiction—we will end up in frustration."

"I went to Texas."

"What?"

"Almost everything you wrote about my grandparents was true: the restaurant; the camping trip; the disaster, but it was a bee, not a boat; my grandmother's death . . . so many things. And so were a lot of the New York bits . . . and Wally. How can you expect me to think it's fiction when he's not? Especially after finding you here . . . in his apartment."

"*My* apartment. When your father arrived in Venice, he stayed at a hotel near the station. Noisy, not very clean. With some rather nasty water bugs that were making him crazy. When we . . . well . . . got to know each other, I saw how he was living and I took pity on him. I invited him to stay with me. He was pleased to do so."

"His search for solitude?"

". . . was *my* search for solitude. It made a better story to give that characteristic to Aidan."

"His quest for self-understanding?"

"He may have been on a quest. He didn't say. He seemed to be. *I* was."

"And were you successful in your quest?"

"Until yesterday. Yes. For seven years. And for seven years before your father arrived."

"You've been in Venice for fourteen years? But what do you do here . . . all alone?"

"Work. Seven years of short stories, the novel, more years of stories."

"Ah . . . yes, you wrote about the work. 'The meaning of my life is in my work,' " he quoted, showing off.

This was going to be tedious, she thought. He's going to review the whole bloody book point by pointless point—if I let him. She decided she wouldn't.

"And what sort of work do you do?"

"I am considering a career in art restoration."

Art restoration. Her mind picked up the idea and ran with it. Her life in art. His. What restoration was he here to accomplish? The icon of his father? Or some earlier trauma? What black hole had been torn into the young life of James? What needed repair? She wondered. He was here on a mission, a self-rescue, to ensure his future by redeeming the past. He would refind his injury and restore it if he could. As she refound hers and rewrote them when she could. She looked up at him and smiled.

"How interesting. What sort of art would you restore?"

He had watched her leave him, travel somewhere within her interior universe, and return with a pleasantry. One day he would travel with her, he decided. For the moment he would be polite, put her at her ease. "I haven't decided," he replied. "I got started late and I'm still in the midst of my studies. There's an institute here in Venice, San Gregorio, where they specialize in water damage. Obviously. But the best schools for general postgraduate studies are in

31

Rome and Florence. I plan to visit them all on this trip, and make some decisions later. So far Venice is magnetic." He paused and sipped his coffee. Then he leaned back in his chair and watched her. "Now will you tell me what you were thinking about so intently before you asked me your last question?"

His interest in her was disconcerting. She wasn't accustomed to having anyone care about her idle musings, only in her carefully constructed fictions. She warmed to him in spite of her resolutions. "I was thinking about the vast silences of time that bookend our lives."

"You know, you really are beautiful." It was the last thing he expected himself to say.

It was the last thing she expected him to say. Aidan had never said it.

"Thank you."

"I've read everything you've written, all your other stories. They're nothing like the first novel."

"There is nothing like the first . . . of anything." She blushed.

Surprisingly, so did he.

"Did you really write it?"

"What!"

"I'm sorry, but in the novel, it's Aidan's voice, it's his story . . . and, well, it says in the novel that he was writing an autobiography of sorts, and a manuscript never showed up among his papers. So I thought maybe that *The Name of the Son* was actually what my father had written . . . or that it was based on what he had written . . . and that you published it after he died . . . for him, so to speak."

"And put my name on it? *Plagiarized* it?"

Embarrassed in the face of her obvious outrage, James

looked away from her, down into his cappuccino. "Not plagiarism exactly." He tried to explain. "Nothing so bad as that. Just a kind of collaboration, maybe . . . or a rewriting . . . an act of love . . . to let it come out into the world. I mean you were a known writer by then . . . all the early stories . . . so you could get it published . . . he was unknown and dead . . ."

But James was talking to foam and air. When he looked up again, Mara was striding away from him across the piazza, into the crowds of Venice.

THREE

Campo
Santa
Margherita

Well that, thought Mara, was *that,* as she hurried back through the bustling center of Venice toward her quiet home in Santa Croce. I didn't ask this disruptive young man to come here. I have tried to be sociable in spite of my own natural inclinations to privacy. But I am certainly not obliged to sit still and hear myself accused. How dare he! He had given her a reason to leave him and she had seized it. What a relief to be done with him!

She hadn't been this angry in years. It was a horrid sensation. She would give it to Gwendolyn, the heroine of her current stories. She began to observe herself on behalf of the character. She was breathing hard. Her heart was beating rapidly. She felt fully, but unpleasantly alive, futilely strong, purposefully going nowhere, as she crossed the Campo San Stefano and mounted the Accademia Bridge, enjoying the hard-slapping sound of her leather shoes striking the wooden steps.

At its summit she stopped to catch her breath and take in the picture-postcard view of the Grand Canal. Lovely. Just lovely, she thought. So what? For what? For whom?

Once she had believed that the beauty of the city had been laid out for her pleasure. She had, when she loved, owned all the grandeur of the earth and sea and sky. No more. Not for a long, long time. Not since Aidan had died. So the anger led to poignant memory and, she observed, to pain and to melancholy. The bridge was not high enough for a successful suicide leap. She was not given to histrionics. But, Mara thought, Gwendolyn was. If hysterical Gwendolyn was to jump off the bridge, it would make for an interesting scene. Who would pull her out? The young Italian who owned the dress shop or a new, plot-complicating stranger? Both? Mara was suddenly eager to return to her typewriter and see. She strolled down the steps off the far side of the bridge deep in thought, James, for the moment, forgotten.

James stood on the top of the bridge and watched Mara's determined descent. He had almost approached her as she stood staring at the water, lost inside herself, but he had found her concentration daunting. He decided to follow her at a safe distance instead.

She had overreacted to the revelation of his harmless fantasy about her fiction. He should have known better. Besides, Mara had to be the novel's true author because Mira, the central character, was a woman's idea of a man's idea of an irresistible woman. He would tell her so if he got another chance; see how she took the criticism. He began to think of her as a woman of unpredictable emotion. Histrionic? Hysteric? Well, undeniably challenging. He had hoped, in time, to feel safe with her. Was that possible? He noted the direction of her disappearance behind the art museum. She must be going home the long way, along the Zattere. He smiled. He would map her soul before he was through with her.

He took the short way through Dorsoduro, stopping in the Campo Santa Margherita for, among other things, some fresh blackberry gelato which dripped, almost immediately, down his shirtfront. In the busy, homely square, he looked around for the Antico Capon and the place where his father had fallen. Or was that fiction? It was a pleasant looking restaurant—half indoors, half outdoors, like most Italian restaurants—with tables and chairs sprawling into the campo. And it smelled deliciously of pizza.

He decided to sit for a minute with a bottle of mineral water, most of which he drank, some of which he used to wipe ineffectively at the blackberry stain on his shirt. He watched the locals and the tourists crossing the market-place, intent on their private concerns. He felt, suddenly, dismally alone.

He remembered a detail from the novel and looked over

to see if there was a tank of brightly colored tropical fish just inside the door of the restaurant. There they were. He thought of his father, now ashes mingled with the lagoon, and his loneliness left him.

He paid his bill and hurried on, so that by the time Mara was making her way down the *fondamenta* toward her apartment, he was comfortably nestled into a rowboat that was tied up a short distance down the canal from her front door. In this unlikely spot he could, this time, observe her approach without much likelihood of her seeing him.

She walked like a soldier, without the slightest swing to her stride. When she had fled the piazza, he had thought that anger was informing her step, but now, with the anger gone from her features, he saw that it was concentration that took the femininity from her. He found it strangely exciting. She opened the street door with the lion-head knocker and the broken lock, and he could just make out her look of surprise at the bundle of red roses he had left lying inside the common entrance hall in front of her private door. She bent to retrieve the roses. She read the card, came back outside, threw them into the canal, threw the card into the canal, bent again—this time to pick a few of the weedy yellow wildflowers—and, clutching these, expressionless, she entered her apartment.

The door slammed behind her. The roses, the card, and an empty plastic Coke bottle floated slowly by the boat that held the astounded James. He was delighted. He reached into the water to retrieve a rose, badly puncturing his thumb in the attempt. He released the thorny stem and the rose drifted away behind the others. Ignoring his wound, he climbed clumsily out of the rocking boat, scraping his knee on the edge of the *fondamenta*. Limping slightly, bleeding slightly, smiling slightly, he made his way in the direction of the hotel.

He had to do some serious thinking about this woman.

Mara wrote. Then she worried.

She had no experience with unwanted men. She had almost no experience with men at all. Real men. Her readers, she knew, would be surprised to know that about her. Her reputation had been made on romance. Her books were not, however, with the possible exception of *The Name of the Son,* formula romances. They were dark, slightly twisted, angry romances. Literate and intelligent, they defied easy classification. Not novels exactly, but groups of stories milling, sometimes rioting, around a single unifying character, this time Gwendolyn. She had hoped that her current collection would coalesce into a second novel. The first "showed promise," the critics had said, and the subsequent story collections had been well-received. Every now and then a fat envelope full of fan letters would arrive from her publisher. She would spill them out and read them with trepidation. Strange women wrote to her about perverse relationships in their own lives, suggesting that Mara turn their pathos and bathos into novels. Strange men wrote, suggesting that Mara have perverse relationships with them in real life.

Mara preferred to imagine her own romances and to live alone. There was so much happiness possible in the imagination. Almost none, in her experience, with a real person. Men had their own needs, their own desires—nothing to do with hers—and she had so few resources for meeting theirs. Love, she was convinced, was better left to the imagination. Hers.

She would not be so unimaginative as to imagine roses. She hated roses. Sibyl, her mother, had loved them and had always insisted on bunches of them, wilting and drooping in the corners of her sickroom. Always bloodred roses. Always sweet-stinking in the damp, thick atmosphere of old woman smells. She shuddered.

The card had carried a quotation from *The Name of the Son.* Had he thought he was being smart? First accusing her of plagiarism, then copying from the supposed fraud? It said:

> *"Venice is a dreadful city in which to chase a woman."* Please forgive my impertinence. Will you meet me for dinner at eight tonight? The Antico Capon, Campo Santa Margherita?
>
> Yours, James

She would not go. She would not ask for any more trouble. Would Gwendolyn go? Most likely. Gwendolyn would go with the intention of falling directly and pleasantly in love with him, and then, knowing Gwendolyn, she would fall indirectly and unpleasantly in love with someone sitting at a nearby table. Fictional characters carried on that way. Mara was not a fictional character. The best course of action, Mara decided, was to write him a terse note and tell him to get lost. But where would she send it? She didn't know where to find him. The Pausania? She was afraid that

39

if she chose to ignore his invitation, he would simply return to her apartment with more demands.

Perhaps it was the time to take that small journey to Treviso. She could spend a few days in a different setting, refreshing her mind in the lush greens and stone golds of the nearby medieval market town. No. She would not be chased away like a hounded animal by this man. Not by any man. She would hold her ground, close her door against him, and write. It felt good to have her writing flowing once again, the characters forming their lives and informing her own. It was strange and magical to Mara whenever, unblocked, they turned from ink to people, with imaginations of their own—demanding people, who lived in her typewriter, waiting impatiently for her to transcribe their adventures. She felt at such times like an underpaid secretary who was slow at dictation but happy to have been hired. What would Gwendolyn be like with a man like James?

Deciding to rest for a while before returning to her work, Mara poured herself a glass of Prosecco and reclined on the velvet couch. She ran her hand over the worn fabric which still retained the slightest scent of his cologne from the day before—the same scent that Aidan had favored. Her hand strayed to herself. What would Mara be like with a man like James?

She remembered her mother coming upon her in a moment of such private pleasure. She was four or five at the time. Her mother was monstrous in memory, all shrieking and slapping, warning her that if she continued such nasty habits she would not be able to have any babies and no man would marry her. Had she believed the warnings? She didn't think so.

She had not sacrificed her sensuality, but she had learned

to be secretive. She was an adolescent before she could begin to fathom why her mother had made such a fuss in the first place—certainly not over a few discreetly pleasurable gestures. She had finally realized that her mother had been terrorized, not by her hand, but by her mind. Mara's mind was a treasury of erotic fantasy. Had her mother known? Mothers have the power to read their children's minds. So her mother had said. Could she? Would she? Had she? She had been witchlike in her ways.

Mara, through all of her own youthful years, had nursed the accursed old woman. Sibyl, her mother had been called. A witch's name. She could curse like a witch as well. She was bitter and demanding and ruthless and greedy. She had died endlessly—transforming, slowly and painfully, into a malignancy of mind and body.

Mara had seen the seasons of her youth, the bright Nebraska days of space and promise, roll away from her forever outside the dark, deteriorated, unchanging house. She would sit by the various windows, watching the land in every direction, in all seasons—snow meadows as far as the eye could see turned to oceans of tender grass. She would watch the grass grow. Green. Golden. Brown. Snow again. In her mind's eye she peopled the vast expanses with families or lovers, emptied it out again and filled it up with soldiers of fortune or grave diggers or witch hunters. She never missed the television that her mother declared she would never buy.

Inside the house, creaking with age and unpleasantness, there was only Sibyl, for whom she toiled. Her devotion to her mother's well-being was not a choice. It was the only life that she knew. The world had offered her Sibyl, and she had, naturally, reflexively, offered herself back. Nothing

41

she did in her sacrifice was appreciated. Her care went unnoticed, except as cause for complaint and criticism. Once, in a rare moment, when Mara had broken, she sought for herself a little mercy, and she had asked her mother if there was anything—any one thing about her— that her mother judged good. Sibyl had considered the question for half a day and then, from the twists of sweaty bedclothes, replied: "Well, Mara, you are very selfish, and that, in this country, in this day and age, is probably a good thing."

Mara had read books to keep herself alive. They had inherited the old house from her mother's brother, Uncle Allen. Allen, newly arrived from England, had been a gentleman farmer, a bachelor, and the sprawling county's most educated man. Over the long years that had enclosed his Nebraska winters, he had made of the once prissy drawing room a large, deep library. It became Mara's sanctuary. Her mother never entered the library, keeping as she did to her bedroom, with occasional summertime excursions to the front porch. It was just as well. Sibyl would never have approved of those who lived within: Shakespeare, Dickens, and Austen were busy writing, writing, writing. Freud and Jung analyzed, Aristotle and Plato contemplated, Waugh sulked, Hawthorne met Twain, Hugo and Flaubert rebelled, Lord Byron rhymed, and Hemingway shot off his short, sturdy sentences. The library was a meeting place for all the greatest minds, and they charitably agreed to accept Mara into their midst for purposes of education. Uncle Allen's taste had been eclectic, and Mara took the benefit from books as diverse as *The Arabian Nights,* the Bible, the *Kama Sutra,* the *Iliad,* and *Grimm's Fairy Tales.*

In time she began to write things herself, never on paper

where her mother might find them—and never certain that they were well enough hidden in her head.

Finally, she had seen death. Ugly and sordid, bloated and bloody death. Mara, revolted, had held her mother's hot, writhing body, had felt the jolt into stillness, and her mother's turning, then, into some *thing,* stiff and cold. It was done. Her childhood was over. She was twenty-four.

She had called the undertaker. She had left a stack of correctly counted currency on the table, lifted a long-ago-carefully-packed suitcase, driven the thirty miles to the nearest depot, abandoned the car, taken a series of trains to New York City, checked into the Algonquin, called a local travel agent, booked the first cruise out of the harbor, sailed to Europe, and disembarked in Venice.

Now, well over a decade later, she smiled in remembrance of her smooth passage. She couldn't have written it better.

For fifteen years she had written well enough. Writing justified, almost normalized, her eccentric life. Writers were allowed to be strange. Writers were allowed to be selfish. It was as if the world had given her permission, in this one way, to empty out her mind for all to see, where in every other instance it insisted upon discretion. So, alone with her pen or her typewriter, she parceled out her secret wishes and fears, her forbidden eroticism, her childhood imaginings and her adult longings, among a host of characters. Then she sent her ornate fictions out into the real world. They brought back money.

Unnecessarily, she was rich. She cared very little about money and didn't need the sums that her writing accrued. She often gave it away. To good causes, without care for the effect. Father Timon was pleased to accept it on behalf of the church. She took her own money from an arrangement the world called a trust—a deaf, dumb, and blind trust. Whoever her father had been, or now was, he had provided well for her. When her mother died, carrying the secret of his identity to her grave, the interest from the trust, many thousands annually, had come to Mara. She could do with it what she willed. The capital, many millions, was controlled by trustees, and that, she had been informed, was willed to her first son. She had been caught at the moment of her mother's death between her father's anonymity and her son's nonexistence—caught for a wealthy lifetime. It was a high-class problem.

When *The Name of the Son* was first published, Mara had hoped it might change her life in some small or, possibly dramatic, way. It had not. Her life had continued as it was before, undisturbed, unnoticed, by the overpopulated world beyond her door.

Until yesterday. Her fiction had finally attracted something besides furtive fan mail and unnecessary income. This time, as she had once fantasized they would, the characters had brought back a real man, a real fan, from the real world. In her novel, the character on which he was based—no, the character based on him—was called Michael. Michael, the son of Aidan. He had been a peripheral character, referential. That would make a good book title, she thought. *A Referential Man.* Michael, the character, had not been fleshed out. He had not demanded to be known. James, the man, did. And James was not safely tucked away behind a typewriter ribbon. He was unpaginated and on the loose. What a damned nuisance. And dangerous! When she looked at him, she saw hurt coming at her. He belonged to Aidan. More to the point, she belonged to Aidan.

Here, on her couch, she imagined James in his bed—a strange bed in an unknown hotel room. She imagined coming quietly into the room while he slept and standing nearby, watching him in the dim light while she slowly removed her clothing, then slipped into the bed beside him, feeling his male body along her side, against her breast and hip and knee—he, barely stirring at first, then moving gently into the awareness of her presence and into her body with the sleepy sensuality of a dream. Now he was Aidan in her mind—the father supplanting the son—the loving Aidan of the rewritten past. She moved gently into the remembrance of his presence and into her body of feeling with the sleepy sensuality of a dream.

Later, in the garden, Mara wrote, and Gwendolyn was satisfied.

Later, in the Campo Santa Margherita, James waited, and James was disappointed.

FOUR

The
Rialto

James slept well that night, wrapping his disappointment in warm, woman-filled dreams. When he woke up, he went to church. He knew he wasn't supposed to. Young, sophisticated, well-educated, intellectual men of his post-Darwinian, post-Freudian, post-Marxian generation rejected religion. He went anyway.

James had no religion, but he loved ritual, maintained a passionate interest in the myths that informed the rituals, worshiped the art and music that were inspired by faith, and had a wish—deeply felt and carefully hidden—for faith itself. Sometimes, standing in the midst of a congregation united in prayer or song, he longed for grace—longed so profoundly and so intensely that he was sure it could not be denied him. Everything in the world seemed natural to him—peculiar perhaps, even absurd, but real, eventually understandable and perfectly natural. There was no space left for the supernatural. So, in spite of his longing for ethereality, he was always spilled back onto the streets without God.

This morning was no exception. He had gone to a special midweek mass on the Isola di San Giorgio, where, in a Palladian church, a choir of cloistered monks had filled the sacred space with heart-holding, heaven-sent chant. He had departed, at the end of the service, shaken, but still secular.

He could not pray.

He could think.

He judged his thoughts mundane. Why hadn't she come to the dinner? He was genuinely sorry to have insulted her. He hoped the note had made that clear, but he had been ready to apologize to her in person. He had thought that the rejection of the roses would have siphoned off her anger so that, on reflection, she would join him. Would she give him another chance to get to know her? Would he, in the knowing of her, begin to feel the surges he felt most sacred—the surges of interest, of love, of desire toward another being?

He had come to the altar of desire before, but communion was always denied. Though life ran through him like a howling wind, though the wonders of art enthralled him and the glories of music enfolded him, God and woman eluded him. At twenty-six he was an agnostic and a virgin.

He thought, perhaps, that he should take a day's vacation from his pursuit of grace and favor. He would wander around this labyrinthine city for a while; he would be a tourist, see the sights, buy souvenirs. He would go to the Rialto Bridge and listen to other tourists misquote Shakespeare and then poke around in the busy market. He would buy a gift for Mara. One she would hesitate to throw into the canal.

The Rialto was a long, long walk from where he stood, and he enjoyed every step of it. He, unlike his father, was endowed with a naturally sunny temperament. In the face of endless personal difficulty he maintained an armor of optimism, shining it up with the polish of curiosity. When he considered the enormity of the universe, the infinite amount of space and time that surrounded him, he found it amazing that he had emerged into consciousness at all, and, because it seemed so unlikely that he would ever do so again, he was determined to savor every moment of his current existence, come laughter or lamentation. He loved extremes. He loved nuance. He loved the accidental world in which he, so ill-suited for it and so uninformed about it, had found himself. This city, with its centuries of whimsical accretions, each more outrageous than the last, amused and delighted him. There, on a small pink house, sat a weathered lion with wings; and there, a great granite serpent made a meal of a monster in front of a shop full of gaudy masks; and there, a tiny boat chugged down the canal, filled with dogs and caged birds, arfing and chirping, while the boatman barked orders and whistled at his lively companions. How, he wondered, had the world looked to his father, knowing as he did that he was about to die? Were the colors brighter—smells more pungent? Did wine have more strength and was meat bloodier? He hoped so. When James arrived, slightly overheated, at the marketplace, he saw that it was stuffed with the *stuff* that had so enlightened Mira the day she had darted away from Aidan, if indeed she ever did.

He could not decide how he felt about Mara. Fascinated, yes. But he had brought his fascination with him. Now that she was real, how did he feel? He felt angry. And frustrated. Why was she rejecting him? Why had she thrown away his roses? Why hadn't she come to dinner? Why was she so reticent, so guarded in the face of him? He wished her no ill. He had, for years, envisioned her as she had written herself: open, sexual, interested in men and the ways of men, though independent of them. She was independent, all right. She was a bloody recluse! Was her present insularity his father's fault? She had alluded to seclusion, even celibacy, since his death. Had she loved him so deeply that there could be no other? Or had Aidan hurt her so badly— by his actions or by his death—that she had become fearful of another attachment? Or, James wondered, was there something in him that she had rejected on first sight? Was it simply that he was his father's son? And yet in the face of the rejection, he admitted an attraction. Because of the rejection? Because he wished to be attracted? Because he *was* his father's son? Because she had been his father's lover?

These apprehensions tumbled around in his mind as he made his way around the marketplace, his eyes drawn this way and that by eggs and shirts, by beads and squashes. On reaching the Rialto, his usual good humor had left him. The market was crowded with people bent on acquisition. He moved among them as unheeded as a spirit. For the first time since he had arrived in Venice he found the foreignness unpleasant. He felt lost, though he wasn't. He located the old church tucked away behind the vegetable stalls. It was locked tight. He sat on the steps, unfocused, letting the scene before him dissolve into a canvas of tumultuous form and colliding color.

In the midst of the chaos, Mara reached for a melon.

Her fingers gracefully tested the smooth surface of the fruit, moved underneath, lifted it slightly, and found the melon acceptable. The vendor, who clearly knew her (or she would not have been allowed such license among the cantaloupes) smiled and took the melon from her to be weighed, holding her hand momentarily as he did so. She appeared pleased by the friendly gesture . . . unafraid of the touch . . . for it seemed neither to ask for nor promise more. Mara paid for the melon. The man handed it back.

James felt his good humor had been handed back as well. A chance meeting was what he had most wanted and least expected. It was the way it would happen in one of her stories, not in life. Of course, he was not being absolutely honest with himself—in truth he had rather carefully considered the possibility that she might avoid her neighborhood market in the Campo Santa Margherita this morning. She wouldn't want to risk running into him. The next nearest market of any size was the Rialto. He knew she worked in the morning and it was likely she would wait to shop later in the day when the crowds were thinner—and so, by such chance, he was here and so was she, and he supposed he had written it so.

"Mara."

She looked up from her purchases and peered into the gloom. She saw him then on the steps of the church. Like a ghost. He was getting up. He was coming toward her. She considered a dash for freedom, but was unable by convention and by character to do so.

"Hello, James." Fortunately my hands are full, she thought, so I don't have to offer him one.

He took her packages. And then, for a moment, her hand. "Let me help you."

"Thank you. No. I can manage myself." But he was in possession of the parcels now, balancing them easily in the crook of his arm, and she felt helpless to reclaim them.

"Why didn't you come last night?"

In fact, she had come. All the way to the campo by the roundabout way, where, from a narrow entryway, she could watch him unseen as he sat amid the tables with a glass full of wine and a face full of anticipation. She had not planned to go, of course. Her intention was to ignore his invitation and write late into the night. But at almost eight she had found herself, once again, without inspiration. Gwendolyn had turned out to be a stubborn woman, voracious for real experience, and she had refused to fork over another sentence if Mara didn't go to see James for her.

So Mara had gone, and stood, and watched, and finally decided to join him. She had just begun to move in his direction when she noticed a young woman approaching across the square toward the restaurant. The woman was very young and very pretty and not very dressed: a T-shirt stretched across her ample breasts, a pair of shorts that barely covered her bottom, sandals. She had stopped to look at the *menu turistico,* and it was then, Mara noticed, that the expression on James's face had changed from anticipation to awe. He was clearly thunderstruck by the sight of the girl. In a moment he had begun a conversation with her, though from where Mara stood, halted in midstride, she could not determine what they were saying to one another, nor did it matter. She was remembering how Aidan had ogled every woman who walked by, evaluating her with the eye of a connoisseur. She was remembering how it had felt to see him do it. No! No, she would not willfully step again into the mouth of that monster—jealousy! Caught in its jaws, she imagined that she would be consumed by it—but the beast had just torn and chewed on her. It had never swallowed. No. She couldn't risk such horror again. Or any other emotion that was dragged along in the wake of love. Mara had returned home then, the roundabout way, feeling old (which she knew she was, at least by comparison to the girl) and heavy (which she knew she wasn't, except in relation to the lightness of youth) and unattractive (which she knew she had no way of judging anymore). Back inside her apartment it was not Gwendolyn who had suffered quietly and alone until sleep overtook her. It was Mara.

"You know perfectly well why I didn't come. You accused me of literary kidnapping."

"You misunderstood me. It was just a romantic notion. You, of all people, should appreciate the idea."

"Why *me* of all people?"

"You know."

"I don't know."

"You're a goddess, Mara."

That stopped her.

It stopped him, too. He hadn't meant to say anything of the kind. He had never uttered anything so crudely self-serving before in his life. There was an awkward silence.

"Whatever can you mean?"

I haven't the least idea, he thought. She caused in him a

possession of spirit. She stood looking at him, annoyed, he was sure, and perplexed. He would have to say something.

"You are the embodiment of romance. You are beautiful, and you are an artist, and you love beautiful things . . . I can tell from your writing and from your home and from the glimpse of your garden . . . and you inspire me to say things I have never said before. I think you must be more than mortal."

I'll be lucky if she doesn't throw *me* into a canal, he thought. Every syllable he spoke sounded inauthentic.

Everything he says feels delicious, she thought. After the days of self-hating and the night of self-pity, it was wonderful to be presented with praise. Was he serious? She considered, there in their silence, in the midst of the noisy, stifling, stinking marketplace, whether she had been too hasty the previous evening. He was a young man, after all, and perhaps he should be forgiven a moment's chance enchantment with a really beautiful woman of his own age. It was only natural. But what if he was like Aidan at heart? He could easily have spent the night with that young trollop (she should be kinder to her sex, she thought—that young female) and then deposit her on the doorstep at dawn, without another thought, ready for a new adventure. Like father, like son? He *looked* so like his father. Never judge a book by its cover? Clichés aside, there was no evidence that he had spent the night in debauchery. On the contrary, judging by the plaintiveness of his first question, he had waited for her to join him for dinner. Inwardly, she shook her head. His head was riddled with romance, fired up with fiction. He wanted a goddess. What chance would a flesh and blood woman have against that? Perhaps Gwendolyn could help her out. Outwardly, she smiled.

"Now it is you who plagiarize me."

"But of course," he said, as he took her point. It's the damn book that has possessed me, he thought. "Aidan sees Mira as the embodiment of Aphrodite, and as all the imagery in *The Name of the Son* is yours . . ."

"If I wrote it . . ."

". . . then you *are* a goddess."

"You're living in that damn book, aren't you, James?"

"So it appears."

She looked around the marketplace, and back into her past. She remembered the terrible fight she had had with Aidan, here, almost on this spot, when he had mentioned his marriage for the first time and she had hit him. *Unforgivable.* She had written it otherwise. But not other, or wisely, enough to repair the damage. Could she go back and cover the same ground again? Did she want to? Should she go there with James? Could he, perhaps, restore her happiness when both art and time had failed? *Never!* "Then let's try something."

"What?"

"Let's go for a ride in a gondola down the Grand Canal." And she took his free hand in her own.

In that moment Mara decided to accept the risk of this peculiar relationship, and with the acceptance, she had felt the fear lift from her. In that moment James decided to accept the good fortune of her favor, and with that acceptance, he had felt his spirits lift.

In that moment they were happy.

They hurried along together toward the canal, but just as they were about to leave the market for the *fondamenta,* he hesitated.

"Mara, wait a minute. I wanted to buy you something."

"What?"

"I don't know exactly. Something luxurious, something extravagant . . . wait. Look. Here are some lovely leather gloves."

"It's August."

"It won't always be August. And, even now, it's often cool at night. Here. Feel this." And he held the soft leather up against her cheek. He felt a slight response to his caress.

"Gloves in August are quite an extravagance."

"Then you shall have them. And a pair for me as well." He completed the purchase, and she seemed pleased to accept the pair he selected and presented. He wondered briefly if he should mention the roses, but decided to leave well enough alone.

They made their way to the great curving canal where the empty gondolas bobbed about waiting to be filled. James felt his stomach lurch a little as he climbed into the unsteady craft. Mara settled comfortably beside him. The design of the boat brought them close together, and he remembered the feel of her body on the velvet couch as it had moved with her sobs against him. The boatman pushed off, at her direction, toward Santa Croce.

"I feel as if I should throw something into the canal," he said when they were well under way.

"Yes. Of course you do."

"I'm not married."

"I didn't think so."

"I could throw in this class ring from Columbia." He held it up for her to admire; the royal-blue stone seemed to pulse in the sunlight.

"Aidan's?"

"Mine."

"Don't. I'll throw something in for us later." She realized that no one but herself and this man would be able to follow their conversation. It depended for sense on the shared knowledge of her novel. The privacy of their communion excited her. She moved a little closer to James. She felt a ripple of sexuality—then, before she could enjoy it, a wave of self-loathing washed through her. She almost fainted at the force of it, but fortunately recovered herself before James could notice her distress. She felt sick. She had to move away. The price was too high. She couldn't do this, not even for the hope of a new novel.

James had felt Mara move closer to him momentarily, and his pulse had quickened. Was it happening? Then, almost in the same movement, she had pulled back. What was she trying to tell him? He couldn't make any sense of her signals.

Gwendolyn was angry. How was she supposed to develop if Mara acquiesced to every slap of neurotic fear? She would have to take matters into her own eccentric hands. Mara felt the emergence of Gwendolyn with a mixture of relief and trepidation. She spoke then, erasing all the warmth of the previous few minutes. She sounded almost angry.

"Let's try to get out of the old plot, James. You ask me five questions—anything you like—about the book. Five." She held up her hand. It was gloved. "You must ask the questions with your gloves on, so to speak—carefully, with consideration as to their impact on me. I will answer them, gloves on—just as carefully, and as truthfully as my memory will allow. You can question my replies, but your questions will all count toward the five. And then we're finished. You must promise me that you won't refer to the novel again. Agreed?''

After the dismal evening alone at the Antica Capon, and the sudden shift in her mood, the unexpected offer was far more than he could have hoped for. He would take what he could get. Why five? He was afraid to ask. She might count it as one of his questions. "Agreed," he said, and he reached to take her hand.

"Gloves on."

He shook his head. She was serious. There was no deciphering her. He put on his own new pair. He leaned back to consider what questions he should ask her as the low, black boat slid silently along the gray-green waters. He looked over his shoulder and noticed, with amusement, that their gondolier was also wearing gloves, white ones, with which to grip his oar. This was a gloves-on gondola. He decided to begin with a question that seemed gentle enough, but he was so at sea with this woman that he couldn't be positive. He hoped he wouldn't offend her.

"Did you love my father?"

She looked into his eyes for a moment, then into a private distance, somewhere over his shoulder. "Yes. I loved him." He thought that that was all she was going to give him, just the terse affirmation of affection. After a pause she continued; he sensed at some cost to herself. "He wasn't an easy man to love. He was searching for something when I met him . . . something that he could not find in me or perhaps in any woman. It was hard to look into his eyes and see in his soul an emptiness that hurt him all around its edges, and to know that I, alone, would never be able to satisfy him. But I loved him and gave him my love against the void.''

Her answer disturbed James. He had known of his father's restlessness, of his promiscuity, but this was the first glimpse he had been given into the eyes of it. She probably knew no more than he about what had driven his father, but she would have opinions about it. He would like to know what they were. Nevertheless, he decided to ask his second question as planned. It, too, promised revelation.

"Did he love you?''

"I don't know. He seemed to. He acted in loving ways. Sometimes. So I chose to believe that he loved me all the time, no matter how he behaved. He never spoke to me of love. Nor did I. I didn't know how to put such feelings into words. I can only do that when I write. I had no experience with men, no way to compare, no way to understand what was happening to me except insofar as I had read the accounts of other writers. I cannot—even now—be sure of our love. But I *felt* loved. Perhaps I made it up. It was enough for me—feeling loved—though not, I know, enough for him.''

One answer was more upsetting than the next. James felt his mind rocking with the boat as it bounced over the wake of a passing motor taxi. He had, for years, found a way to forgive his father. He had decided that choices made from love, even if the love was not for him, could be forgiven. But what if his father hadn't loved her? What if Aidan had deserted his family, not for the enormity of love, but for the littleness of lust? It was not a welcome explanation. With effort, he asked his third question.

"Did he love me?''

He saw the question soften her features again. Perhaps she did care for him a little. "James, I wish I could say what you want so much to hear, but I was telling the truth when I said he would not talk to me about you—or your mother. Oh, he slipped occasionally; enough to give me some idea of the forces with which he struggled. But I *know* nothing. I don't even know your mother's name. It wasn't that he lied. He told me he was a married man with a son. It wasn't that I didn't ask. Perhaps he assumed he was protecting me, but I was not protected, I was hurt. I felt he didn't trust me, that he didn't want to risk such intimacy. Perhaps if he had lived longer . . . anyhow, I can only think that he must have loved you—both you and your mother—very much, or he wouldn't have been so troubled by my curiosity. He was determined to protect your privacy at all costs."

"My mother's name is . . . was . . . Renata Raye."

"*The* Renata Raye?"

He nodded, smiling sadly. "Some people have mothers who are housewives. Mine was a household word."

She was stunned by the news. An anonymous woman, the unknown wife, had suddenly taken shape and form in her mind. The beautiful face of Renata Raye had floated from movie screens and magazine covers throughout her youth. While others aged, Renata Raye had grown more luscious, more curvacious, more talented. She had been Aidan's *wife*? How could Aidan have escaped his wife's limelight so completely? How could she not have known? If she wrote such a happenstance, her readers wouldn't believe it. She wouldn't believe it! The famous Renata Raye had been the unknown Mara's unknown rival? It was absurd. If Renata Raye had not been enough for Aidan, how ridiculous had it been for her, Mara, to try? And then . . . how long ago was it? Four years? Five? There had been the sudden, shocking suicide.

"I was sorry to hear of your mother's death," she managed to say. She found herself moved, again, by the sight of his unhappiness. She wanted to hold him and comfort him. She knew this was a ridiculous idea under the circumstances. And was that all she wanted?

"Thank you."

They rode in silence for a time, letting the sounds of the city splash against the side of the gondola. James realized it was crazy, but he wanted this woman to hold him, to comfort him. That was not all that he wanted. He could feel the heat coming off her body all the way along his side.

"James, a question comes to mind that you may want to ask. Let me speak of it first. It will save you a question."

He nodded.

"Aidan always wore his wedding ring. He was in terrible distress about his infidelities. So was I. But in the brief time that we were together, *I* learned about love—a kind of love stronger than any force in the world. Stronger than the judgments of reason. Stronger than right. Stronger than wrong. Stronger than pain. I was held in the power of it one time only, and I am sorry for the pain it has caused you or caused others, but I am not sorry for the experience. I could not appreciate life—not art, not music, not literature, not poetry, nor could I hope to write anything of lasting value—if I had not known such passion. I would have no way to understand you, or anyone else—nor could I find forgiveness in my own heart, without having loved so profoundly, just once."

Again he wanted to touch her in some tender way. He

felt that now, in this moment of revelation and remembrance, she would accept his touch. But the force that had kept him from intimacy for so long stayed his hand. He tried to touch her with his eyes. He hoped she could feel his forgiveness of what she had been, his yearning for what she was now. Was this longing made of love? It had no urgency. It felt tentative and fragile and very precious.

She could not read his emotions as he looked into her eyes. But she was glad of the silence. In the silence, she remembered Aidan. He had possessed such a lust for life. Not just women, but art, music, literature, poetry. Mundane matters, too, food, wine, even the weather, relishing sun and storm. He had sucked up the world as he had sucked up her will. His own will he had kept untamed, untrammeled. He went his own way in the world. Covered by a carapace of the commonplace, he had been deep and rich and exotic. No one had been able to own him. Not Mara. Not a legion of other women. Not even Renata Raye.

"Do you have another question?"

"Yes, but the next one is very difficult. It seems too personal."

"We made an agreement. You ask five and I'll answer five, but I appreciate your choice to keep the gloves on. It's all right. If I wrote it, I can talk about it."

"You wrote that you had met him, the first time, when you were very young . . . sixteen . . . in New York City. Did he really . . . I mean . . . was he . . . the first?"

She did not respond. Now it was he who could not read her expression. She did not appear to be distressed. But the pause gave pause. Had he, in spite of her assurances, been too bold?

"I didn't meet your father in my youth. I met him here, and I was thirty-two years old. He was my first lover. Also my last lover."

"Then you were never a—"

"No. I made it up."

"Then there was never a—"

He should have known. The youthful indiscretions of Mara's fictional self had been the major flaw in the characterization, the weak point in the novel. He had never believed in Mira's imprudent past—though he had had his hopes.

"I believe you have asked your five questions, James, and been given your answers. Now we are finished."

What did she mean by *finished*?

"We are almost at my home." Again a silence prevailed, each lost in the revelations of the other. Mara, sitting slightly on an angle, could see the seriousness in him, a seriousness that gave his familiar features a fine, hard-edged look that, if she were a different kind of writer, she would say thrilled her. She noticed his long, dark lashes, his soft facial hair. What would it feel like against her skin? She shivered. He seemed unaware of her observations and her oscillations.

As the boat drew into the last canal, she spoke again, her unpredictable formality returning. "I find I have once again been made very tired by our interaction. I will pay the gondolier to take you to wherever you are staying. Don't protest. I am very rich. Where are you staying? Oh. But, of course. Doubtless the Pausania." She directed the boatman to the steps near her apartment and carefully stepped up onto the *fondamenta*. "Please take this man to the Pausania Hotel." The abruptness in her manner was abrasive. But

James, who had hoped to be invited in, offered no protest. He, too, was once again tired. She turned away, then turned back to look at him. He did not look at her. Was he angry with her? Sad? Shocked? Glad to be rid of her? She could not tell. He was as deep and as hidden as she was. He was a match for her.

Just as the boat began to slide away, she stepped back to the edge of the canal. She knelt down and tossed away a small metal object, not into the water, but into the bottom of the boat. James, startled, leaned forward to retrieve the gift that had fallen so unexpectedly at his feet.

It was the key to her apartment.

FIVE

The Zattere

Gwendolyn was delighted with Mara's impulsive gesture, but Mara was appalled. Whatever would happen to her now? She entered her apartment with a spare set of keys and walked straight through to the garden, hoping to save herself with the sun.

She sat in the far corner beside the hibiscus and the bleeding hearts. Perhaps Aidan would help her. Breathe, he would say, just breathe and accept what is happening to you. She sat with her head between her knees, feeling the heat on the back of her head and neck, but it did not reach inside, into her head and into her chest, where she was full of horror. *What have you done? You know you can't do this. Get away. Change the locks before it's too late.* He likes me. Is it so much to ask? A little comfort, a little romance, to be touched again after so many years? *Too much. Too much. You're better off alone. He'll see that you're tainted, that you're evil.* No. I am not evil. *You are, or you wouldn't feel like this. You slept with this boy's father. He was a married man. The only love of your life, and it was evil. His wife committed suicide. Do you think you are blameless?* It wasn't my fault. I didn't know her. It was years later that she killed herself. It couldn't have anything to do with me. *You took her husband. He died in your arms. And then you wrote about it. You twisted it and turned it from what it really was to what you wanted it to be, and then you sent your dirty little novel out into the world where she could read it. Read it and weep. Read it and kill herself.* No! *You should kill yourself.*

"Enough!" Mara stood up. And then she threw up. And then it was over. She hosed down the garden then, and fed Wally, and made a cup of tea. She would be able to write now. Gwendolyn would be eager for the next chapter. None of Mara's characters gave a damn how much Mara suffered. They had their own lives to live.

Slowly James removed his gloves. Then he spoke to the gondolier, correcting the destination from the Pausania to his hotel near the railway station. He had actually considered moving to the Pausania Hotel, but it was too expensive, and he had grown uncommonly fond of the barren little room with the angel on the wall.

He slipped the key into his pocket. He kept his hand in the pocket, the palm pressed against his hip, touching the hot metal with the tips of his fingers. How was he to understand this unexpected offering? Five questions, she had said, then we're finished. Then the key. He didn't get it. He didn't get her. Did she want him or not? Did he want her? Yes. Would he dare to touch her? If he touched her, would the fear overtake him? Before he met Mara he had hoped that with her range of sexual experience she might be able to help him. If the panic came, maybe he would be able to talk about it and, with her, begin to understand what happened to him when he was with a woman. Now he knew she was less experienced than he. She had known his father, and his father only. Still, she had helped Aidan to live. Or so she had written. His father was dead. To try to make love to her would be an awesome risk. How humiliated he would feel if he failed again, failed with Mara. Through the lining of his pocket he felt the warmth of his own flesh surrounding the key. He let his other hand trail in water, and he wished for, and feared, the night.

After writing, Mara decided to walk. She chose a familiar route out along the Zattere, behind the Salute, to the tip of Dorsoduro, where she could stand with the breeze wrapping and unwrapping around her and look out across the basin to the Piazza San Marco. It was a classic picture with the sun setting behind the palazzos on the Grand Canal. Usually it left her cold. Being in such a beautiful place all alone was chilling. But tonight she felt fortunate.

Would he come to her? He could not misunderstand the offer. Could he? *She* could. One moment she felt a surge of desire, in the next, one of fear. Once in her life, and only once, she had felt love strong enough to overcome consequence. She had accepted this singularity of experience, and although she mourned, she had lived without longing. Perhaps the mourning simply took its place. Until James. She did not know how to be slow or how to be subtle. She had developed no feminine wiles. There had been no dates, no dances, no boyfriends to flirt with or girlfriends to talk to when she was growing up. Everything had been her mother.

It was Sybil who had taught her to read and to write and to manage elementary math. But what her mother had taught her best was shame—shame for her illegitimacy, shame for her body, and shame for her feelings. The authorities had caught up with them in time, and Mara had been sent off to the local elementary school, too old and too warped ever to fit in. Placed in rows or circles with other children, she ached for invisibility. Both community and competition were cruel to her reclusive soul. She didn't belong with others. She belonged in the sickroom or the library or on the sagging front porch. She had always hurried home directly after the last school bell, where her mother waited, demanding perfection in her homework and in her housework.

"Well, Mara, you are very selfish, and in this country, at this time in history, that is probably a good thing."

Her mother's indictment had blighted her adolescence. How could she be less selfish? She subscribed to the best newspaper that was available in the county. She read up on world events, registered to vote, and sent her allowance to

67

worthy causes. She banished the words *I want* from her vocabulary. In time she cleverly turned Sibyl's accusation to her own advantage and used it to gain an evening out each week for Red Cross meetings. The attempt was hopeless. She was as ill fit for committee work as she was for a camel. The other young women, tight with familiarity, watched her social awkwardness with a kind of awed disbelief. She sensed their pity; there, but for the grace of God, go I, they thought. So she started going to the movies instead, where she could sit alone in the cool darkness, collecting flickering fuel for her fantasies. She began to envisage not the nearby Nebraska fields, but different vistas altogether. She saw *How Green Was My Valley* and wanted Wales. She saw *Heidi* and thought to surround herself with Switzerland. She saw *Summertime* and fell in love with Venice. She fell in love with the movie stars, too. Cary Grant, Jimmy Stewart, Spencer Tracy.

But without a father's smile, a father's touch, Mara was frightened by real men. Her imagination, nevertheless, was unstoppable. Mara's first love had been the postman, a weathered and beaten man whom she found roughly romantic although she was forbidden to speak with him. So she made him up, made up his life. She gave him an attractive wife rather like herself. She provisioned them with an adventurous life together: a crippled child to care for, a perfect child to amuse them, and a dog that saved them all from a fire. The poor Nebraska letter carrier had become, decades later, the wholesome Charles of her third book of stories.

Her mother had different ideas about the postman. Men, Sybil had assured her, were evil. Mara, Sybil had pointed out, was the living proof. Past the accusation her mother refused to answer any questions about Mara's paternity. She would glare or grimace at the child's natural curiosity. "He has had no truck with you," she once declared, "so you will have no truck with him!" But often in Sybil's grumblings Mara had picked up crumbs of information. Once in her sleep her mother had moaned out the name Michael. From that night forward Mara had claimed that name for her father. Sometimes he was the profligate son of a wealthy and famous politician who had traveled west to make his fortune in the outback of America. Sometimes she believed him to be a munitions manufacturer who had met her mother on a businessman's tour of the Nebraska missile silos. A man who made millions because men made war. And sometimes there was no elaboration at all. He was just Michael. He was just Dad.

Mara knew now that her mother's bitter rage had been fed by the financial arrangements her father had made on behalf of his illicit family: a modest living for Sybil, a fortune for Sybil's daughter. She had never had a chance at love.

Until Aidan.

And now, James?

Mara walked home in the failing light. Wally would be waiting. Then she would be waiting.

James watched the sun set from the terrace of a trattoria on the Dorsoduro side of the Giudecca Canal, where he thought more of Mara than he did of the food. If he was right about the effect he was having on her, she should be walking somewhere in this neighborhood this evening.

There was a good chance that she would pass the trattoria. He had planned to work his way through the novel, location by location. But he had recently realized that Mara was now caught up in his quest unawares. She didn't know she had joined him in a mental lock-step through *The Name of the Son*, but the evidence was there. They had met at the apartment where the first chapter was set, and then again at the second, San Marco. She hadn't come to the Campo Santa Margherita, or so she said, but even there he thought he had glimpsed her retreating into the twilight. Even without her physical presence at the campo, she knew that *he* was there. And then they had met—not entirely by chance—at the Rialto market. When she had innocently suggested the gondola ride on the Grand Canal, he had been dead certain. If the mind worked as he understood it, Mara would soon find herself out for a walk along the Zattere, the location of chapter five. Maybe tonight. He was enjoying the discovery that the strange ritual of his itinerary was now being shared by the woman who had written it.

There she was! His heart pounded with excitement. At the sight of her? At the confirmation of his peculiar prediction? He didn't know. She seemed lost in thought. And he watched her with pleasure, noting the way her body moved through this now familiar foreign landscape. He wondered if she would sense his eyes upon her, but she walked determinedly onward and did not appear to be aware of his presence. She was going home to wait for him. Would he have the courage to follow her? He wanted to. He wanted to leave his fear in the past and come to her as his father had come. He wanted to be where his father had been, feel the soft folds of the flesh that had held him. He wanted to touch where Aidan had touched, move as Aidan had moved. It wasn't incest, he assured himself. She wasn't his mother. She was just a beautiful woman. He wanted her. He wanted to be like Aidan. To be like him, in her.

He wasn't ready.

Night came, and Mara, alone and tense, found little with which to distract herself. Writing had failed her. Gwendolyn had disappeared into a hotel room, fully intending to consummate a dysfunctional relationship, and was now nowhere to be found. Mara, unlike herself, had been unable even to read.

For a long time she had sat in the garden, letting the darkness caress her skin, glad that tonight it did not engulf her soul. What would it be like to be touched by a man again? Would she remember what to do? Aidan had taught her. But Aidan had taught her what Aidan had liked. With him it had been easy. She needed only to respond. Would she feel as she had felt in Aidan's arms? He had been so confident, so commanding. She remembered the way he had taken hold of her arm when they walked together or when he wished to turn her toward him for kissing. He had held her as if he had owned her. She had had no trouble responding.

But James was different. He had presented himself with such assurance, such insistence, that at first he had frightened her, but now she knew that under the appearance of confidence he was all uncertainty. Would the confidence bring him to her, or the uncertainty keep him away? And if he came, which would prevail? Whatever prevailed would be different from her imaginings. Of that she was sure. There was no way to prepare herself. What would she feel? She had loved Aidan. She didn't love James. Was it wrong to want a man she didn't love? *It's wrong to want any man.* What if she fell in love with him, or learned to love him? *You'll be sorry.* What if he didn't love her? What would become of her then? What if he did love her? *He is going to die.* What would she do when he died?

She heard a rustle in the bushes. A sliver of light caught the glint of Wally's solitary eye.

"Prowling, are you?" The cat disappeared into the blackness. The fireflies were out.

A new anxiety assailed her. What if she forgot Aidan? She could never *forget* him, of course. But what if her memories, now unsullied, became mixed up with memories of James? She had created a hundred love affairs over the years, with every kind of man; in her mind she had made love in every kind of way. Those imaginings gave life to her life as a writer. But the memories of Aidan were real, separate and apart from all the other images of love. They gave life to her life as a woman. And because there was only Aidan, they were pure, imparting a purity to her. She had deified him. Now was she to defy him and lose what was sacred—to lust? *You should be ashamed of yourself.*

James decided he would go to her. Perhaps if they didn't talk, if he just held her, she would somehow understand him. Perhaps if they talked, if he just held forth about himself, she would understand him. And help him to enter into a new understanding of himself.

Midnight came.

James did not.

Mara closed Wally out for the night, then allowed herself a second glass of wine. She climbed into the freshly made bed, the bed that had protected her and Aidan from the world. Her eyes traveled over the carved bedposts for the millionth time. The creatures there crawled and cavorted as they always did. The monster bed, he had called it. The last time she had been in this bed with a man he was dead. Was it so wrong to wish for a living man? *If wishes were horses then beggars might ride.*

Of all the ways of being alone, waiting was the worst. Well, he hadn't come. Maybe James was dead. She shouldn't have tried. She wouldn't again. She felt worn and wilted and melancholy. She felt as she had felt on the nights Aidan hadn't come home. She knew she was not enough for him. She didn't know why. She gave him everything she could think of: her love, her home, her mind, her body. But still he prowled. Sometimes he brought something to earth and then he didn't come home and he didn't explain. They would go on the next day as before. But in between would lie the night; his had been rich with the pleasures of the body, hers impoverished by the tortures of the spirit. When he died, the torture had stopped. She had felt, alongside her grief, relief. And then guilt. Dead, he was hers alone.

In time she tossed and turned herself toward sleep, then found she was sinking slowly into a warm fog of fantasy—Aidan, and James, and the fictional men of her stories—letting her feelings thicken and form into dreams. She sensed the tender presence of James standing next to her bed, a small votive candle cupped in one hand, a cape draped about his shoulders. He looked like a priest. He didn't speak. She smiled up at his image wavering in the candlelight and she searched out the glittering blackness of his eyes before she realized she was not asleep. She was not alone. He was present—not a dream—standing, capeless, in the gloom.

He didn't move. She was afraid to.

"James." He looked so young, so strong, so sure.

He uncovered her then—first the light blanket, then the sheet. He took hold of the hem of her nightgown and slipped it off over her head in one graceful movement. Before she could respond, he blew out the candle, re-covering her in darkness.

She felt his weight on the edge of the bed, heard him slip out of his shoes, and then he was beside her, the varied textures of his clothing rough and soft against her nakedness. He smelled of the night air, dark and cold. She was trembling.

He lay on his side. He moved her body so that she was close up against him. Her head rested on his upper arm. She was aware of the muscles there. He began to stroke her with his free hand, his left hand. She started. He wore the tender kid glove of the afternoon. She felt his fingers move along her hairline, then slowly, gently down across her forehead, stopping to know the worry lines then the softness of her eyebrows. His breath, next to her ear, was light and even. There was no urgency in his touch, but there was tension in it. She knew that there had been no sudden shift of feeling in him since last they had spoken, no crashing wave of passion had swept over him, washing away the concerns that lay between them. He had brought himself to her unprotected, full of wanting and conflict.

With growing excitement, she felt the soft leather continue its progress down across her face, lingering over eyelids, nose, lips. She allowed her consciousness to condense at the place where his fingertips met her skin—her pleasure increasing as her neck and shoulders, her arms, wrists, and hands gave up their secrets to his touch. She was certain that if she opened her eyes she would see a soft, warm glow emanating from her flesh—a pulsing trail of light, tracing the travels of his hand across the surface of her body. Her body, not Gwendolyn's.

He moved his hand down, over and around her breasts, causing her to gasp and arch her body to meet his touch.

"Sssh," he breathed into her ear. She felt calmer, smoothed out into an expanse of receptivity. Mara felt the long gentle caresses from her breasts to her navel—hypnotic, magnetic, lulling her into strange love with him.

His leg moved across her body and he lifted himself up and over her in a gentle maneuver that brought him to her other side, and then he slid down her body so that his head rested on her hip. His breath now rustled her pubic hair. He lay his right hand, ungloved, cool and new, flat against her stomach. His familiar left hand slid beneath the small of her back, down and under her thighs. She opened to him now, eager to be known by him.

But instead he moved up to kiss her. A deep and passionate kiss. His breathing had changed. Hot and rapid. He seemed to be struggling for air. She had heard this kind of breathing before. He pressed against her in his excitement, clinging as Aidan had clung.

"I must go."

"No. James. Why? What's the matter?"

"I'm sorry. I'm so sorry."

He rolled himself over her body again, this time as if it held no feeling. He bent down to retrieve his shoes, and then he was gone into the night . . .

Stunned, Mara sat up and switched on the light. She had never been so confused. She stood up weakly, and, after slipping into her nightgown, walked to the back door through which he had fled. She leaned out into the night air. There was no sign of him. She wouldn't have written this.

She shook her head as if to clear it. Then she stepped back inside and shut the door. She locked it with the inside bolt, against his key. She poured herself another glass of wine and drank it straight down. Still feeling shaky from a mixture of excitement and shock and loss, she returned to the bedroom. There was no votive candle. That much had been dream. His right glove lay on the floor beside the bed. That much had been real. She reached down for the fallen glove and climbed into the bed with it. She slipped the glove onto her own hand and replayed the evening's lovemaking in her mind, letting her hand drift across her body. Later, her frustration relieved, she fell into a deep deathlike sleep.

Torcello

James sat in the sanctuary of the ancient cathedral on the overgrown island of Torcello far out in the Venetian lagoon. He stared at the wall of mosaics that depicted the Last Judgment and decided to become a monk. He knew he had no faith. He knew he had no calling. He didn't care. If he was destined to live a life of celibacy, it shouldn't be wasted. He should turn his neurosis into an asset. Live a life where purity was a virtue, not an eccentricity.

He studied the masterpiece before him, looking for the

telltale signs of restoration. Here and there he could detect recent handiwork. Surely the head of the angel on the right was modern, though beautifully done. What did modern man know of the angels? The medieval men who had created this mosaic so many centuries ago could *see* the damned angels—undamned angels, he corrected himself. Except the devil. That black angel had been sent to Hell because he refused to worship man. The fellow had a point, but it hadn't been a good idea to argue with God. James could find no God with whom to argue. What the hell was wrong with him? He looked at the rendition of Hell on the opposing wall. It was all disconnected bones and body parts. Disconnection *was* hell. His mind, his soul, longed for union. His body refused to cooperate.

What a fool he felt. His fantasy had been one of conquest, of her, of himself. But rounded, fleshy, breathing, responsive reality had defeated him. He had suddenly felt too shy, even in the darkness, to take off his clothes. In anxiety and haste he hadn't even remembered to remove his second glove. He had hoped he would be able to have another gloves-on conversation, tell her of his difficulties. He hadn't been able to utter a word; and silence hadn't worked, either. What must she have thought of him? He hadn't been able to stay in the bed. Was it the monster bed of the book? It had been too dark to tell. It felt so. She had been willing. He should have gone on. In. What must she be imagining in the wake of his unexpected, unexplained, unforgivable flight? He shivered. It was cold in here, even in August.

He left the dark cathedral and wandered out behind it into the brilliant fields of wild grass and wildflowers. There was so much beauty all around him. He was convinced that his body had been built to celebrate it. What else could sex be for but for celebration? But his body refused to join him in his worship of the world. In defiance of his mood, James had brought his sketch pad and pastels along with him. He found himself a comfortable place to sit in the high grass, surrounded by black-eyed Susans and Queen Anne's lace, where he set to work capturing the colors of creation. It was the best he could do by way of celebration.

His difficulties with desire had been foreordained and foretold. The children of movie stars were expected to be nuts. There had been no lack of money in his home, no lack of sophistication. He suspected that his mother had sent him to his first psychoanalyst as a prophylactic measure. He was six years old. He wouldn't talk to the prying, peering, old witch doctor. He thought she dressed funny. He thought she had a dirty mind. When she offered him toys instead of talk, he had seized on them with relief, playing quietly in the farthest corner while she watched and winced, made notes and noises, and periodically murmured to his mother about male role models and father figures. Mother gave him Cary Grant. And Jimmy Stewart. And Spencer Tracy. Friends of the family. He saw more of his mother's leading men than he saw of his father, who would not move to Hollywood, but chose to stay in New York where he could oversee his flourishing extermination business. James had assured his father that there were plenty of bugs in California, but his father was unmoved.

James remembered his father's rare visits to the West Coast with nostalgia. Aidan was a quiet, private man. He was unlike the other men in his mother's life. Aidan was solemn, the others insouciant. Aidan was often ill-tempered, the others cheerful. He was interested in art and music and books and flowers and his business, none of which he talked about, all of which he shared with James by simple association. He would walk silently through museums or gardens with his son in tow, or sit working at his accounts and papers while James watched over his shoulder. He did not go to the movies.

Years later James had learned about the women. Aidan had loved the ladies far more than art, music, books, flowers, business, or his marriage. It was not, finally, business affairs that had kept him on the East Coast, but the affairs of the heart, and the resultant agreement between Renata and Aidan to live apart. James once asked his mother why they had stayed married. Everyone he knew in Hollywood divorced, sometimes seasonally. She had smiled, rather wistfully and replied that Aidan didn't wish it. What about her? Did she wish it? No. She had said no. That was all. With one shining star after another to choose from, she had remained married, however distantly, to a man who killed cockroaches for a living. James had developed first the fantasy, and then the conviction, that his father held her with some extraordinary sexual power.

He put aside his drawing and removed a heavy tortoise-shell comb from his pocket. It had been his father's. He combed his hair. He then took out a worn gold wedding band. That, too, was Aidan's. He sat looking at the ring and the comb.

As beautiful as his mother had been, it had always seemed to James that it was Aidan who looked the part of a lover. He was tall and lean and dark, with strong Arab features: a well-defined chin and jaw softened with a salt and pepper beard, a large sharp nose, and narrowly set dark eyes through which he watched the ways of the world, especially the ways of women, with interest and appreciation. He moved gracefully, powerfully, through the world. He combined his intelligence with his reticence, so that however you made him up in your mind, he seldom said anything to damage your fantasy. To James he was the soul of romance.

James had missed him terribly during his growing-up years. Still, he had always known his father was there. *There* was faraway New York City, but *there* was also a place of unwavering acceptance. Whenever he telephoned, his father listened. Whenever he wanted to visit Manhattan, his father encouraged him. On the rare occasions when his mother allowed him to go, he was delighted to be in his father's home. Unlike his mother's spacious, perfectly ordered house and manicured gardens, Aidan's apartment was cramped, dilapidated, and dusted over with the black salt of New York City air. Its walls had been remodeled into library stacks, its floors covered and covered again by Oriental carpets. The shelves contained, besides books, a collection of precious objects from his father's travels: ivory goddesses and silver birds, ancient Japanese paintings, and deep blue enameled dishes. Each one had a meaning for Aidan, which he would sometimes, though rarely, share with James: this olivewood carving acquired from an old man in Turkey with a fish tattooed on his nose; this porcelain teacup given as a remembrance from a woman in Malta who danced with a snake . . . As he spoke he would pace, carrying the object around with him, putting it down randomly at the end of the story. Teapots ended up in the bedroom, African masks in the kitchen, and candlesticks in the bathroom—where they often remained for years. While his father worked quietly at his severely disordered desk, James would sit amid the jumble, rearranging, straightening, repairing, and restoring his father's apartment in his mind. His mother complained that James was obsessional when he returned from his father. Besides, he was a delicate child, often ill, and she thought it best to keep him at home, in the warm weather, near his doctors. But seldom near herself. She had her work.

Aidan had always been *there* until shortly before his death, when he had suddenly disappeared for several months. Then the news had come of his heart attack and death in Venice. What had he been doing in Venice? What story was *there*? The question had haunted James until the novel had arrived. Then the novel had haunted James.

And so James was here. In the unlikely fields of Torcello, the birthplace of Venice, looking at his father's possessions. Trying to restore order in his mind.

A furry caterpillar worked its way up a tall stalk of grass, unaware of the transformations before it. A butterfly lit on James's knee, then departed on its own flight of fancy. Grasshoppers hopped and bees buzzed. Insects had delighted his father in fiction. They had frightened his father in life. Aidan's phobia of insects had been a mystery to James until this summer, when he had traveled to Texas, to his father's childhood home. There he had found the story of his grandfather's death. Stung by a yellowjacket on a camping trip. A rare reaction. He laughed out loud. In the novel, Mara had made such a muddle of all that.

Mara enjoyed the long, slow boat ride to Torcello. She had stopped in Burano, with its little rainbow-colored houses, for an excellent lunch.

Earlier, she had awakened with Wally snuggled up in the

bend of her knees. He must have slipped in unseen when James escaped from her apartment. She was glad of the small, furry bit of company and gave the old cat a tickle. He blinked his one eye at her, covered it with a paw, and went back to sleep.

She had, in the light of morning, decided to put her halting love affair behind her. Surely James would not return after such a scene. She found that she did not miss him, or hate him. And more surprisingly, she did not hate herself. She found no fault with her own behavior. She had been welcoming, responsive, clean. There must be something wrong with the boy. Strange to think that there was someone in the world who was more troubled by sex than herself. She had puzzled over his distress for a while, then began to recall the masculine feel of his shirt and trousers, the soft-sensual feel of the glove. The boy had shown the makings of a lover. She wondered how he was. Relieved, most likely.

Well, he was gone now, so he was hers now. Mara was now free do with him as she willed. She would distort him and elaborate him into a curious character. She was too annoyed with Gwendolyn to present James to her. No. He would go into the next book. She wondered what it would be about.

Mara sighed. She was alone again. The punishing voices were silent. She was better on her own. The sunlight and its play across the waters, the breezes and the blueness of the sky, were pleasures that did not confuse or disappoint her. Ever. Now, as the vaporetto neared the dock at Torcello, she felt fresh, and rested, and ready to write. She had brought pen and paper with her, and she planned to spend the afternoon writing in the fields behind the cathedral.

James returned to the quiet campo in front of the cathedral and bought some lace from an old woman whose face was as intricately lined as her complicated work. She displayed her lace in a simple fashion, laid out on an apron spread upon the ground. The other vendors, in makeshift tents, had more wares on display than they could possibly have produced in a lifetime. James admired the old woman for her lack of pretension—for knowing what she did well and what her limits were. There was, he mused, plenty of time left for him to be old.

He went into the bar of the *locanda* and ordered a beer. He hadn't had a beer since leaving the States, and the familiar taste was welcome, bringing with it a rush of home-sickness. It was, he thought, time to stop chasing dreams and head back to his studies, to his work, to his home. The desire for monkhood had passed. He sat for a while recalling the smooth feel of Mara's sensuous body, first through the thin skin of the leather glove, then against his naked hand. How he had wanted her! He had kissed her very well. And then the panic had pushed through him with a greater force than he had ever known. Why? Why couldn't he go on? He knew he wasn't gay. He never looked at men. Not in that way. He looked at women. He recalled the young woman with whom he had chatted in the Campo Santa Margherita on the evening he had waited in vain for Mara. Her breasts, barely concealed in the damp, white T-shirt, had made his body sing. He remembered her beautiful bottom as she meandered away from him. But he knew that if he had abandoned his plans with Mara and gone off with the stranger into the night, he would have found himself, eventually, in the same unsatisfactory scenario as the previous night. Experience had taught him that looking was allowed—and fantasizing. Touching was all right, if he stayed on the surfaces. Even an occasional kiss. But a passionate kiss, or an exploration that carried him into a woman, was forbidden. His sexuality was limited to two dimensions. Length and width were his. Depth was not allowed.

He looked at the drawings he had made in the field, of the field. They were adequate, he thought. They had perspective, movement, depth. But he could not walk among their flowers. They were not fields. They were drawings. Illustrations. Illusions. Images. Two-dimensional fictions. So were his women. He had hoped to make the leap from fiction to reality with Mara, who was both.

Mara strolled along the canal that led into the heart of Torcello. She considered stopping for a beer at the *locanda,* but was afraid it would make her too sleepy, and she was determined to write. The stimulation of the previous night must yield up its chapters. The Italian shopkeeper who had kept Gwendolyn occupied in the hotel room needed to be fleshed out a bit, perhaps given a fetish . . . not shoes. Lace would do. Not very original, but Venetian and sexy.

The canal ended at the grassy campo, quiet now in the midday doldrums, the lace sellers gone. The cathedral was closed to accommodate the afternoon siestas of its keepers. It stood like a great stone barn, its outer walls a shell against the elements, which safely held within a display of mosaic art, extreme in its drama and fragile in its beauty. She thought perhaps that she would stop in on the way back and pay her respects to the round-eyed Madonna, who, embedded in the wall opposite, had been forced to sadly contemplate the Last Judgment throughout the centuries. Mara thought she might need cheering up, all things considered.

Torcello was a happy place for Mara, rich in memories. Aidan had loved the mosaics and had brought her here several times during their shared summer. Nervous of the insects, he had resisted her desire to walk in the fields beyond. Once, she had succeeded. It was afterward referred to as the I-told-you-so-picnic. Safe, she thought, in the middle of a wide expanse of blanket, she had opened the picnic basket to tempt him with ripe cheeses and ripe fruit. As she reached for the wine a bee had flown up her skirt. She had instinctively swatted at it before Aidan could stay her hand, and the nasty little beast had stung her on the inside of her thigh before dropping, still kicking but dying, onto the blanket. Aidan was far more upset than she, and Mara had finally calmed him down by insisting that he alternate the ice pack with kisses. When the crisis had passed he had hurried them out to the canal, where they had eaten their lunch on the move, rather uncomfortably, for the swollen sting had brushed against her other leg as she walked. He hadn't relaxed till they were on the boat, moving faster than insects toward Venice.

Today she was unlikely to irritate the insects. She hadn't brought a lunch or a blanket. Nevertheless, she had dressed defensively in blue jeans and a long-sleeved silk blouse. She planned to nestle like a small animal into the high grasses, and there she would bother nothing but her brain.

James made his way back along the canal that would take him out to the vaporetto landing. He smelled faintly, pleasantly, of beer from the bottle he had spilled over the counter and into his lap. He had decided to stop at San Michele on the journey home. He wanted to expedite his visit to that location, and he calculated he would have a little over an hour on the cemetery island before it closed. The San Michele chapter was the strangest chapter in Mara's novel, and he didn't think there would be anything to be learned of his father there, though Brother Sebastiano, if he was a real person and still living, might remember something. It was unlikely. What in the world wasn't?

His discouragement had not left him, and he was sorry that Mara was no longer walking through the book as he was. There had been no sign of her on Torcello. Perhaps she would come tomorrow. Or perhaps she was really lost to him now. He had hoped, if she was still with him, that a surprise encounter on this romantic little island would help him set matters right. He would have to talk to her sooner or later. He would have to explain himself. But how would that be possible when he couldn't explain himself to himself?

Mara decided that she didn't understand anything about writing. Here she was in an inspirational spot, comfortably settled, fully equiped to write, with a head loaded with recent experiences from which to choose, and with a manuscript housing a group of fully developed characters with whom to work. But nothing, not one acceptable sentence, would come. Her mind, against her will, kept running back to James and to the previous evening's events, but rather than finding herself swimming through deep fresh material that would result in a wonderfully original chapter, she found herself lost in a lagoon of languid alliteration that resulted only in frustration.

Shouldn't she be angry with him? Or at least insulted? Instead she was possessed of warm, soft feelings and a kind of tender concern unknown to her experience. She was worried. Not about the problems he had brought to the doorstep of her life, but about *him.* Perhaps her concerns were something like the moods of a loving mother toward a troubled son. Unselfish.

She felt a need to commune with Aidan about these recent shifts in the ground of her life, and the emotions that blew upward from them, like the winds of San Michele. She would stop at San Michele on the way home. He always seemed so close to her there, as he sometimes did in the garden. She glanced at her watch. One boat had just left, but she could catch the next one if she rushed to the jetty. She hurriedly picked a handful of wildflowers. The Madonna would have to do without a visitation from her. But Aidan would have one.

James threw some wildflowers over the side of the vaporetto onto the placid water of the lagoon. It was disconcerting to think that his father rested here, mixed into the watery world over which he now traveled. But he was glad that Aidan had arranged for his own cremation and burial at sea. There were no bugs in the depths of the sea.

When he was young James had been embarrassed by his

father's occupation. When the other children in his school-
room reported on the exploits and adventures of their Hollywood parents, he had been glad of his mother's
continuing fame, about which he spoke, behind which he
had hidden his father. For James, it was the only chink in
Aidan's shining armor. Why, he wondered, had such a
cultured man chosen such a depressing career?

Although he was never fully to understand Aidan's
choice, he had come to accept it, when, during one of the
rare New York visits, his father had taken him to the plant
that housed the tools of his lethal trade. James, then an
adolescent, had felt a reluctant fascination as he realized the
level of technology and expertise involved in the control of
insect populations. He had walked with amazement
through the eerie, underground storeroom that held the
vats and bottles and drums of various poisons: pure, combined, diluted, condensed. Would he have been more or
less fascinated if he had known his mother would one day
choose to poison herself? The drums were brightly colored
and tightly sealed. In this one corner of his life his father
was precise and orderly; no toxins spilled from his plant, he
assured the worried James.

Next he was shown the astounding array of complicated
equipment needed to mix and dispense the poisons. And
from there they went into the laboratory where a dozen or
more chemists were at their work with complete concentration. It was creepy. At the central office the best available
computers, slightly ahead of their time, hummed with rele-
vant information about the lives, especially the love lives,
of every known species of insect. Research was leading to
new ways of interfering with the reproductive cycle without
environmental hazard. James imagined tiny little condoms

for termites and locusts. Ultrasound was the wave of the future, his father was explaining. James wondered what his current shrink would think of his father's obsessive need to prevent the birth of baby bugs.

Everywhere his father went he was greeted with respect and affection by his employees, and James was observed with the respectful interest due to the heir apparent. The company had grown to a nationwide concern by that time. Although James knew that he would never follow in his father's footsteps, that a life in business would never satisfy him, he was not above being impressed by his father's accomplishment.

When James was older still, he realized that his father's work had another benefit. It allowed him the anonymity, the privacy, he so greatly valued. Even the snoopiest of tabloid reporters was uninterested in the life of an exterminator. They left Aidan alone, concentrating on his wife's eccentricities and on her real or imagined lovers.

James watched as the boat pulled closer to the high-walled island of San Michele, wondering what, if anything, he would find there. He was the snoopy reporter now. He dropped the last of his flowers into the water, hoping his father would forgive him for this invasion of his private past. And for the attempted invasion of his mistress.

"James!"

"Mara!"

"What are you doing *here*?"

"I'm sorry."

"That was the last thing you said to me last night, now it's the first thing today."

"I mean it."

"What else do you mean?"

"What do *you* mean?"

"Why do you keep following me around? What is it you want from me?"

"I . . . I wasn't following you. I was following the story. You're doing it too. That's why we keep running into each other."

"What are you talking about?"

"The Name of the Son."

"In the name of God, I've had enough of this! I've had enough of you. Why don't you go home and leave me in peace?"

"I will. I promise. I just have to finish what I came here to do. Please, Mara. Can we talk?"

"We are talking."

"I mean . . . about last night. I would like to try to explain."

"This can't be a good time." She looked helplessly around at the tombstones. "This can't be a good place. I'm angry at being taken by surprise again. And I'm angry about last night as well, though I wasn't aware of it until a moment ago, when I saw you step out from behind that hideous angel."

"Please."

"Look, I have no wish to autopsy our tryst. There is nothing to say about it. Nothing at all."

She stood staring, glaring at him. Her mind beginning to run into and after the night before.

"Mara, you're doing something you do sometimes. You're here but you're not here. You're thinking something. It looks terribly important when you do it. But then you don't say what it is you've been thinking. Would you, this time, tell me?"

"I couldn't do that. I could never do that." She appeared frightened at the prospect.

"Why? I so want to get to know you better. If I'd known you better, then maybe last night would have been different. Would you help me to know you?"

"I've never told anyone my thoughts. Not even Aidan. I don't like most of them."

"I would like them. They're yours. They are part of you. Let me know what goes on behind those serious eyes of yours." He reached over to touch her between the eyebrows where the skin was furrowed from thought and worry. She jumped away as if burned.

"Don't touch me!"

"All right," he breathed, knowing now the seriousness of her injuries.

"I can only reveal my thoughts when I'm writing. After I've structured them and given them to a character. Polished them. Censored them. Whatever they need." But he could see that in spite of her protests, she was wavering. She wanted to be known.

"Try, Mara. Just now you started to think about us. Tell me. Uncensored. I won't reject your thoughts, I won't reject you, whatever you think."

She was silent.

"You're wondering if you can trust me. After my behavior last night, you're positive you can't. But even my departure has a logic to it if you take the time to discover it. Can't we try to understand together?"

He guessed that she was gathering her courage. He relaxed a little. She was going to try. Try to be closer. It would be arduous. It would be awkward. It would be worth it. He would make it so. She took a deep breath then.

"We shouldn't have tried," she said. "We're not in love. And we're not casual people. At least, I'm not. Didn't you believe me when I said that your father had been the only man in my life? Does that sound casual? How could you do what you did? How could you climb into my bed and then leave me without a word? I should have kept myself to myself. I shouldn't have pretended that I could be easy. Well, it didn't work out. It's happened to other people before. Doubtless it will happen again. But not to me. I shouldn't have let it happen at all, but for the likeness you bear to Aidan—that was probably wrong of me; and Gwendolyn's crush on you, I can rewrite that; and what seemed to be your interest in me. Were you interested in me? I'm not used to men being interested in me. I'm not used to attention. You were interested in me—in the marketplace and in the gondola. Or were you only interested in him? I thought it was me. That's why I had the courage to throw you the key. And then you didn't come. Do you know what that was like? Do you know what went through my mind? I had visions of your revulsion. I was so ashamed. I had visions of you dead, floating in a canal somewhere. I am ashamed of that, too. And then you *did* come. After I had despaired. After I had finally gotten to sleep. Before I was awake enough to realize you were there, you *were there.* And I felt your hands on me and that was wonderful. You were touching *me,* not the pages of that damned book for once. But then I thought you were not really touching me at all because you had your glove on and I thought maybe you didn't want to touch me, to get your hands dirty on a woman like me . . . and that was an awful feeling . . . hideous . . . but it went away very fast because it felt so good to be touched . . . even with the glove . . . especially with the glove . . . and then with your hand . . . I *felt* things. Can you imagine how powerful a moment's touch is to a woman like me? I suppose not. I haven't been touched in seven years! Do you know every cell in your body changes in seven years? So you could say I've never been touched. You know, I once read a book about babies. Do you know that babies who aren't touched die? *Morasmus* it's called; dying for the lack of touch. I understand that. I've imagined I might die from it. But I'm better off without it. And it said that if a mother doesn't feed a baby when it's hungry, then the baby will hallucinate a breast for itself. Think of that: infants, all those sad little babies . . . hallucinating . . . fantasizing what it is they need! It's what writers do, you know: sitting alone, making up what we haven't got hold of. But can you imagine what a poor hungry hallucinating baby must feel like when Mother finally puts a big beautiful breast right into its wet empty little mouth? What an impact that must make! All that warmth and taste and texture, after all those thin pathetic shifting dreams. That was what you were to me last night—all warmth and taste and texture. And then you were gone. Without a word. That was contemptible. Was I so awful? Was I repulsive because I'm so much older than you? I'm not pretty anymore. Not like that girl I saw you talking to in the Campo Santa Margherita. I used to be pretty. Like that. Before Aidan. I'm not anymore. I'm sorry. Did I do something wrong? Was I inept in some way? You knew I hadn't any sexual experience, except with Aidan. I don't have any idea how much of that sort of thing carries over from one man to another. Couldn't you have taught me? I thought we were doing things right. What didn't I do right? Didn't you know I liked it? Should I have said something? What should I have said? That it felt good? That I wanted more? That I loved you even if I didn't? I didn't. I don't. But even so, even without loving you, it felt right. It *felt* right. To me. But how could I know if it was right for you. It wasn't. I know that now, of course. You made that perfectly clear. You bastard! I'm sorry. Was it so bad for you that you couldn't even speak of it? You crawled across me like I was a big dead fish. You ran away. Ran. Away. After you left me, I felt awful. Don't you care how I feel? I haven't begun to know how I feel. I only know that I don't feel very good about any of it. Or about you. Except a little while ago on Torcello I felt very warmly toward you and I couldn't understand why. And I came here to San Michele to sort out my feelings in this quiet place. Not to see you. What are you doing here? Why are you following me? What do you mean we're following the story in the novel? I don't know what you're talking about. And I don't care anymore. And I don't want to see you, and I certainly don't want to talk about any of it. So there is nothing at all to say. You see, I told you, there is nothing at all to say.''

"Wow!"

"That's what you have to say?''

"Well. It's amazing. All that in your head and you weren't going to share any of it?''

"It's angry and it's ugly.''

"It's real. And I'm the person who made you think all those thoughts. It's right that I should hear them. Right for us. Thank you for telling me.''

"You must hate me now.''

"I don't hate you. I like you better.''

Mara burst into tears.

James stepped forward and took her into his arms, holding her gently while she cried.

"At least this time you are crying about me," he said.

He waited until she began to calm down before he spoke again. "You were wonderful last night. You were wonderful to invite me, and wonderful to be there. You looked wonderful, and you felt wonderful, and you were wonderful to be so willing. I wanted you very, very much. My wanting was in my touch. Couldn't you feel it? Even through the glove I forgot to take off? And then I left you without warning. I'm so sorry. I was a perfect bastard."

"Yes, you were," she sniffed, pulling slightly away. Not all the way, he noticed. He began to feel a little safer.

"Maybe it didn't have anything to do with you—my leaving. Maybe it had to do with me."

"What do you mean?" She was wiping away her tears, and with them, it seemed, her anger.

"Maybe I have a problem—a hang-up."

"Do you?" She seemed taken aback. "I think I thought that you might have some kind of inhibition, but I didn't take myself seriously."

"You should have. I do."

"You should have told me."

"I know. I should take my own advice."

"Is it because I was your father's lover?"

"No. I don't think so. It's happened before. Last night I was feeling anxious, but I thought because you had been so inviting, because you were so lovely, that I would be able. And then, I couldn't. I was too embarrassed. I realized that I hardly knew you. I thought I knew you. Even before I met you I thought I knew you, but I didn't. I had only my fantasy, my hallucination of you; a fiction based on a fiction.

I could talk to that fantasy Mara. I could make love to that fantasy Mara. Maybe. Sometimes. My success depended on the fantasy. But then I was with you, really you, and I was overcome with shyness and then with shame. And now with remorse.''

"I'm sorry." She had thought only of herself. *Selfish.* She should have thought about him.

"Yes. So we're both sorry. Maybe we could sit down somewhere and talk for a little while after all? I'd like to be closer to you. Now that you've taken such a risk with your thoughts.''

"There's only the headstones here. If we go out through that gate to the main part of the cemetery, there are some benches near the monastery.''

"Brother Sebastiano?''

"No such person. But there is a Father Timon with very sticky fingers whom I visit there occasionally.''

"Let's stay here. It's private, and as deserted as you described.''

The air between them now was clear and mild.

"We could sit on your father's grave," she said.

"What!" She watched an appalling look cross his face like a fast-moving cloud shadow blotting a brillant landscape.

"I didn't mean to be disrespectful. I often come here, just to sit and talk to him.''

"Do you mean to tell me that my father is *here*?''

"I thought you knew. Didn't the authorities inform you?''

"Only that, according to them, his remains had been disposed *according to the customary.* Neither Mother nor I inquired further. I suppose that sounds heartless, but, well, he was dead. What did it matter?''

"It mattered to me. He wanted to be cremated and buried at sea. That's what he told me during one particularly long, dreadful night; but he had made no arrangements, nothing was in writing, and the Italians didn't consider my report of his wishes of any value. So he was buried here." She walked a few more steps into the overgrown arrangement of tombstones. James followed her. "He was fortunate to get a spot. The early Venetian Protestants were buried here before the room began to run out. I don't know where they put them now—perhaps out there on the other side of the wall with the Catholics, although it doesn't seem likely. The few remaining spaces here go to people like Aidan: foreigners, non-Catholics, those who die alone in Venice without relations or arrangements. I shall be buried here. Grim, isn't it?"

He surveyed the rundown section of the cemetery in which they walked.

"Yes. It looks like something out of a horror movie."

"There isn't any money for upkeep. The two Protestant churches in Venice are impoverished. Father Timon accepts my donations readily enough, but I think the money ends up as fertilizer, out there in the Catholic flower beds. There's no more room on the island. After twelve years the bones are moved to a boneyard farther out in the lagoon. Unless the grave is endowed. I've endowed Aidan's grave for a hundred years. They can't move him until the money runs out." She stopped suddenly at a relatively well-kept plot that was marked with a white marble headstone. James read the inscription.

AIDAN SA'ID
August 1, 1932–September 24, 1983
Imagination and memory are but one thing

He felt, suddenly, quite overcome, but with what emotion he was unsure.

Mara stooped to brush debris from the grave. A small, disgruntled, green lizard rushed up and over the headstone. "Here," she said, as she sank down upon the grave. "I always imagine he is glad of the company. I think he would be pleased to know that you are here."

James sat down beside her. He felt close to her again, as he had in the gondola, and in the bed. He could hear the rustle of the lizards in the dry leaves all around them. For a while they did not speak.

"So many memories come rushing up from the past," he said.

"What is it that you remember?"

"Shall I tell you?"

She nodded, curious to know what this new place in his life would evoke within him.

"You'll tell me what you think about it?"

"I'll try."

"I'm remembering my mother." Mara was taken aback, but she was determined for the moment to be more concerned with James's needs than with her own. "Don't you think that one of the world's best-kept secrets is how often adult people think about their parents?"

"What was she like, your mother?"

"My real mother? I don't know."

He noticed that she had gone a little pale. "I don't think I remember much about my real mother at all. I think of her as she was in her movies—always beautiful, perfectly dressed, willful, smart. She turned down unflattering parts. I saw all of her films, of course. Sometimes in the movie theatres, sometimes at home, in the screening room where

I could watch my favorites when she was away on location. I suppose I was lonely.

"There was one that was released when I was about twelve, one that held me in a kind of fascinated horror. It was called *What Women Want*. It wasn't as rotten as it sounds, and mother was astonishing in it. Maybe you've seen it?"

"No."

"Anyhow, there was this one love scene that shook everyone up. Me, worst of all. It took place in a dressing room. Mother played a woman who goes backstage in a theatre to seduce the leading man—and she did. The dressing room became an undressing room. The sexual tension built slowly, relentlessly throughout the scene; more and more of her body was exposed. And then there was a heartbreaking fast fade and cut that just barely saved her from pornography—and me from insanity. I watched that film over and over and over, always with growing anxiety at the approach of the love scene, then a terrible embarrassment when it came on screen, and then a kind of numb relief when it was over. I was obsessed with it. I was watching it for maybe the fortieth time when an unexpected thing happened. I was in a second-run house somewhere in downtown Hollywood. It was a seedy, tacky place, and I was sitting alone near the back, absorbed in my anonymous ritual, squirming through the love scene as it neared the climactic moment, when a man sitting near me suddenly stood up. I had noticed him before, at other showings of *What Women Want:* an odd little man, bald but for a few sparse reddish hairs. He was wearing a checked suit. A fan, I had thought. As he jumped to his feet, he yelled an obscenity, and then he threw a rock through the screen. The people sitting next to him screamed and scrambled away. I wasn't afraid of him. He was crazy, I supposed, but a weak, pathetic kind of crazy. I sat back to see what would happen. There was some matching commotion in the projection booth, maybe in response to the melee in the theatre or maybe something else, but just at that moment the film jammed. There, frozen on the screen, twenty times larger than life, was my mother; her bare breasts stared out at the milling audience like two dead eyes—and there, where her throat should have been, was a black, jagged-edged hole. Her expression, caught as it was in pretended passion, appeared agonized to me. I was just as paralyzed as she was. The film, caught in the heat of the projector bulb started to bubble and burn, causing the image on the screen to oscillate and distort. As the film was burned away, the great black hole in the center of the screen turned white and spread outward, wiping the picture away. I sat, staring at the empty space that had been my mother, for what seemed an eternity before I could move. Then I ran from the theatre out into the street, where, in the sudden glare of daylight, I was barely missed by an oncoming car."

Mara had taken his hand sometime during his narrative. He noticed it now, warm, in contrast to his own, which was as cold as marble.

"I wouldn't see her movies for a long time after that. Now that she's dead, I watch them sometimes. But never *What Women Want.*"

"What did he yell?"

"Who?"

"The fan."

" 'Whore!' " She turned to look at him, and he saw concern for him in her eyes. "I've never told that story to anyone."

"Perhaps you needed to tell him."

"Perhaps I needed to tell you."

"What would you like me to understand from your story?" she asked gently.

"That, like you, I sometimes get confused. That, like you, I am more accustomed to illusion than to reality. And that, like you, I am real." He reached over and touched her, just between the eyebrows. This time she did not flinch. She moved her head slightly forward, pressing into his touch.

"I know you're real."

"How do you know?"

"I can feel you." She continued to look into his eyes. Ever so slightly she increased the pressure of her hand. It felt electric; the current, unbroken, ran from his finger down through her body into her hand, into his hand, and back up through him. "Touch," she said. "I think it is touch that stands at the border between fantasy and reality. If I made you up, like the Michael in my novel is made up, I could see you in my mind's eye. Right there, where you are pointing. I could move you around, hear you talk, make you dance. But I could never, ever touch you. As I do now." She moved her other hand tenderly down his arm, along the line of his body. "You're very real to me, James. I'm glad we're real. I'm glad we don't fade out. I'm glad a projectionist can't stop us."

"I don't want to stop." He kissed her then, pushing her gently down onto her back.

"I don't want you to stop either."

He began to loosen her clothing, and she moved to help him.

Whore! "If we do this, will you think I'm a whore?" she asked him between insistent kisses.

"No matter what we do, no matter what you write, I won't think you're a whore." He uncovered her breasts.

"What are we doing?"

"We are making love."

On Aidan's grave! "Here?"

"There isn't enough love in the world, is there? It can't be wrong to make a little more of it."

It is wrong! "But James—"

"Even here. Especially here."

You should be ashamed of yourself. Go away! This is right for him, right for us.

"Will we really be private here?"

"It's after four. The cemetery closes at four." Gwendolyn, please come and help me silence the voices. "No one will come."

"Mara, don't say that. I have some hopes about coming." And he smiled at her. Silence. She smiled back at him. Thank you, Gwendolyn. And she slipped his hand into her jeans. He stopped suddenly. "Will we be able to get out?"

"Yes." Was she really free for a time to give herself to James? Silence. "Yes."

And there, on his father's grave, James began to add a new dimension to his life.

EIGHT

Scuola Grande di San Rocco

"Who's Gwendolyn?"

They were on the vaporetto, moving slowly through the gray evening back toward the heart of Venice. It sat before them like a huge ship sinking into the depths, all indistinguishable lumps and lopsided towers, half in mist, half in water. They stood side by side, closely together, with their arms across each other's backs.

"She is the harrowing heroine of my current work of fiction. She loves you."

"Is she? Does she? Is that harrowing?"

"You know, James, you about drove me crazy with all your chatter about *The Name of the Son*. But now I find I like your interest in my work. People are interested in me sometimes because I write. And occasionally I meet someone, or I get a letter from a fan, who actually enjoys the writing and can discuss it with some intelligence. But to find a man who likes me, and my work—it's unprecedented."

"Aidan?"

"He never read any of my work."

"You mean I've actually gotten somewhere that my father didn't get to first?"

"Yes." He seemed pleased. "By the way, what did you mean when you said we were following the story?" she asked. "I was too angry to care, just at that moment."

"When I arrived, I planned to visit all the places in the book in the same order they were written. I noticed early on that you had begun to do the same. Think where you've been this week."

She did. "Then we must be going to the museum next. Or is it San Rocco? I don't remember."

He smiled. "I enjoy knowing your novel better than you. San Rocco. We'll go tomorrow. All right?" She nodded. "Tell me more about Gwendolyn."

"She's a problematic character. She is difficult to make out—headstrong, impulsive. Much of what she does makes sense only to her. She presents quite a writing challenge. If I say too much, she loses her mystery—too little, and she loses her credibility."

"I would think the more you tell us, the more mystery she would have. I mean, if she's at all like you. Is she?"

"Well, she does things like . . . like what we just did."
She blushed.

"I hope Gwendolyn does them as well as you."

The blush became a warm glow lighting up her features,
as if from the inside. "You were wonderful, James."

"You were wonderful, too. But, as I told you, you were
wonderful last night, so that was no surprise. I think I'll
have to send you flowers on this day of the month, every
month, for the rest of my life."

"When are you leaving?"

"At the end of the book."

"Where will you go?"

"Into the future for a while. I've lived in the past for a
long time."

"I'll miss you."

"What makes you think you'll be given the chance? What
makes you think you won't be going with me?"

"You said you would *send* flowers, not *bring* them. It's all
right."

James noticed that although they were jammed against
the railing of the vaporetto by the strenuous tourists of
Venice, he felt absolutely alone with her. It was this sense
of privacy that she had conveyed in her novel. It was a way
she had of being in the world—alone, or with one person
only.

The boat docked at the back of the city, and they decided
to walk back to the apartment together hand in hand.

"That is where I had the tombstone carved," she told
him, pointing into a small shop full of marble slabs and
dusted everywhere with gray dust. "It's from Hobbes's
Leviathan."

"It's a beautiful inscription. Do you believe it? That memory and imagination are the same?"

"Phantoms, both."

"But surely memory is rooted in reality."

"And where are the roots of reality?"

"In the past."

"And where is the past?"

"Mmm."

"Phantasm. The psychologists tell us that we are formed by our past, that our present being is the result of the twists and turns of our childhood experiences. But where *are* those experiences now? Nowhere. They exist only as memories in our present mind. What if we were to change our minds? Change our memories? I think that if I rewrite my childhood often enough, each time a little better, in time I will become a different person."

"You want to be a different person? Don't you like who you are?"

"Sometimes. Sometimes I hate myself."

"It's wrong to hate yourself."

"That's the wrong I'm trying to rewrite."

"I hope you'll save all the good parts." He pulled her closer. "Seriously, though, the past must be considered real. For instance, the love we made on San Michele—I'm certainly not ready to consign that to fantasy."

"Do you feel it now?"

"I do, Mara."

"I do, too."

"Then we have made something real."

"For as long as it's present."

"I'm glad you are letting me know you, Mara."

"And through me, him?"

He looked surprised. "I'd forgotten about him. Surely he is past."

"A memory. A phantom. We can't touch him."

"He can touch *us.*"

"No, James. You're using a figure of speech. We can't touch him. He can't touch us. We can think of him, bring his image into our mind, and when we do, we feel things. We feel touched from the inside out." And she gave his hand a gentle squeeze.

"I want to touch you again. As I did on San Michele."

"Soon. Tonight. Do you want to stay with me? We could get your things from the hotel."

"All right."

"But let's not go straight home. Let's go to San Rocco this evening. The sooner we get through the old book, the sooner we can write our own."

"Did I come for that?" He wondered aloud. "To be in a novel? It's a kind of immortality, isn't it?"

She didn't answer. Once again he saw the faraway look in her eyes.

"Mara, tell me."

But she would not.

She could not. Suddenly, at the mention of immortality, she was remembering the night, seven years before, when Aidan had died. He had struggled for breath, struggled to hold onto her at the same time. She had tried to leave him, to call for help, but he had fought to keep her in the bed, and she had acquiesced. Should she have done so? Might he have lived a little longer if the doctors had come? There was no way to know. He had fought death differently than her mother had. Sibyl had been weak and only half conscious. Aidan was strong and alert and in agony. He knew exactly what was happening to him as his chest spasmed and exploded, as his lungs filled with something other than air. And he had been enraged. Sweating and thrashing, he had gripped her shoulders until they bruised, trying to hold himself in life. And then he had cried out and died. She had lain for a long time with his weight upon her, staring at a large black and white moth that was clinging to the ceiling. After what seemed a lifetime, the moth had twitched once and fallen to the floor. In the bed there was only her own warmth between Aidan's body and her own. Then, hurting and exhausted, she had climbed out from under him and begun her life without him.

There had been an emptiness carved into the world that night, from which she never thought to escape.

"Mara, you've gone quite pale. Please tell me what you're thinking."

"I can't go through it again, James. I can't. You'd better go back to the hotel. I need to be alone now."

"I won't rush you. I can wait. You needn't talk until you're ready. We needn't make love until you feel safe again. I just want to be with you."

"No."

He couldn't fathom the change. He felt the beginnings of anger like a small animal scratching in his chest. Their lovemaking had made him different. He was vulnerable to her shifting moods in some new way.

"Can you wait to be alone until after we visit San Rocco?" He was playing for time.

"All right." But she seemed to be alone already. She was walking along beside him, but she had gone somewhere untouchable. Her hand was inexplicably cold in his. He let it go.

She led him without conversation or hesitation to the old scuola and, once inside, James, in spite of his distress, was taken aback by the paintings. The cavernous building was badly lit, and a few of the magnificent canvases had been botched in restoration, marring his experience to some extent, but the overall effect was awesome. Tintoretto had painted the whole damned Bible for them. Bigger than life. *This* was immortality.

"Mara, please tell me what has happened." They were standing in the Sala dell'Albergo on the second floor. Tintoretto's masterpiece, the *Crucifixion,* loomed above them. "Why did you suddenly feel that you can't be with me anymore?"

"Some things are better left unsaid."

"Not between us."

"It would be too brutal to speak of it. Why won't you let me protect you, protect us, from my thoughts?"

"I don't need protection from anything that is you."

"You will be hurt. I don't want to hurt you."

"Your silence is the worst hurt of all."

"All right, then," she conceded. "It's on your head."

She led him to the wooden bench that ran around the wall facing the painting. There they sat, and without taking her eyes from the cross, she began to speak.

"I used to dream sometimes that Aidan came back to me. He would arrive with a smile or a frown in some unlikely happenstance—once as an overgrown choirboy, once as a politician, and in one dream he stepped out of the Renoir painting, *Dancing in the Country,* and said to me, 'Welcome to Venice.' Of course, I never thought I would see him in reality. When you arrived, so unexpected, so glorious in the morning sun, I thought for a moment that I was living a dream. Aidan resurrected. Don't you think the whole myth of resurrection must have come into being from the dreams of left-behind lovers? But there is no such thing as resurrection. You are James. I have had a difficult time leaving my imaginary world for you. I have not been graceful. Reaching out and pulling back. Starting and stopping. I'm sorry. I thought for a while . . . in the marketplace . . . and in bed . . . and on San Michele . . . that I could make the leap . . . take the risks that any lover has to take: longing, jealousy, rejection. But I am unable. To live again, to love you, would mean to mourn again. I don't want to watch you die. It is that I cannot do again.''

''Die? Why should I die?''

''I know your father's blood disease was hereditary. You know I know. It's in the novel. When he first told me about the illness, I took the time and trouble to educate myself. It passes from father to son. You have it. You know it. And you know you will die soon. Aidan lived to be fifty. He's the only person known to have lived so long. He was destined to die by thirty, and so are you.''

James was silent for a long time. He was staring at the *Crucifixion.* Christ appeared both in pain and at peace to him.

''I told you it was terrible. I shouldn't have said it. I'm sorry for my weakness.''

Still he was silent, looking, looking into the depth of the painting, its two dimensions made three by genius.

''Mara, I'm not dying.''

''There's no cure.''

''I'm not sick.''

''It's genetic.''

''I'm adopted.''

"No!"

She stood up and stared down at him. She pulled her arm back as if to strike him. And then she fled.

James ran after her, out of the small upstairs room that held the masterpiece, across the upper floor, down the marble stairs and toward the main door. He didn't know why she had bolted. Only her *no* and her footsteps echoed around the empty rooms as they ran through the chapters of sacred history. On the front steps he slipped and fell, rolling painfully down three ungiving steps onto the pavement, where a long-haired boy helped him up. He didn't think she had seen him fall, for she had been well ahead of him when he went down. Now she was lost in the warren of alleyways behind the scuola.

Damn, he thought. Venice is a dreadful city in which to chase a woman. And Mara, though worth the chase, is really a dreadfully troublesome woman.

Nevertheless, he must find her. He had been inside her. He felt warm and confused. There was only one place left to go. The Fondaco dei Turchi. Perhaps she would be there, too. He limped off hopefully.

But the museum was closed.

He started to walk back in the direction of Mara's apartment, stopping on a small bridge to let his thoughts catch up with him. Why had his assurance that he was not going to die caused her to run away? He had expected her to be relieved, happy—for him, for them. Instead, all the color in her face, as though riding outward on her cry, had left her. Could she only love a dying man? What else had he said? The news that one is adopted can be upsetting. He had been shocked and scrambled for a long time after his mother told him that she had not given birth to him, but rather that an agency had given him to her. But what could that remote happenstance mean to Mara? His remarkable, inexplicable likeness to Aidan remained. Perhaps she could only love him for his genes . . . the little flecks of Aidan that she imagined had grown up into James. Damn her. He could make no sense of her.

A gondola slid silently along the canal and beneath the bridge on which he lingered. Here, in this quiet part of the city, far from the eyes of tourists, the gondolier appeared tired. And suddenly James was overcome with his own exhaustion. He turned away then and walked wearily toward his own abode. He had had enough. He needed to rest. He wanted to sleep off the sun of Torcello, the sex of San Michele, and the inexplicable abandonment by Mara in the Scuola Grande di San Rocco.

He wanted to stop wondering how Mara was, where she was, who she was.

He wanted, he realized, to go home.

But where was home?

Mara, having eluded James, walked the short distance to her apartment, determined to escape pain.

She sat with Wally for a while in the gathering darkness, running her hand idly through his soft fur. Aidan did not come. Nor did the persecutory voices. They seemed to attack and berate her only when she moved toward a man, not when she moved away. She didn't know why everything had changed within her, why the thought of James was now intolerable. When she remembered their lovemaking on San Michele, she felt perverse, dirty. There was a smudge of dirt on the sleeve of her silk blouse to prove it. Grave dirt. She went in and showered for a long time in the strange little shower stall with the high window that overlooked the garden.

Outwardly clean, she dressed quickly and packed a suitcase. Then, after stopping in at the convent near the end of the canal where the nuns promised to keep an eye out for Wally until her return, she left the city.

She did not go far. Just far enough out of the novel so that James would not know where to look for her. She took the slow boat along the entire length of the Grand Canal, past the riverbanks of palazzos, now dark, shuttered against the night. The vaporetto then made its sluggish way out across the lagoon to the Lido, and there she checked into the old Hôtel des Bains. The real hotel where the fictional character, Aschenbach, had come to die, dreaming of Tadzio. It was her kind of sanctuary.

She did not unpack her writing. Gwendolyn could die for all she cared.

James awoke in the dead of night, enveloped in flame. He leaped from the bed, thick smoke filling his lungs, before consciousness cleared the air and he was able to lie back down again, without his nightmare.

He often dreamt of fire. He knew his mother's death would haunt him as his grandfather's death had once haunted Aidan. He should have known how fragile she had become, how unhappy. He had been young when the news of his father's death had reached them. He was resilient in his own way. But his mother had never been quite the same again. Estrangement had suited her. Mourning didn't. In the years that followed, she had gone on with her work, of course. But Hollywood was changing, and she was changing, too. The roles were fewer and less flattering as time passed. There had been a man. Not the first. Not a star. A rather pudding-faced psychologist who seemed quiet and quite kind. James was not privy to particulars and so he did not know who had lost interest in whom, but he judged from the depth of her melancholy that it was Renata who had been rejected.

For some time before her death she had complained of feeling unwell, though her complaints were shifting and indeterminate—headaches, shortness of breath, dizzy spells—and could not be diagnosed. He remembered one dark night in New York City, where she was unhappily located for her latest film. James was walking with her on Fifty-seventh Street. It was midwinter, and she was bundled up against cold and recognition, when, with frightening suddenness, she had been subject to a particularly severe asthma attack. He had hurried her into the warm air of a nearby hotel lobby, where she gasped and coughed until he was able to find her inhaler deep in her oversized, over-stuffed bag. He had, in his haste, punctured himself on her nail file and bled into the purse and onto his shirtsleeve. When she had recovered her breath and her heartbeat had returned to normal, she had held his bleeding finger tightly in a handkerchief and spoken to him softly.

"In the moment when you took my arm, James, and led me into this lobby, I saw myself in a preview of my old age. I could not get any air into my lungs and it made me sick. I was cold and stooped and unsteady, afraid I would faint or slip on the ice and go down. I'm only fifty. I look forty. With makeup and the right lights, I can still appear thirty on screen. But in that hard, cold moment I felt eighty. I don't think I can face growing old."

He hadn't taken her seriously. He should have.

Later he heard from her friends that throughout the long winter her depression had grown steadily worse. Back on the West Coast she had become uncharacteristically reclusive. He had been away in France, taking the first of his tentative courses in art history and restoration. On a field trip to Chartres that was part study, mostly pleasure, he had been one of the last to receive the news. He had stopped for a drink and a meal in a smoky little inn near the edge of the quiet village when his mother's picture jumped from the front page of the wrong kind of newspaper, a steady, serious journal that carried news of international interest. Renata Raye's suicide had been spectacular—as befitted her career, some of the more lurid tabloids were to proclaim. First the poison cocktail, then the Molotov cocktail that had sent her remains and her mansion up in sky-soaring flame and smoke.

Homeless and parentless, James had faced the world in the form of the press when he returned to Paris and then to the United States. In very short order he and his mother were old news. But it had taken him the better part of a year to recover his usual good spirits. Friends told him that this was to be expected after such a shocking loss, but because he had known her so vaguely, and because most of what he knew and loved still remained to him, on film, he felt that his mourning took an excessively long time. It was at the end of that gray-black year that he had decided to go on his quest, and at the moment of his decision the world had regained its normal hues.

The sound of the water lapping below his window was comforting after his incendiary dream. The angel stood peacefully at the end of his bed. He closed out women from his mind and so drifted back into quieter sleep.

In the huge, strange hotel room, Mara found she could not sleep. She was unsettled by the absence of her customary evening routines; she missed the company of Wally as he wove his way through the garden's greenery in search of Aidan, finding only memories. Or so she imagined. This aloneness was not a liberating aloneness like the isolation on Torcello. Had she been free only yesterday? Sex changes everything, she thought. This is a crushing loneliness.

She got up and went to the window. The bedroom was located on an upper floor facing the night-shrouded sea. She could hear the gentle waves, smell the salt air. The sea brought her no comfort, though it should. She had read somewhere that it should.

She wondered how James was sleeping. Had sex changed him, too? Until yesterday he had been a technical virgin, or so he had said—many sexual experiences, but no intercourse. Mara had never been technical. She had been a virgin, and then she had not been.

Sex had changed all of her feelings then, too. Sex, she had discovered, was much more powerful but not anywhere near as interesting as she had imagined it to be, in spite of Aidan's expertise. That aspect of their alliance had been both a gratifying surprise and a stunning disappointment. She had imagined the pleasurable intertwining of bodies as a magnificent art form of infinite possibility. An erotic *pas de deux*. A free-fall through sensuous skies. A deep dive into the soundless depths of bliss. Her mind wove variations of ecstasy. Aidan played, albeit beautifully, only the major themes. But the shock of his touch, the closeness of his body, the movements of muscle and breath, the rough masculinity of him even in tenderness—these were better in reality than in imagination. And because she loved him, the simplest touch was pleasurable. Perhaps gymnastics were for the less in love. Now, she knew, she merged her exotic fantasies with the more mundane memories of their lovemaking. In gracefully retouched retrospect, their sex had become exceptional.

Similarly, the sex on San Michele had been exciting in content, but not in form. She and James had made simple, furtive choices, no doubt determined by time and place. Except for the lizard that ran up her leg, their lovemaking had been ordinary in its organization. She laughed as she remembered the lizard. How shocked James had been to look up from her warm thigh to find himself eye to eye with the cold-blooded little beast.

Her sexual experiences were, on consideration, not much different than the rest of her contacts with *real* life—powerful in their sensual impact, but much less creative than she could arrange in her mind. For instance, what would she have done with that lizard? She laughed again as the ideas came. Gwendolyn would never forgive her. Her readers would squirm a little, and read on with more ruthlessness. But James had merely brushed it away. She could forgive him on the grounds of his inexperience. But so, she thought, would Aidan, and he had accrued experience past calculation. Perhaps the lack of interest in sexual experimentation was hereditary. A family trait toward the commonplace.

Oh, but they weren't related after all! James had said he was an adopted son. If this were true, the resemblance was shocking. How, she wondered, did he explain his appearance to himself? She would never know. By the time she returned to her home, he would be gone. He would go to that awful museum in the Fondaco dei Turchi and then come to find her in the garden—and then, when she didn't turn up, he would leave. End of book. End of story. He had found what he was looking for, no doubt. His sexuality. Such as it was.

And what was to become of her? She didn't appreciate being opened up again, reminded of the textures of love. Thankfully, she had escaped the rest of the terrible slide into the jaws of jealousy and despair. The thought of embracing James again was abhorrent. When had that happened? On their walk to San Rocco, when she recalled his father's death, she had pulled back from him in a kind of anticipatory fear, but it was the news of his good health that had shocked her into full retreat. Perhaps it was only the illusion of Aidan's resurrection, his reassemblance, that had drawn her into the arms of James. Would she be punished? What was she facing now? Would she be alone again or would her betrayal of Aidan usher in a grand era of unloved lovers? She did not know. She did not know what to think. She did not know what to do.

She could write. She could gather up the recent rearousal from her body, harvest the reawakened feelings from her spirit, store them up in the silo of her mind and, when

needed, pitch them back out into her work. But for whom?
Her sigh of submission melted into the sea sounds outside
her window. Resigned, she removed her manuscript from
the bottom of her suitcase. Gwendolyn was waiting. She
was feeling friendly toward Gwendolyn at the moment for
her help on San Michele. Perhaps she deserves an adventure, thought Mara. So, pen in hand, she prepared to explore the erotic possibilities of love among the lizards.

Waking at dawn, James decided he would go to church. If
woman would have him, why not God? As he brushed his
teeth and trimmed his beard, he realized he was very, very
confused. Why did Aidan's face look back at him from the
mirror? A good match on the part of the agency? The small
genetic pool of Arab families? What kind of Arab family
gave up a son for adoption anyhow? There was no one left
to ask. He understood his parents' choice—not to have
children of their own. They had not wanted to pass along
the deadly gene. In that, they had been successful. As if to
spite his childhood frailty, he had grown up healthy as a
horse, with a determination to live to be a hundred. His
emotional frailty seemed now to be mended as well. That
had taken someone from outside the family. Mara.

He wanted to be with her again.

Now what was he to do about all that? After the sex he
was sure he had fallen in love with her. Now he was sure
he was not. It seemed to him that she had stepped from the
pages of the novel to do his bidding, and now he found
himself left with her, unplotted. He would have to write her

in or out of his life in some way that made stylistic sense for them both. He nicked himself with the razor.

He wanted to be with her again.

Holding a tissue to his cheek, he went to the window and looked down into the granular green water of the canal. The color of Mira's eyes. He thought about sex. A natural mystery, a greater mystery than God. Why then, why there? He had felt the strange power seize him in the cemetery— the force that had led him to Venice, that had possessed him in the apartment with Mara and on San Michele, determined to make a man of him—it seemed to push upward through the earth itself. He knew there was an explanation, a psychological force, an inspired fantasy at work within him. Empowered, he had kissed her and touched her and kissed her ever more intimately and touched her ever more intimately and entered her and moved within her and left her, spent. He had done it all very well. Perfectly, but for the lizard. But he had so gracefully brushed it from her thigh that she probably hadn't even noticed the momentary distraction. He thought. Had she laughed? No.

He knew, in spite of her erratic behavior, that she must be very appreciative of his efforts, after so many years of celibacy. Perhaps it was their sexual success that lay behind her need for flight. It was possible that she feared some form of emotional dependence after their erotic encounter. He decided fear was the most likely explanation for her sudden change of heart. He was glad that he was not frightened. He was sure now that his phobia was a thing of the past—a memory, a phantom, a dead thing no longer in existence—and that he was free to go forward, in and out of other adventures. It would be appalling to find himself dependent on Mara for continued sexual success. The thought was chilling, and he quickly dismissed it. He would not fear the ghost of inhibitions past.

He wanted to be with her again.

It had seemed right, a matter of course, for him to fall in love with her after making love to her. What had she said? We are not casual people. That was true. They had talked quietly together for a time, upon the grass, among the leaves; and then, at the sound of evensong, dressed hurriedly. As the bells rang from the church tower, they had left the island on the last boat.

Now he found that all the unexpected turmoil on their homeward journey had left him—even in the new light of morning—disgruntled.

Even so, he wanted to be with her again.

He changed his mind about going to church. He would go to the museum according to plan, and then to her apartment. They would sit in the garden, with Wally and the winged creatures of the evening. They would talk again of their lives. Sunset would come. Sense would be made of nonsense. She would come around. The years of her abstinence would work on their behalf. He would reach out to her with a tender gesture and make of himself her reality. He would be with her again. Then, tearfully, they would part. Or decide to get married. He hadn't the least idea how these things turned out.

Mara walked along the empty beach. Here, in the seashell-colored dawn, the usually bustling Lido was bereft of the tribes of tourists who would, later in the day, inhabit the rows of rented seaside shacks—the cabanas, as the beastly hot, ugly, tin boxes were called. She wondered why people did that. What were the pleasures of perspiring proximity? She stretched out her arms, enjoying the space and the solitude.

She stopped and watched the sea where small lumps of water shuffled about, trying without success to turn into waves. The sand underfoot was cool and slightly soggy. She thought she should throw herself into the sea, but then remembered that the water here was badly polluted. She was not suicidal. She just wanted something to happen. She just wanted something to change. She wanted something to enter her life in a way that brought transformation, not tribulation. She wanted to be swept up, swept away, tossed on currents of light and air. James had only weighed her down. It was discouraging.

She waded into the foamy edges of the water, then, having had enough of the elements, she turned around abruptly and began to make her way back across the sand to her hotel. It was then that she saw him, alone—a familiar figure far off down the beach. The experience was entirely different this time. There was no shock in it. No surprise. He turned slowly and looked at her. She at him. He did not look young or especially strong. But he did look confident. As if, in spite of all reason, he had every right to be there. She stood unmoving. He did not approach. She knew the distance was necessary. She did not know how she knew.

She took him in with her eyes for a long time. He was a sight that made all of life worth living, and removed all fear of dying. She could sense the acceptance in him. "It's all right then, about James?" she asked him, speaking softly, knowing he would hear her. He nodded. "He's not . . .

ours?" Again he reassured her. She wished she was close enough to see his rare, good smile. Close enough to touch. "There will never be anyone else," she whispered.

But, of course, they both knew that.

James looked at the uneven stitching up the belly of the dead, stuffed water rat and felt slightly ill. The Museum of Natural History in the Fondaco dei Turchi was gruesome. He went around stoically, noting all the nasty details of chapter nine: the crocodile, the African spears, the grizzly little dead man in the glass case. What was he doing in this beastly place? Life had leaked out of his quest. He was just going through the motions now. He decided to leave the museum as quickly as possible and go have it out with Mara.

It was then that he was seized with the notion that he was being followed. He listened, but could not detect footsteps. The museum was empty at this early hour but for the overweight lady on the ground floor who had both sold and then taken back his admission ticket. But he was filled with the certainty that he was being watched. He had never felt this feeling before, though he had read about it. It was uncanny. He walked into the next room and stepped carefully out of sight around the corner. He found himself in a rather long, narrow exhibition hall full of stuffed seabirds. There was no sound. Nothing moved. Yet he expected the appearance of his pursuer momentarily. Who could it be? Perhaps it was Mara. She was the only one who knew his itinerary. Impatient, he leaned his head back around the corner, but the room behind him was vacant. He walked on, unsure of the way back out. On either side of him were glass cases containing rows of mounted bugs.

The knowledge came to him on a wave of shock. He stood, trying to sense the presence that, unseen, stalked him in this place. It was a quiet person, masculine, sad. It was his father. It wasn't possible, yet he was sure of it. Could there be ghosts? Who did he think he was, Hamlet? The feeling was familiar—a variation of the powerful emanation he had felt most recently and most strongly in the graveyard. Had he gone mad? Mara had said that she sometimes felt Aidan's presence, but he had taken that to mean some strong mixture of memory and imagination would, in times of need, collude with her consciousness. This present sensation felt external to himself, though perceived with his intuition only.

It came closer.

He started to sweat and then his knees went weak. He sank down until he was sitting on the floor, his back pressed to the wall. His heart was pounding wildly, causing his head to throb and his eyes to focus and unfocus in a steady pulsation. What was his father trying to tell him? What was it that he needed to know? His mouth was dry with fear and he felt nauseated again. Was he ill? A black doubt entered his mind. Maybe he was not adopted. Maybe his mother had lied. Maybe he was ill with his father's illness after all. Was this what his father had come to tell him? The room began to turn and grow dark. The presence was directly overhead. He forced himself to look up.

What he saw were the butterflies, untouchable, mounted inside the dusty glass cases on the opposite wall. Their fragile wings seemed to be beating slightly, up and down, up and down, in rhythm with his own heart. James watched them in amazement. Up and down, up and down, went the tiny, gloriously colored wings, banishing his fear.

He sat in communion for a while.

"I love you, Father," said James. "I wanted to be with you again." Then he slipped softly into unconsciousness.

The speedboat, as if held up by wings, skimmed across the lagoon like a giant dragonfly. Mara, elated, sucked in the unusual sensations of speed.

She was on her way home.

Her novel was done.

Her second novel. Was. The second novel. Done.

The arc of the Gwendolyn stories had melted and merged into a beautiful new shape. The shape of the past two weeks had been lost altogether as nights and days ran into one long orgy of work at the Hotel des Bains. She was returning from her labors, tired but satisfied. She had written out the entire book in careful, legible longhand in deep blue-purple ink. She now looked forward to the hypnotic task of transcription and the simple, pleasurable puzzles of the rewriting.

She was happy. Happiness had made her feel homesick again. It was an intense, bittersweet sensation now. The open, ornate apartment would be a welcome sight after the days surrounded in staid decor. Wally would be waiting and he would greet her with great good cheer. Wally would be glad to say good-bye to the nuns—however sacred their hearts—and return to his scandalous life with Mara as housekeeper. She would feed him something special, and then take her typewriter out to the garden, where the essence of the day would enter into her work.

A spray of water catapulted over the windshield, covering her and the boatman with wetness and laughter. She glanced at the suitcase that held the novel. It was safely tucked into the dry hold of the boat. They were heading across the basin toward the channel between Dorsoduro and La Giudecca, the logical way to the back canals of Santa Croce, so she redirected the driver, suggesting the longer, slower journey along the Grand Canal. The sunny, sunburned man shrugged and cut the engines to a safer speed, turning the boat in the direction of main street.

Mara stepped back and sat down, enjoying the sights inside the boat and out. As they passed beneath the Accademia Bridge, she looked up and remembered herself standing there not long ago, furious with James for his accusation of plagiarism, struggling with Gwendolyn's desire for a dramatic leap into the canal. She almost expected to hear the impetuous female plop into the water alongside the boat. But, of course, Gwendolyn was no more. As they neared the Rialto, she began to think more seriously of what was awaiting her.

The ideas that had overtaken her on the Lido and the long hours of hard work had strengthened her. Her flight from James now seemed weak and wrongheaded to Mara. What had she feared? In the unlikely event that he had remained in Venice, and if he came looking for her, she would deal with him. She would invite him in or send him away, according to the dictates of the moment. Her dictates. Her moment. How quickly, how thoroughly, a man could take you over, she thought. While you are pleasantly distracted with their beautiful profiles or the hairline on the back of their necks, they picked up your autonomy and hurled it heavenward into the tumultuous winds of emotional involvement. She would not be so careless again.

The boat slowed once again as they passed the steps of Ferrovia. Mara watched the newly arrived passengers as they stepped from the dry-landed station of train tracks and ticket booths out into the wet world of wallowing gondolas. You could tell the first-time tourists from the sudden change in their faces. Their chins dropped.

Mara's attention was caught by the struggles of a man working his way up the station steps with two large suitcases. He gave the impression that the bulky cases enclosed gravity itself. Leaving Venice was never as easy as arriving, she mused. There was something familiar in his movements. An awkwardness. Then she saw. It was James. She was near enough to call out. She didn't. A baggage handler approached and took the bags from him. Enlightened, he stopped and turned to survey the city. She could see the movement of his shoulders as he sighed. He did not see her. He turned back and followed his luggage into the station.

Mara leaned back against the cushioned seat of the motorboat. The chapter of her life entitled James was over.

James tipped the porter and checked his bags into the left luggage bins. The dirty, diesely smell of the trains reminded him of the natural world beyond the waterlines of Venice. He looked forward to the great religious art treasures of Rome. They would restore him. And someday he would restore them.

The previous two weeks had been weird. He had taken long contemplative walks through all the art of Venice and he had slept deep regenerative sleeps. He had attended church daily. There, the familiar rituals had begun to sound a new, soul-felt, music within him, for he now knew that he was part of the mystery and that he was surrounded in miracles, of which a museum of natural history could contain but a few. Periodically he would stake out Mara's apartment. Usually Wally joined him on the floorboards of the borrowed rowboat to indulge in a little stolen affection. Their three eyes would stare collectively at Mara's closed front door for an hour or two, then Wally would reluctantly return to the sanctuary of the convent courtyard and James would row back to his hotel.

Time had run out. His appointment at the institute in Rome could not be postponed. He could come back, of course, but he knew it would not be the same. His last encounter with Mara belonged to this journey.

He went to buy his ticket.

He glanced at his watch.
Damn Mara!

The motor taxi pulled up in front of her apartment house and Mara stepped up to the *fondamenta* with relief. Now that she had seen James depart from Venice, home was sanctuary. The driver lifted her suitcase up and over the side of the boat to her. As Mara reached for the handle she noticed his hand in the driving glove, strong and brown, the palms and lower fingers covered with soft kid leather, the fingertips bare, and her heart clenched suddenly in unexpected longing for James. The spasm may have caused her to falter, or it may have been a sudden swell engendered by a passing vegetable barge that gave the small craft a lurch; whatever happened, it happened too fast for Mara to be certain, but just as the boatman released his grip upon the handle and before Mara's hand was firmly in place, the suitcase fell heavily between their outstretched arms into the canal. It splashed down and then floated uncertainly, half in and half out of the water. Before Mara or the driver had time to react, another swell caused the taxi to crash toward the *fondamenta,* crushing the suitcase between the boat and the wall. Mara saw the crack appear in the case and watched, horrified, as it quickly filled with water.

"My novel!" she cried, as it sank out of sight.

"Signorina . . ." The boatman prepared to leap into the canal.

"Never mind." She knew it was lost. She ran for the apartment. Once inside the entrance hall she leaned against the heavy door and in semidarkness she began to cry. There was no saving it, of course. Had it been typewritten, maybe. But the work of the past three years, magnificently enlarged, beautifully synthesized, and carefully copied over onto the thin blue-lined, yellow sheets, was now nothing more than disintegrating paper and currents of purple-blue ink.

She stumbled into the kitchen and, still sobbing, began to prepare some coffee. She could reconstruct some of the book, maybe most of it, in time. But it would never be the same. The inspiration of the previous weeks would not come again. Some patched-up, sewn-together version of the book would appear some day, she supposed. But the heart of it, the soul of it, would be missing.

The doorbell rang.

She thought it must be the postman with the accumulated mail of the last two weeks. As she made her way to the front door, she tried to dry her tears, but they kept coming. Oh, what did it matter! She opened the door and James stood before her. Through her tears he appeared to be drenched.

"There may be time to save it," he cried as he made his way past her, dripping and slipping, through the apartment. He was indeed soaking wet. "Hurry!" He was clutching her muddy suitcase to his chest.

He ran out of the apartment into the back garden and tore open the case. Throwing soggy clothing aside, he pulled out the ruined manuscript. It was, as she had feared, unreadable. Without wasting any movement, he reached for the garden hose, turned it on and adjusted the head to a fine spray.

"What are you doing?"

"Do you have any clothesline? Clothespins?"

"Yes, in the shed."

"Get them. String up as much of the line as you have. I'll hand you the sheets. Pin them up. Don't let them overlap or they'll stick together."

She did as she was told. And for a few minutes they worked silently, urgently, together. One by one he peeled off the sheets, sprayed off the smears of ink and mud, and passed them to her.

After about fifty of the blank pages were fluttering uselessly in the sunlight, she could contain herself no longer. "James, this is pointless. There is nothing on the pages. I can't read a word."

"I'll explain later. When I'm done. I need to concentrate now. Meantime, when the pages are dry—be sure they are completely dry—you can take them down to make room for more. You'll have to put something heavy on them so they won't curl up too badly."

An hour later the task was accomplished.

"Could I have some of the coffee I've been smelling?" he asked, looking up from the work for the first time. "And a towel?" He was almost dry, but he used the towel to remove the bits of mud and canal debris that clung to his clothing and hair. "Thanks."

She looked at him full of questioning that barely masked her despair.

He smiled. "Have you any lemon?"

"For coffee?"

"For restoration. I need a spray bottle, too. Like one you would use for ironing or cleaning windows, and a candle, and some matches."

Without questioning him further, she went to get the things he had requested. He was clearly doing whatever it was he was doing in his own way, in his own time.

"Now watch," he instructed, "first the mixture . . ." He mixed some lemon juice with some water and poured it into the spray bottle. He sprayed the mixture lightly over the surface of one of the dried pages. ". . . then the flame." He blew gently on the paper until, once again, it had dried, then lit the candle and moved its flame close to the surface. Slowly, as the searing heat scorched the paper, her handwriting, now a light brown in color, began to appear. "There," he said, smiling with satisfaction, "it will be tedious work, but you'll have it all. The lemon juice will adhere in the creases made by the force of your pen into the paper. Be careful not to hold the candle too close to the paper or it will go up in flames. You'll get the right distance with a little practice."

"I don't know how to thank you."

"You already have," he said, looking deeply into her eyes, recalling the intimacy on San Michele. "I'm just glad I came back for one more try at saying good-bye. I'm on my way to Rome. I've decided to study there in the hope of working in the Vatican collection someday. I feel at last . . . a vocation."

She looked down at the fragile paper he had placed in her hand. "God, if there is a God, bless you, James."

"There is. He does. What is it called, your new novel?"

"It's called *The Name of the Father.*"

"Well done, Mara. I wish you every success."

There was a formality in his reply that seemed to settle over them, making her feel suddenly ill at ease, anxious to have done with the parting.

He looked himself over. "What a mess," he declared. "But there is no help for it. My train leaves in fifteen minutes. I'll have to restore myself in Rome. Good-bye,

Mara. I know as I look back on us, through time, I will begin to love you. Perhaps I already do. The more time there is to look back through, the more love I will feel. When I'm filled with love, shall I come back and see how we fare together? I will want to be with you again."

The formality was dispelled and her mind flooded with vivid imaginings. She could not think clearly. She had no idea how to reply.

She knew exactly how she felt. She reached out and took his hand, enjoying the feel of the familiar skin, now softened by the hours of work in the water. She drew him near her and they shared a tender kiss. There was more in the kiss than friends would share; less than lovers.

"What a wonderful kiss," he pronounced. "I would like another one of those some day." Then he backed away. "Good luck with the work, Mara. Send me an autographed copy."

"I will."

"Say farewell to Wally for me."

"You can say so yourself." She pointed upward to the beam where he was perched like an owl.

"So long, old boy. Keep your eye peeled for my return." Wally swung his tail in friendly response.

James was at the front door. "Say good-bye to Gwendolyn for me."

"I can't. There is no Gwendolyn. I've changed her name."

"You have? To what?"

"To Mara. What does it matter?"

"It matters to me."

And he was gone. The heavy door closed behind him. Mara walked slowly back into the garden and watched the pages drying gently in the breeze. Wally followed her out and leaped up onto the wall, where he stretched out in his rightful place in the sun.

She was exhausted, but she knew she could not rest until the lengthy task that loomed before her was put, like a shadow, behind her. She rolled up the sleeves of her mind and went to work with the mental muscle she had developed on the Lido.

Epilogue

It was a week later when Mara once again finished *The Name of the Father*. She had slept little and eaten less, but she was, in the moment of its completion, revived and refreshed by the sight of the neatly typed pages. Her first task was to take the carbon copy to the convent, in a plain brown wrapper, where the nuns agreed to keep it in a safe place. The hand-written copy—drowned and dried and sprayed and scorched—she put in the bottom drawer of the claw-footed dresser alongside Aidan's neatly folded shirts and the old notes that he had made for the book he was working on when he died. Then she wrapped the original and addressed it to her editor in New York. She would hand it to the postman the next day.

She poured herself a glass of wine and sat down on the velvet couch to rest. Wally was darting about after a fly. "As flies to wanton one-eyed cats are we to the gods," she mused, but Wally refused distraction from his prey. Her eyes wandered around the familiar room, catching on the spine of a book tucked amidst the others on her bookshelf. She got up and took down the volume—the first novel: *The Name of the Son,* the book that had brought James into her life; and into her heart and mind and body.

She stared at the cover of the book. What world lay within? It had been seven years since last she looked. *Memory and imagination are but one thing,* she thought.

And then she opened the book.

THE NAME OF THE SON

by Bess Arden

FOR MY SON, MICHAEL

*It is a wise child
who knows his own father.*

—

HOMER

ONE

❦

The

Arrival

had come to Venice, not to die like stodgy old Aschenbach, but to refind in self-sought exile, to recapture in self-imposed celibacy, my long ago lost love of woman. I would die soon. The doctors assured me of my impending death (if such news could be called assurance), but I was determined to die at home, in New York City, in my own apartment, in my own brass bed, in love with, but if not so, nevertheless inside of, a passionate woman, who, at the moment of my breathless demise, would discover that life could suddenly become very heavy. I had always intended to ejaculate into eternity.

Now, only a few months after my arrival, I stand, alive, alone, in love, here in the small brick-walled garden behind my Venetian apartment. There are gardenias at my feet. I stand here now as I did on the day of my arrival, though I was certainly not in love then. The gardenias had not yet bloomed. Let me tell you the story of these summer months, so different from all that I had planned. Let me tell you of my life, however short, in Venice . . .

It was late afternoon on the third day of June when I first made my way into this garden. I stood, breathing deeply, savoring the peculiar, damp, spiced air of this exotic city. The deliciously mingled atmospheres of East and West, the strange miasma of foreign culture was a comfort to me, and thus coddled, I allowed myself to feel the fatigue of my long journey.

The previous evening I had set out from New York, leaving my hectic business office in Nell's capable hands. Nails, I call her. I trust her. She was once my lover, and left-behind lovers always have something to prove. In her case, competency, she thinks. But she's wrong. It was tenderness she lacked, though I will never tell her so and risk the ruin of my office, which has never run better. I kissed it, and her, good-bye without an iota of regret.

A swarthy terrorist-in-training disguised as a taxi driver drove me to the airport in, or more precisely, in spite of, the angry rush hour traffic. At the departure gate I felt worn out before I started out, and I hoped for a smooth flight. I dislike turbulence.

My mind, on the turbulent voyage to the end of its life, needed a place conducive to contemplation. The actual decision to go had been made in a cheerless coffee shop in midtown Manhattan, where I had retreated to warm myself after a chilling encounter with Sonia. I was sitting quietly with a rather nasty cup of coffee, nursing a chest tight with unhappy sensations, when I noticed an attractive woman making her way through the tables in my direction. She was of a type I would have once been drawn to. Lively, open good looks with a strength in her well-proportioned, youthful body. She was preparing to sit at a nearby table when without warning the short, mean-faced proprietor began to shout at her for failing to close the rest-room door. "Careless bitch," he had yelled, "whore!" And worse. In the heat of the unexpected attack, so crazy and so venomous, the face of the woman turned waxen and seemed to melt away, leaving only wide, hollow ghost eyes staring around the restaurant, dragging below them the ruins of her form and features. She seemed to have forgotten where she was. I waited for her to rally—to spring to life and fight back like a hardy New Yorker—but instead she turned and hastened to the door, taking half of her humiliation with her, leaving the rest to drift across the remaining patrons like a toxic cloud. Because I had failed to intervene, because I had not gone after her with offers of solace and comfort, because I had remained, impotently sitting—blindly staring, silently criticizing *her,* as well as *him*—I knew that something was broken inside me. I felt I had to get away, and I followed her out of the coffee shop on the first step of my journey. She was long gone, of course.

It was strange to think I would never see this hapless woman again. She would never know me. She would never know that she had reset the course of my life. She would lick her bitter wounds alone or recriminate with her cronies, while I, unbeknownst to her, went home, and told Sonia, and packed my bags. I would leave America. I would go to Europe, where a patina of civilization still coated the thin, beaten surface of daily life. I wanted to immerse myself in the oldest, most worn and tired of cultures. And I wanted to be alone.

"Italy!" Sonia protested when she heard of my plan. "What kind of a place is Italy? If you vote the wrong way they'll shoot you in the knees." She was wearing a Batman T-shirt, a black wing beating on each tiny breast.

"Venice isn't Italy," I responded, feeling dead calmness for the first time in a long time in the face of her. "It was a republic for a half-dozen centuries before Columbus bothered to be born. And I'll be visiting, not voting."

"Communist!"

"At least in Italy there is a wrong vote." What was I doing in another pointless argument? It was suicidal.

"You've never forgiven me for my father," she declared. Her father is a senator. When I failed to take the bait, she snorted and left the room.

I left the country.

I wasn't a communist. I didn't know what I was anymore. I had never felt comfortable in America, though I was born on the outskirts of Austin. My parents were from Lebanon, by way of France. They were quiet, Christian, desert-seeking people. The hot, dry vastness of Texas swallowed them up and spit me out. My name is Aidan Sa'id and I do better in cities.

For the last twenty years I have lived virtually, if not virtuously, in Times Square, on the top floor of a hotel converted into a residence for theatre people: actors who wait tables, aging dancers, magicians who have failed to materialize their own success, cat ladies who were once chorus girls, and diligent unknown writers. They endlessly amuse me and unfailingly irritate Sonia. When we could afford a second apartment, I bought one for us on the Upper East Side, where she calmed down for a while and I shriveled up with boredom. I soon went back to the hotel for the majority of my living, leaving Sonia to her own vices and devices for long stretches of time. We were not separated, but apart. I have often been happy, in my way, at the hotel, though I am referred to by the other tenants as "the dark at the top of the stairs," in response to a naturally serious countenance—or, perhaps, as some creative form of prejudice. I have very dark skin, a great scything nose that precedes me into trouble; and my hair and beard, though carefully trimmed, are Arab-curly. Taken together, my visage suggests a barbaric character. I am a gentle man by nature, but in the occasional rage—usually with the landlord on behalf of the rent-besieged tenants—I don camel's-hair robes and call upon my looks to appear ferocious, like a wrathful, tribal princeling. It was time to leave my fabulous and forlorn neighbors to their imaginary lives for a while, to discover if there was anything real in my own.

On board the plane I was forced to slide my lanky body over the legs of an unaccommodating couple who were four knees deep into a private argument. I was not comfortable flying this tightly packed. In better times I flew business class, but now doctors and lawyers fly first on my nickel and I, in an ill-considered decision to economize, had put myself into coach. I worried about the ambiance of the flight ahead. I dislike the proximity of strangers.

The man seated next to me appeared to be about seventy. He was a prim, soft-spoken being with a cultivated New

England accent. I liked him. He was being badly embarrassed by the behavior of his younger, angrier wife. She was fighting with him, and with a succession of flight attendants, over the continued possession of an oversized, overstuffed carry-on bag. The woman raucously opposed its removal from her lap up into an overhead compartment, while her husband became noticeably smaller and redder. I wondered how these two antipodean creatures had mated in the first place.

The agitated man suddenly turned to me as if he had read my mind, and spoke rapidly, angrily, under his breath. "I was a bachelor until I was fifty," he said, as his distracted wife, having lost the battle of the bag, began to remove various revolting items from its depths. The man continued his alarming confession: "The priests say that when you marry, the two of you become one. But the priests don't know dick about it!" The woman pulled out a pair of rubber thongs and bent to put them on while the bag was being stowed away. "Nothing could be further from the truth." He was silenced then as his wife sat up abruptly and began to complain about the choice of in-flight movie.

I was blackly amused. Had the man flunked first grade? Everyone knew that one and one made two, and usually a miserable two. Look around. Certainly you should know it by fifty. I am fifty. For a moment I felt sorry for the poor, duped Catholic. Why had he succumbed to matrimony so late in life? Had he fallen in love? With her? There was no accounting for love. Look what love has done to me. Most likely the loneliness had gotten to him.

Men and women, I thought. Men and women. I was glad to step out for a while. There would be no woman to abuse or confuse me in Venice. No mother, grandma, auntie, cousin. No playmate, girlfriend, lover, mistress, wife. I couldn't recall a single significant moment in my fifty years when I had not been concerned with them—how they looked, what they thought, what they did, what they thought of me, what they didn't think, what they didn't do to my mind, to my body. And I had begun to resent them, resent the hold they had upon me. I was escaping from all of them now. No new fantasies, anticipations, longings, dreads, excitements, woes, or regrets would plague me. I would blind myself if I had to. Live as a monk. Surround myself in solitude. Think of myself alone. Alone, maybe I would find my own ironic way back to the joy of them— simply remember what all the fuss had been about.

The seat belt sign flashed on. I was off.

Fortunately, the flight didn't lend itself to further conversation because, unfortunately, it was turbulent. As the plane twisted and turned toward Europe, I withdrew into myself, the woman threw up over herself, and the old man was left as lonely as ever.

I was greedy for fresh air and needy of sleep when we finally landed, smoothly, thankfully, in Milan. I dozed fitfully on the bus to the train and on the train to Venice, waking to the sight of passing fig trees and the curving gray-green vineyards of Lombardy. Awake, I worried. Why had my life turned out so dismally different from my youthful imaginings? Why had my work gone so stale? I'm the best theatrical manager in the business, and I was no longer able to get through an opening night without being bullied by boredom. A hit . . . a flop . . . every show was a show and closed when it did, and what did it matter?

And when had I begun to notice that everything broke? Suddenly it seemed that there was nothing I owned, nothing I cared for, that wasn't cracked or chipped or marred or stained; snagged, stretched, dented, peeled, or disintegrating. When had I begun my futile search for repair? When had I begun to hunt again for the fresh young females, all of whom failed to restore me, while Sonia and I struggled through all the requisite tortures—the confrontations, separations, reconciliations, the long serious mind-numbing talks?

And, in the midst of the turmoil, the physicians' decrees: "You are going to die," they said kindly. "Avoid stress."

It was dangerous to give a damn about Sonia, but I did. I do.

I was hot and depressed and irritable when the train finally arrived in Venice. I emerged from the noisy station out onto the steps covered in tourists and sunlight, and I stood awestruck, looking out over the Grand Canal. It was then I remembered why I had traveled so far, so urgently.

As the glittering, watery magic of the city rose to meet me, I realized that this fantastic floating miracle could never be imagined before you saw it, or fully believed while you were in it, or remembered accurately when you left it. Venice exists magnificently apart from the everyday consciousness that comes and goes, here and there, in ordinary reality. Venice would not go with you, but waited, patiently, to open herself to you in a triumphant and glorious welcome upon your return.

Revived, full of the pleasure of reunion, I found the right quay and crowded myself onto a churning vaporetto. I was deposited one stop later, at the Piazzale Roma, within easy walking distance of the apartment.

I followed the intricate map over three small bridges and, turning right, I found myself on the designated *fondamenta* of a sleepy canal: the Rio Santa Maria Maggiore, a grand name for such a small tributary. A huge stone gargoyle on the corner house caught my attention—a gray, angry face full of warning. It made me laugh.

I had rented the apartment sight unseen. The description had been satisfactory and the terms of the rental were favorable. I was to look after a small garden. The thought delighted me. The neighborhood in which I found myself was quiet, seedy, working class. Pale paint—yellow, pink, rose—peeled from the facades of the canal houses that stood, baking, in an unbroken row, three stories high and a few feet back from the bottle-green canal. A collection of small boats, including one blackly gleaming gondola, bobbed just below the level of the sidewalk. Desultory pigeons, sacred in Venice, poked about without much reward along the pavement, while above them, on a flower-bedecked window ledge, a caged bird sang a fat, sad song of captivity. Everything seemed quiet, tentative, expectant.

I found the right number, noticing, just outside my door, a tough, rubbery weed topped with a yellow flower that pushed itself up through the cracked concrete in a wild, forlorn attempt to retake the city for nature.

I entered the shuttered building through a heavy wooden door, pleased by the shine of the big, brass lion's head door knocker, and found myself in a large common entrance hall of white stucco with a rose marble floor. Straight ahead, through a grillwork door, I glimpsed the garden, quilted in color; and to my left, up a single high step, was the door to my apartment. Around the walls of the foyer, just below the level of the step, I noticed a watermark from a winter flood.

I unlocked this door with the rusty, old church key that

the landlady had sent and stepped up into the front room. Inside, it was dark as night.

A wave of homesickness washed over me and receded as suddenly as it had come, leaving me stunned by its unexpected force. I must make this place my home, I thought, come hell or high water.

I made my way to the front windows and opened the bulky wooden shutters. Bright sunlight bounced off the canal and into the room where, after glancing off the tiled floor and around the whitewashed walls, it danced upon the ornate wooden furnishings, animating nymphs and angels and assorted animals that were carved into every surface on which I was to sit or sleep or stack things away. I knew the heavy, overly worked furniture would be considered ugly by those with modern tastes, but I've always been partial to anything with a claw foot. I liked this wooden menagerie.

The rooms ran one after the other, from the large living space in which I stood, to the back garden. The bedroom, central in position, without windows, beckoned. The bed was a masterpiece of mythology run amok. The animals carved into the bedstead included centaurs, winged lions, and fire-spitting dragons. Serpents with claws wound up the bedposts to the feet of falcons with human faces. No demon would dare enter this room in the night. I would be safe in this bed. A refuge, I thought, then felt a soft feather of fear brush up my spine.

The kitchen was a comfort, large and clean and it contained another collection of carved chairs around a table of beautifully inlaid wood. I would write here, I decided. There was an ancient stone fireplace in one wall and, by contrast, a modern set of kitchen appliances on the other. The refrigerator was stocked with a few essentials in thoughtful anticipation of my late afternoon arrival. The bathroom, a narrow addition off the kitchen, was brightly tiled, with one chin-high window in the shower stall that overlooked the garden.

I felt greatly relieved and somewhat self-satisfied as I unlocked the door that led from the kitchen out into the greenery. I stood there relishing my situation. The apartment was far better than I had dared to imagine. I could settle in with the prospect of doing exactly as I pleased.

I had done it.

The journey had gone well—taxi, plane, bus, train, boat, feet. One person, unaccompanied, could move without complication through the world. One person could arrive precisely, at the right time, in the right place, unmolested, unencumbered, and unembarrassed. One is one.

My eyes moved over the garden and I began to see places where I would weed and prune. Something was wrong. I was alone in the stillness I had sought, but I felt unalone. I felt I was being watched.

I peered into the shrubs and flowering plants, assuring myself that I was indeed unaccompanied. The garden walls on all three sides were of unbroken brick and very high. I raised my eyes up the back side of the house. The shutters of the second- and third-floor apartments were closed, their occupants having fled to the coolness of the mountains for the summer. I was, as I had been promised, all alone at the bottom of the house.

I looked into a small toolshed in the far corner, finding a couple of folding canvas chairs, a rickety table, a ladder, some candles, a few tools, but no visitors. The feeling of another presence would not leave me.

Was it a wish?

I unfolded one of the lounge chairs and sat down with a sigh. Looking up, I searched the deep unsullied sky. Not a bird flew. Along the top of the walls, high above my head, the branches of mulberry and chokecherry trees from the adjoining gardens rustled in a slight breeze.

Then I saw it.

There, among the branches, partially hidden by the leaves, was an eye. Tiny, dark, singular. I was badly startled. It took me several moments to make out the shape of a scrawny, gray kitten, and longer still to realize that the second eye was not closed or hidden, but gone. My heart sank.

Venice, I knew, had thousands of wild cats. I had even anticipated, not without pleasure, that some of them would be residents of my garden, but I hadn't thought of this. The remaining eye looked bad, rheumy. I stood up slowly and approached the wall for a closer look. The animal arched as if to hiss or flee, but stayed, staring back at me. Perhaps it was too weak for unnecessary movement. It continued to eye me, as though I were a mortal enemy.

A silky, cold sweat covered my body as the pain doubled me over. It was familiar pain, radiating out from the center of my chest and rolling along my arms, up through the back of my head and down into the pit of my stomach. How sick I felt! It was happening more of late—and was gaining in severity. Shaking, I could only sink back down into the lawn chair and hold my head in my hands. I rocked myself back and forth, breathing, waiting for the pain to pass. I needed rest. I needed to think. I needed to know, if only for one instant, why I lived before I died. I needed not to worry, not to be caught up in the cares of the world for a while, just for a summer. Yet, within minutes of my arrival, the world had summoned me. Life, in the form of a suffering cat, had demanded my involvement. Life had hauled itself up to the top of my garden wall and sat, like a Cyclops, awaiting my participation.

I have learned to endure my personal suffering in silence. I take considerable pride in my courage. But I cannot bear the suffering of others. Both the meant and the meaningless cruelties of life are a torture to me. My tender barriers of self-involvement can too easily be torn asunder. A kitten can do it. And then the pain will flush through me. I try not to let my weakness show. I hide my vulnerabilities in silences and distances. I wrap myself in cynicism like an assassin's cloak. When I am forced into closer, always painful, contact with others, I bear up.

I was tired of bearing up. I had come here for respite, for refuge. I needed to heal, damn it, or I was done for.

A butterfly lit tenderly on my knee, then fluttered away, leaving the beginnings of calmness in its tiny wake. I concentrated on breathing slowly and deeply, as I had taught myself to do long ago, and in a few minutes the shaking and sweating stopped. The pain was lessening. I wiped my face and looked up at the kitten. It was now relaxed, and sat watching me balefully from among the foliage as before.

"All right, little one, all right," I said, "we'll see what we can do for you."

I thought, perhaps, as I warmed the milk, that I should let the creature die. At best, it would have a rugged street life, always at a disadvantage with only the one eye in this tough, cat-scratch-cat world. But I knew I could only do as I was doing. I had lived with disadvantage all my life. A disease that promised early, painful death. Better to live.

When the milk was warm, I rummaged through my bags

until I found some antibiotics among the medications I was loath to take. I slit one capsule open, letting the pale powder shower onto the surface of the milk. I didn't know how much I should use. If the dosage didn't kill the little beast straight out, I would repeat it at subsequent feedings. I took the saucer and reentered the garden, and with the aid of the ladder, made my unsteady way up the wall. The kitten arched, hissed, and disappeared in a rustle of waxy leaves.

"Here you go, *gatto*," I called, reaching up and sliding the saucer onto the top of the wall. The ladder tottered on the uneven flagstones, and I braced myself with my free hand against the rough surface of the brick. How cool it felt. How real. I leaned my forehead against the wall for a moment.

"You will be the death of me, cat."

I retreated slowly down the ladder and returned to the kitchen. I opened a beer for myself and leaned in the doorway, my eyes fixed upon the top of the wall, watching the place where the kitten had vanished. In a moment it returned, saw the saucer, and jumped back.

I laughed. "Now, we're even."

The kitten slowly approached the dish, sniffed at it, backed away, approached again, sniffed again, and looked around suspiciously. Finding itself alone with the milk, it began to lap hungrily, seemingly unaware of the antibiotic.

The instant in which the kitten accepted the offering, I felt my entire body relax. I had not been aware of the level of my tension until it drained away from me, and I knew I could delay sleep no longer. Too exhausted to unpack or undress, I fell heavily onto the velvet couch in the front room, untroubled by the light. Avoid stress, I thought. And then I was asleep.

TWO

Piazza
San
Marco

I rolled over into sensibility, bringing with me the imagery of the night. In my dream I had been all alone on the deck of an abandoned ship in the midst of a dreadful storm. I was relieved to awaken on dry land, although the unfamiliar couch seemed to undulate with the remembered motion of yesterday's travels. I lay quietly for a few moments and recalled a long ago fishing expedition taken with my then young son, Michael. I had become seasick and Michael had become disillusioned. The sight of his steady father heaving helplessly into the sea had left the boy moody for days. I am a constant disappointment to my child.

I opened my eyes to the morning, deciding that I didn't like the way my mind worked. I lay thinking about my thoughts as I have often done before, usually diminished, sometimes dazzled, by what my brain, unbidden, tosses up upon the shores of consciousness—unfortunately usually, mostly, junk. This morning's flotsam of upset stomach and upset childhood was typical, and utterly failed to meet my standards of mind. Where was my richness? Where was my complexity? Where were the great leaps of imaginative thought that I needed to give meaning to me? I didn't want to start my day thinking about Michael, for if I did, I would soon be ravaged with remorse, gravid with guilt. If my sabbatical went as planned, I would write for him, tell him of myself as I discovered myself. But I would write in the afternoons when I could bear the sadness with a stronger heart.

I remembered the kitten. Suddenly worried, I got up and went quickly to the back door. The coolness of the early morning air slapped me sharply in the face. Now fully alert, my heart pounding a little too fast for safety, I peered around the glistening garden and along the top of the walls to see if my ward had survived the night.

The little cat sat on the wall, watching me like a bird. Sunlight sprinkled down through the treetops and I could feel my heart begin to steady itself. The kitten let out a tom-sized wail of wanting, and within minutes I was dressed and out in the watery world in search of supplies for the two of us. I quickly located a nest of necessities—three ancient mildewed little shops that appeared to be leaning on one another for support. Within them I was able to find chocolate and cheese, salami, bread, oil, pasta, and olives, none of which I should eat, all of which I would, as well as vinegar, wine, salt, soap, and cat food.

With the feline fed, I took the time to undress, shower, redress, and unpack. I hadn't carried many belongings, but those I brought with me I enjoyed in a private way. They were well-cut, well-woven. I favored rich blends of color. My personal kit was well-chosen: a light cologne, right for a man in summer, a heavy tortoiseshell comb passed down to me by my father and his father before him, a razor designed for sleekness or slaughter; even my polishes, for shoes, teeth, jewelry, were carefully considered. My watch was Swiss and accurate, my rings expensive and tasteful. This habit of particularity in objects drives Sonia crazy. She finds it unmasculine. It is soothing to me. Knowing that I will die soon, that I will suddenly and forever not be here, evokes in me a desire to leave behind good things, clean and simple and well-ordered.

I soon set out at what was a New Yorker's pace for the Caffe Florian, working my way through mazes of twisting, cobbled alleys and over a dozen bridges. I was delighted to find that I could remember my way around. The market-places were already vibrant with activity, and bakeries were redolent with the hot smells of fresh bread and sugary pastries. Energetic restaurateurs were setting out napkins and silver on little tables along the canals, where, later in the day, they would serve appealing-looking pizzas but fail to provide their perplexed customers with the hacksaws needed to cut them. This was a city where an observant pedestrian spent a lot of time watching people eat—or try to eat.

Feeling splendid, I entered the great public irregular

retangular square of the city, the Piazza San Marco, the meeting place of all Europe, where it was believed, if you sat long enough, you would eventually see everyone you had ever known, though I have never recognized a living soul there. I wanted to experience the full force of the piazza's magnificence, so I had purposely come into it from the far side, opposite the facade of the Basilica, the monstrous Christian knockoff of the Dome of the Rock, with its famous replicated stolen leaping bronze horses.

As I crossed the piazza I felt myself drawn into the vitality of Venetian life as it opened and expanded before me. It seemed a thousand people and a million birds danced together in the luminous morning light, surrounding themselves with countless marble columns, supporting grand and ancient arches, curving to meet the brick-red roofs and silvery domes where golden spires sprang into the cloudless sky as if to celebrate their hot, dry existence—here, in the midst of the sea, in this delta of architecture, where water should wave and seaweed sway.

I sat down at one of the small, white tables in the outdoor café. It tilted slightly, predictably, on the uneven pavement. I ordered a cappuccino and slipped a book of matches under the short leg. I dislike unsteadiness. It was too early for Florian's orchestra to begin its daily duel with the Caffe Quadri's band across the piazza. Just as well, I thought. I dislike dissonance.

I unfolded a copy of the *International Herald-Tribune,* purchased along the way, and enjoyed the lightness and crispness of the paper. It was yesterday's news, but no matter. Today would be yesterday's news tomorrow. I read it with intense but detached interest—like an astronaut who has left the world for a while, knowing he will attend to mundane matters when he gets back home, ideally with a fresh, new perspective, but for the time being released to float in a space of different dimensions and different requirements.

My cappuccino arrived, and its dark sweet aroma, its delicious milky flavor, enhanced my experience of foreign freedom. I drank the coffee and savored the day, encountering, within myself, what might have been the beginnings of happiness.

And then a dreadful thing happened. Looking up from the foamy dregs in the bottom of my cup, I noticed a young woman at the far corner of the piazza. She was moving straight toward me, walking slowly, arrhythmically. The curious hesitation of her stride engendered within me a lurch of excitement that I could ill afford. She stopped, backed away, and began another approach, reminding me of the kitten as he encountered the saucer. Closer now, she seemed to be looking over the café. Her eyes ran over me without recognition. With relief I decided that her advances had nothing to do with me. I looked away with determination, returning my attention to the newspaper, but again her uneven gait caught the corner of my eye, and my attention was fishhooked back to her tentative progress.

She wore a thin white dress that the breeze from the lagoon pressed provocatively against her body, accentuating her narrow waist, the curve of her hips, her ample breasts. Her hair, long and loose, was red-gold, framing a simply beautiful face. Her only adornments were mother-of-pearl earrings; blue-gray-green and iridescent like her eyes, they seized and reflected the available light. Her skin was marble white, as if she lived her life beneath a parasol or deep below the surface of the sea. She wore no makeup, which gave to her features an innocence younger than her years would bear. As she moved ever closer, I put her age relievedly, regretfully, at thirty. She was too old to have retained the upsurging power of youth that had once, so often, dragged me like a full moon tide off into bliss and pain. Her maturity released me to myself again. My virgin solitude was intact. I felt like someone who had just been missed by a car spinning out of control. It had been a very close call. I turned away and ordered another cup of cappuccino.

But still . . . I could not help noticing how she moved to and from the café several more times. She did not sit down. Instead she drifted about the square wistfully for a while before being drawn back into the crowd. Gone. The distraction had been, blessedly, brief.

My chest felt tight.

I didn't need her. There was enough woman trouble back home to end a lifetime. The pain of them had accumulated over the years, overproduced, pumped into my life by my dysfunctional heart, just as my dysfunctional liver overproduced and pumped out cholesterol into my arteries. Sonia was sticky in my blood. Clog. Nell, too. Clog. And Melodie, Kathy, Carla, Sonia, Lynn. Clog. Clog. Clog. Clog. Clog.

The woman in white, had she been younger, had I engaged with her, would have added to the buildup, increased the internal pressure, though at first sight she had washed through me, promising a purification of my heart and soul. A cure. Now she was lost among the crowds.

The pleasure had drained from the morning. The piazza had become just another overtouristed Italian square, dirty with pigeons and a few stray sea gulls. My second cup of cappuccino had failed to arrive. I put down more than

164

enough lire to cover the bill and left the café.

I walked unhappily in the direction of the clock tower at the opposite corner of the piazza before realizing I was being drawn into the wake of the woman. This was where I had last seen her. I was appalled. I hadn't yet been in place for twenty-four hours and I was already beginning to stalk. I will not do this, I declared to myself. But would I listen?

Forcing myself to turn away was like forcing myself against a law of nature—gravity or entropy. I faced Florian's again and, exhausted, made my retreat back to the same seat from which I had sprung. The clock struck noon. The band began to play. My second cup of coffee arrived as if I had never left.

"Excuse me." It was a woman's voice.

I looked up into a manifestation of my homeland. It wasn't the woman I had watched drip away and run away in the coffee shop, but it could have been. She was younger than me, dressed in pale blue synthetics that were creased from traveling; she was shod in soft, fat, running shoes. She carried a large fake leather bag on a shoulder strap, which she firmly clasped against her chest in anticipation of the imminent arrival of pickpockets.

She spoke with a y'all-know-I-could-only-be-from-Texas twang. "Do ya know the way to see the Michelangelo's David?" She was polite and well-intentioned, searching for what she had been told was important in the entirely wrong place. In seeking help, she was innocently exposing her ignorance and leaving herself vulnerable to humiliation. I felt followed. Cornered by my culture. I could hurt her. I had no wish to hurt her.

"The David is in Florence," I replied. It was the simplest truth.

She looked at me curiously for a moment, and then slowly, as the idea made its weary way into her head, she nodded and grinned. She was not humiliated. Not even embarrassed.

"Why, silly me!" she declared in a moment of dazzling self-clarity. "Why, so it is. Well then, can you tell me what's to see here? I've lost my group, don'tcha know?"

I subdued an evil impulse to send her out into the lagoon to look for obscure inscriptions on the cemetery island of San Michele. Goodness reigned.

"You might try the Basilica there," I suggested, pointing. She seemed to notice the awesome structure for the first time. "There are some lovely mosaics inside."

"Why, I'll just do that," she said. "Thanks, mister. Have a good day." And clutching her plastic pouch, she went off. I watched her go—another woman glancing off my life into her own improbable future, trying as she went along to See Things. Perhaps back home over a barbecue she would remember me. "The day I lost the group," she would say, "in Venice I think it was, I met the nicest man. He tried to be helpful, but y'know he sent me into the most godawful, gloomy Catholic church I ever *did* see."

I decided to go into San Marco myself after I finished my coffee. I would gaze again at the gleaming mosaics and the marble floors of many colors. Before an altar to someone I would light a candle to something.

But I never got there. A surge of unfathomable fatigue pulsed through me. Perhaps I had not recovered from my journey, or maybe it was the shift in time. Whatever it was, I went nowhere.

I sat and thought about women. In my convulsive youth, I had often had three women a day—girls, they were called then—and every one was a treasure to me while I held her. I loved the smoothness of them, the many textures of their skin and hair, their secret smells and the soft sounds of their pleasures. I marveled at the variety of their responses, the uncharted currents of their intellect. I knew I would never marry. No woman could ever replace another woman. They were each a solitary splendor; meaningful, magnificent in their own unique way. I knew for certain that no one woman could ever replace them all.

And I saw for myself a way to enjoy centuries of life in the space of a decade. I would cherish each of the women I touched, and I would keep on touching more and more of them.

Then Sonia touched me. It was as if the hand of a goddess had reached down and swept the mortals from my bed. I was hers. As long as her eyes had shone at the sight of me, I never looked away.

I have never been able to understand why she blinked. For a long time I was convinced it was something I had done, and I flogged my memory, trying to recall my crime. But I was innocent. I had been (astounding myself in the process) faithful. I had loved her. I had sacrificed for her. I had given her a son. But she no longer loved me, and I died in a manner that no doctor had ever predicted. I tried to go back to promiscuity, now adultery. I took small comfort in it, fearful that I had been stricken by some strain of latent middle-class morality, but in truth I was still in love with Sonia. Michael, you cannot imagine my unhappiness.

I hoped to love again, but found no one. Alluring young women seemed shallow to me now, older women dangerous. Sex reduced itself to ritual; orgasm, to a sigh of despair. In time I couldn't perform at all, because my body knew it was playing in a theatre that had long ago gone out of business. But I never thought of stopping. I found women who wanted to be touched, but not entered, and I went on with the rites, not knowing what else to do, pursuing the lost lust of my youth. And I stayed with your mother not for the good of you, or the good of her, but weakly, shamefully, because there was no other place to go. She seemed to want me near her, though not in her. Perhaps she found some enjoyment in tormenting me. Torment was the rent.

The shock of finding her with Mallory should have killed me. It's always strange to think of Mallory as I saw him then, bare bottom up, astride my wife. I could never bring myself to hate him. In that instant he became all butt and balls to me. Not hateful, just slightly ridiculous, and less slightly, sickening. I think she hated me for not hating him. Instead I hated her for letting herself be seen.

From that day forward her life became one long complaint against me. I could do no right in her eyes. Perhaps she thought if I was vile enough, wrong enough, mean enough, selfish enough, she would be able to overlook her own unimaginative sins. From the remembered body of Love there emerged the ever-present Goddess of Strife. She sucked up the days of my life like my mother's old Hoover sucked up dirt. On bad days I thought she should have it all. I thought I should empty into that all-taking-ungiving lap everything that I carried in my pockets, followed by the pockets themselves and the clothing they attached to, then my internal organs, the meager contents from the belly of my brain, and what shreds of my soul remained to me. I could then float lightly down to her feet and die.

Now I want to live.

A crease of clouds folded the sunlight to the far side of

the piazza, throwing the buildings into contrasts of brightness and shadow. I saw the woman in white. She was approaching again, rippling across the square in the changing light. This time she did not hesitate, but chose a seat near to my own and sat down. She jumped visibly when the waiter arrived, but placed an order and then seemed to relax a little. She looked around tentatively at the other patrons. Our eyes met. Hers were deep, wet, still, and I responded with a wish to play in those cool waters. She turned abruptly away from my gaze and I felt the loss.

She took a sketch pad and pencil out of a small straw bag, looked in the direction of the Basilica and began to draw. When her drink arrived she didn't seem to notice, so intent was she upon her work. Thinking that it was safe, I watched her for a long time. But it was not safe. She was mesmerizing, distressing: she evoked layers of desire, anxiety, anger, fear. The accretions of experience.

The waiter brought me a bill and I paid him and left without looking back. I hurried in the direction of the clock tower. The way was now clear into the narrow shopping alleys of the Mercerie. There, quality and kitsch vied for attention in successive windows. There was nothing here I wanted. I was drawn to the woman, drawing, at Florian's.

I went home. I took the long way back over the Rialto Bridge and through the heart of Cannaregio, each step forward a victory. Once in the sanctuary of the apartment, I began to set up the space in which I would write. I planned to write an account of myself, a kind of autobiography. There was never enough time to write. Now was the time, or never. The increasing angina, the sudden losses of energy, were a signal that I was catching up with my prognosis. The internal clock was winding down, and would soon

169

strike for the last time. At. My. Heart.

If the heart is the place where hope is nestled, there was a place left within it for Michael. Michael Renoir Sa'id. Michael, a name whose meaning is a question: who is like the Lord? Yet it is a solid, popular, masculine name that made of him an American. Renoir was a conceit of Sonia's, partly in deference to her own Gallic blood, partly because when we married her parents had presented us with a small, lush painting by Renoir, and the picture was Sonia's most prized possession. I felt that if she wanted to bestow some of her good feeling on the boy, it could do him no harm, and although I have never cared for Renoir's work very much myself (and resented the extravagance of the gift), I liked the films of his son, so I went along with the name, for I had the last word—Sa'id, the Smith of Arabian names, that made him forever my own. He is a child who will one day do great things, though at present he is a strange, gawky adolescent hiding the spots on his face with his nose in a book.

I had never done right by the boy. Thinking he should be spared the sadness of his parents' marriage, I had sent him relentlessly, endlessly, away—to schools and camps, on group vacations, to Sonia's parents. In trying to protect him from the heat, I had left him out in the cold. Or perhaps I sent him out of sight because I could not bear the guilt of knowing that I had passed on to him the disease from which I suffer. It is a terrible thing to know you have given to your child that which will one day kill him.

Whatever the sorry reason, he has never known me. He has grown, with his mother's help, to revile me. And yet I love him so. If I am able to write, maybe he will come to believe he was wanted and cherished. Maybe he will be able to forgive me for never knowing what in the world to do with him.

But will I be able to know and forgive myself? I wondered if writing the journal would guide me to the meaning of my life? Would it be the last thing I ever did with the remains of my life? Or would it *be* the remains of my life? An artifact to leave behind. Better than neatly folded shirts.

Weeks went by quietly, and the solitude began to work a spell upon me. My heart beat at an even pace. The bouts of pain were less frequent. I slept well, with nights full of unremembered dreams. In the mornings, after breakfast in the garden with the skittish kitten—well-fed but still untouchable on the wall—I was able to think, and in the sultry afternoons, while Venice slept, I was able to write. As evening approached and the Venetians sprang to life again, I retreated into contemplation, and began to know myself.

Almost everyone knows the ache of loneliness, and most of us can distinguish it from the sad-sweet melancholy of being alone, but for the first time in my life I found the refreshment of reclusiveness, and it was filled with many flavors. Admittedly, the first taste was of anxiety. Would I go mad? But the isolation lent itself to sanity, serenity, simplicity—to a unity of self—an unaided, unassisted life that began to strengthen me. I enjoyed the marketing, cooking, cleaning, and gardening that alternated with the attempts at the writing. I didn't feel competent in any of my pursuits, but I felt *potentially* competent. I found wells of resource within myself, brimming with waters not yet drawn.

There was, now and then, a dreary day of restlessness, when nothing seemed to interest me; when listlessness, boredom, apathy, and languor could be distinguished, one from the other, in the subtlety of their substance. But the majority of my days were relaxed, tranquil, pure.

Only one moment of each day was predictably awful—the moment when the last rays of the sun left the city and I was forced to turn on the lamps and then fasten the shutters against an onslaught of mosquitoes. The only American convenience I have wished for in Italy is a window screen. Here, the heavy black wooden shutters closed me in, coffinlike, for the night, and I felt utterly abandoned by life. I could usually rally and do another round of work, but occasionally I fell into a lethargy of despair and then into sleep.

Sometimes, hoping to cheer myself, I would close the shutters early, leave the apartment and go walking out to the Dogana at sunset, where the water lapped languidly at the foundations of the buildings, and the great crescent of

173

the city curved out and away from me toward the Lido. But there, too, I was prone to sadness. I longed for love—and love, in my mind's eye, always took the shape of Sonia's young body when she still loved me, before Michael was grown, before Mallory had groaned upon her. I would think, if Sonia loved me now she could be here beside me, and together we could enrapture ourselves with the romance of Venice. But Sonia, evidently, could live quite well without me. If she longed for me, there was no sign of it—not a call, not a letter. I refused to plead anymore. She must come to me, or never come with me, again. On those despondent evenings, everyone in Venice seemed to be part of a couple, or a family, and I, alone, walked alone.

At such times the quiet of the city consoled me. In the backwater where I lived there was seldom a sound louder than a cat's cry. The blaring beat of America seemed far far away. No one shrilled at me, on purpose or by mistake. In the stillness the words began to come, the struggle to capture myself in words was truly in progress. Barrenness gave way to the satisfactions of the work. My minor message to the world began to take shape, and, once or twice, at the arrival of truth, I accomplished joy.

I was distracted by the butterflies. They had begun their campaign against my concentration one morning by sending a solo scout fluttering right through the apartment, in a straight line from front window to back garden. I didn't recognize it. I followed it.

Butterflies had been my youthful passion. Before women. It had been years since I had taken any notice of them, but this lone messenger was a blue beauty, flying back memories of my earliest years, when I would lie in the high grass of a Texas summer, watching, waiting, enchanted with the glory of them. I never collected. I couldn't have brought myself to pierce their light, lovely bodies with a cold, steel pin, to see their angel wings flail and be still. I soon knew all the local species, and I was book-smart about hundreds of others not yet glimpsed. Their lovely Latin names, strung together, made up a liturgy, sacred in my mind: *Duomitus leuconotus, Composia fidelissima, Polygonia interrogationis, Automeris Io.* It was a secret love. I was afraid of the derisive laughter of the rougher boys. Nor would my parents have understood my unprofitable pastime. My hardworking parents had hopes for me and they were increasingly worried about their dawdling, dreaming child. Son of exiles, I was to be someone someday. Was I? Here in an exile of my own devising, chasing butterflies and literary allusions?

A month to the day from my arrival in Venice I identified a Mourning Cloak *(nymphalis antiopa),* and later that day I almost died. The Mourning Cloak is a dark butterfly, brown with a yellow border. Who had thought them up? Who had sent one to me on that day? It was the first of its kind that I had seen in Venice, and I was happy enough about the sighting to take myself out for a celebratory lunch at the outdoor tables of the Antico Capon in the Campo Santa Margherita.

On the way to the restaurant I did my shopping for the day, pleasantly picking out speckly brown eggs and green vegetables and sun-yellow butter in the busy stalls of the marketplace. At the restaurant I ordered some stuffed mushrooms, a sausage pizza, and a bottle of Prosecco, the sweet, fizzy local wine that I had come to enjoy. Everything I had purchased or ordered that day, save the vegetables, was forbidden—fat villains, out to get me from the inside out. Daily, I measured the known quality of life against the unknown quantity. Daily, butter and eggs won out over three or four possible extra minutes.

While I waited to be served, I watched the life of the campo. Young children ran about on the pavement; dogs, too, muzzled by local law, ran playfully after them. The children threw balls to one another and for the dogs to chase, knowing the muzzles would keep the balls in play. Overweight grandmothers kept an eye on the youngsters and on their knitting and on each other while they gossiped. Tourists shuffled along, tiredly following the black and yellow signs to San Marco in one direction or the car park at the Piazzale Roma in the other. The local faces had grown familiar to me in the short time I had lived among them, and I was growing comfortable here. The heavy concerns that I carried about in my own country felt lighter here. Perhaps the writing helped. The pressures of work and women and what-to-do-about-my-life, about lawyers and doctors and about Michael, all seemed localized and distant. I *knew* I couldn't leave my problems behind, but I *felt* as though I had.

What I had begun to realize about myself was that I worried wherever I was—about wherever I was, about details, niggling little nothings—practically all of the time. I had always thought it was women who worried me, but here there was no harem to harass me. It wasn't women. It was me! I could drive myself crazy all by myself. It was a disheartening discovery. I worried in lists: about the wrinkles in my trousers, about whether to weed the garden again, about whether I had gotten enough sleep, about what would happen to me if the cut on my finger developed an infection. I worried about how the little cat was faring when it rained—and if he was getting enough calcium. I was not living a liberated life of glorious adventure. I was being carried along on an endless undercurrent of apprehension. What was the source of my constant disquietude if it was not to be found among the females? Surely it couldn't be death in disguise. Doom didn't niggle. And I had learned to look death in the eye long ago.

I glanced over to the ice cream parlor on the far end of the campo in anticipation of another forbidden pleasure. The gelato there was made fresh each day: blueberry, dark chocolate, *zabaione* . . . She was there. The woman in white, only now she was in fiery red. I watched her as she handed some lire across the counter and received her double cone. Weeks had elapsed, yet she seemed to be wandering alone as before, with the same skeptical, elliptical walk. Her hair was piled up in waves, held in place with a silver filigreed clip.

Perhaps she sensed my eyes upon her as I had once sensed the cat's eye on me, because she wheeled around sharply and began to survey the side of the campo where I was sitting. She came toward me again as she had done at Florian's. This time she didn't stop, and I felt my blood begin to pick up speed—but she walked right past me, as if I didn't exist, her eyes beyond me, and I turned around to follow her gaze, wondering what drew her attention. Fish.

A dozen or so brilliantly colored tropical fish flashed in a large, lighted tank just inside the restaurant door. She peered into the aquarium the way Sonia peered into the windows at Tiffany's. As I watched her, watching the fish, a small smile on her lips, the cone moving to and from the smile, I began to feel my emotional feet slide out from under me. I recognized the feeling as I was pulled deeper and deeper into it. I had felt it once before when I first saw Sonia. It was an unearthly love. I knew I must flee at all costs, return to my precious privacy. I must not allow her to breach the walls of my seclusion. I had work to do, thoughts to think, a life to relive. How could I ever know what had happened to me if *she* was happening to me? I started to get up, keeping an eye on her, as though she were a mortal enemy.

It hit me then. The worst agony of my life. Square in the chest. The intensity of the pain was unprecedented. This must be the end, I thought, I must be dying now. I reached for the medication in my pocket. Too late. The pain turned cold and pressed in on me and out of me at once. It pushed me forward and I keeled off the chair, plunging into a night-black hole where the pavement had been only moments before.

The next thing I can remember was the blackness receding, breaking apart into blood redness, then into pinpoints of white light dotting the familiar surroundings of the restaurant which seemed to swirl above me. She was kneeling next to me, her face close to mine, her fingers in my mouth pressing a nitroglycerin tablet under my tongue. Her other hand held my wrist. I knew there were other people hovering about, but I couldn't make them out. I saw only the concerned face above my own, and the movement of her breasts beneath her dress.

She leaned closer and spoke into my ear. "You're going to live," she said.

"Pain."

"Yes," she said sadly. "With pain."

She moved one hand under my head, and, with the other,

brushed at the crowd of curious Italians, like flies.

"He's going to be all right. *Va bene. Va bene.*" The strangers began to move away as I found the strength to prop myself up.

"How do you know?"

"Know what?"

"That I'll be okay."

"My mother had a heart condition. I nursed her for years. Since I was very young. I know what to do, what not to do."

"Had?"

"She's dead. She was struck by lightning."

"I'm sorry."

"I am, too. Here, let me help you." She supported me while I sat up, first on the pavement, then slowly up onto the chair. She handed me the vial of tablets she had removed from my pocket and sat on the edge of the chair opposite me. The pain was still intense, but lessening, and for a time I could only sit, self-involved, struggling with the shakes and the nausea. She waited patiently until I regained some composure.

"Perhaps I should see you to the hospital or call someone to take you there."

"No," I declined, "you were right the first time. I'm going to live."

"How bad is the pain?"

"Very bad." She looked concerned again. "But it's easing. You've been a wonderful help." And her eyes misted over. She seemed a long way off.

"Will you stay with me for a while?" If I had had any extra breath left in me, I would have held it while I waited for her reply. She nodded affirmatively, and I was frightened by how aroused I felt. Given the precarious state of my health, it was dangerous. My fall into unconsciousness had pitched the last of my resistance into the blackness. When I returned to the light, I was hers. Could she sense it? Would she care? Would life be worth living if she didn't? Who was she? Had I indeed gone mad?

I reached tentatively for my wine. I needed to clutch at some kind of a life preserver to carry me through the rapid surges of my emotions. She, too, reached for the glass, as though to prevent me from taking a drink. I prepared to protest, but instead she took a small sip, then pushed the glass to me, then poured some for herself. She raised her glass to me.

"To life."

"To the woman who saved my life."

I knew we were being watched with interest and some concern by the other patrons, but I felt alone with her nevertheless. The waiter arrived, and, with unusual grace, set down the sizzling pizza, announcing it was now to be courtesy of the management and he hoped that the gentleman was feeling better. I was. The rich aromas of cheese and garlic seemed a summons to life, the vision across the table a summons to love.

We sat eating and drinking, quietly, as if we had done so for many years. I was surprised at the strength of my appetite.

"I saw you some weeks ago at Florian's. You were sketching there. But for a long time you walked around the café as though something was troubling you. Do you remember?"

"Yes. I wasn't sure I had the right to sit down there."

"Whyever not?"

"Because it was Florian's," she replied as if that answered the question.

"I don't understand."

"I first read about it when I was a child. It has always held a special place in my imagination. George Sand sat at Florian's. Mark Twain wrote at Florian's. So did Henry James and James Fenimore Cooper, Proust and Goethe and Ruskin. Lord Byron lingered there over his verses. Turner sketched there, and Monet. I didn't know if I had the right to associate with that company of ghosts."

I could picture them in my mind's eye as she talked . . . the lot of them, drinking cappuccino and looking over each other's work. I thought of the woman from Texas asking me, "What's to see here?" I felt sorry for both of us. There was so much we had not seen.

"You're an artist," I said lamely.

"I'm a writer."

"The sketches?"

"A hobby."

"What do you write?"

"All kinds of writing—short stories, poems. I support myself with nonfiction pieces, research projects. But I'm here in Venice to try to write my first novel."

"I am trying to write, too," I blurted out to her. As soon as I said it, I wished that I hadn't.

"About your life?" she asked without missing a beat.

"Yes. I suppose so." I was really embarrassed now.

"That will be an interesting pair of books, Aidan," she said. She appeared to be savoring some sort of private joke. "My book and yours."

I was stunned. How did she know my name? It was a

moment before I realized she must have read it off the prescription on the bottle of medication. "What will your novel be about?" I asked her, recovering myself.

"I don't suppose anyone knows what a novel is about until after it's done, but I think I'm writing about how people we barely know . . . people who only come in contact with us for a day or an hour or a minute, or stay with us for one night, can affect our lives forever after . . . not always happily."

"Like the woman in the coffee shop."

"Or the man in the coffee shop."

"You tell me your coffee shop story. I already know mine."

She laughed. "If you promise you won't steal it."

"You should do the promising," I said. "You're the professional." I prepared to laugh along with her, but at my words her expression had abruptly changed and become serious. "I was only kidding," I rushed to explain. "My writing is just an amateur account of my life, about trying to live in the face of death. Your story is safe with me."

She was silent for a moment. Her smile was wry now. "My coffee shop story is not a very good one. Not yet, anyway. But I'm working on it. I met a man in a coffee shop when I was only fifteen. We spent a night together. I fell in love, but I never saw him again."

"And he never knew that you loved him?"

"No." She looked serious again, then brightened. "But if I'm lucky I might be able to center a novel around him. I don't have the ending yet." Again serious, again bright. What was she thinking about behind those rapid changes of expression? I was in the grasp of womanmind once again.

"You look pale suddenly," she observed. "How are you feeling?"

"Done for." The physical pain had faded away, leaving a warm weakness in the fragile hollow that held my heart.

"Shall I walk you home?" she asked, concerned again. For me.

"Nothing would make me happier." I meant it. I didn't. I did.

"I would like to make you happy." Did she mean it? What if she didn't? I felt my composure buckling and cracking as the weed of desire pushed upward—strong, beautiful, unnecessary. Yet nothing had ever seemed more necessary than the presence of this unsought, unknown woman. I fought for normality.

"What is your name?"

"Mira."

"I've never heard that name before. Is it short for Miranda?" Again the somber cloud moved across her features.

"No."

"Then perhaps it is short for miracle." I expected her to smile at that, but she remained serious. "When you save a man's life, Mira, you become responsible for it."

"And when you don't save it?"

That gave me pause. "Yes. Well. Then."

"I mean a character in a novel might do something entirely different. She might run about calling for help like a frightened child. She might not know about the medication and give you mouth-to-mouth resuscitation . . ."

That sounded very appealing to me at the moment.

". . . and you would have died," she continued, "or she

might have known what to do and not done it."

"Why not?"

"Because she hated you, or she loved you, or both."

"But you don't even know me."

"I'm talking fiction, but, even if she didn't know you in the story, she might not want to get involved—or she might not feel she had the right to intervene in someone else's destiny. If she was evil, she might even withold the medication . . ."

"I'm glad you felt you had the right to intervene."

"I'm glad we're not fictional."

"So am I."

I left a tip for the waiter, and we began to walk the short distance to my apartment. All the way home I was stepping through clouds to the cobbles. She had taken my arm so lightly, so naturally, I felt it as an angel wing.

Once we were inside and alone I asked to hold her. She assented and moved gracefully into my arms, allowing me to kiss her, responding with a gentle openness. I was firm where I had been soft for so long. She felt it and stepped away.

"It's too soon," she said. "We need to know each other better."

"You've brought me back to life—two different ways in a day. What more do I need to know about you?"

"Perhaps that seems enough for you," she replied, "but there are things you need to remember and I need to forget."

"What things?"

"Another time. Soon." And she kissed me lightly on the forehead.

"I may not have another time left to me."

"You need to rest."

I felt like a petulant child. I tried again. "I don't want to rest . . . to go to bed. It's the middle of the day. Unless you would reconsider and join me."

"No."

There was an edge of anger in her voice that brought me back to my senses. What had I been thinking of? We weren't in the sixties. Girls were women now. With rights—and wrongs. They worried about diseases and relationships. But there are other senses, and her body—when I held her—had been so responsive.

Before I could apologize, she spoke again, without irritation.

"Look, you go shower and get ready for bed. I'll stay with you until you're asleep."

I did what I was told. How had we arrived at such intimacy, and she at such authority, so rapidly? As I was undressing I took the pill bottle from my pocket. The prescription had long ago worn off it. Had she gone through my wallet? When? I felt a crawly feeling in the pit of my stomach, then stepped into the shower, where the warmth of the water soothed me. Don't worry so much, I lectured myself.

I found her in the bedroom. Prim, on a chair carved with a dozen dragons. She had placed a glass of water on the nightstand and had moved the telephone to within an easy reach. She actually tucked me in. And I actually relaxed. She was right about the depth of my exhaustion. This was no time for a reentry into sex. But I fought sleep, unwilling to let her go. What if she never came back? What if I never found her again?

"Where do you live . . . here in Venice?"

"The Pausania Hotel. Do you know it?"

"Yes. It's expensive to live in a hotel."

"I know. I have a benefactor." My heart sank. "It's not what you think. I'm here alone." It rose again, buoyed with possibility.

"Look. I don't want you to leave me yet. Will you tell me the story of your novel? I mean, more of it."

"You want me to tell you a bedtime story?" She laughed her delightful laugh again.

"Yes."

"All right," she agreed, "but not that one. If I tell you that one you won't be able to sleep."

"I want that one. It's about you."

Her green eyes searched my own, coming to some kind of decision. "Okay. If you insist." She sat down on the edge of the bed. I loved seeing her there.

"I insist."

She spoke softly and smoothly in a true bedtime-story voice. "When I was fifteen years old my mother died. Like I told you . . . in the park near our house, under a tree. She had always warned me not to stand under a tree in a thunderstorm, but she did, and she died. My fathers were already dead. Real father . . . stepfather. I had no brothers or sisters, and when my uncle Jesse sold the house for me, I had enough money to skip town and make a shaky start for myself in New York. I had always been very good in school, but academics held no interest for me. I wanted to be an artist . . . a writer . . . a painter . . . a romantic. I was very sure of myself for my age, and very lonely. One day in the coffee shop near the Art Students League I noticed a man noticing me. He was maybe thirty, or thirty-five, but he seemed much older to me . . . and very distinguished.

He had a beard, well-kept, and wore good clothes. He seemed to be gentle . . . the way he spoke to the waitress . . . the way he moved the silverware around while he waited. There was a glint of gold on his left hand—which didn't stop us. He picked me up, or I picked him up, and we spent the night together at some quirky little hotel. I was pretending to be older and more worldly than I was. I let him lead in everything for I knew nothing. He was very experienced, and I had been right about his gentleness. He took my virginity with only the slightest flash of pain. He was genuinely upset when he realized what he had done . . . asked me why I hadn't told him that I was a virgin. I hadn't told him because I didn't want to stop him . . . but I didn't tell him that, either. Falling in love is such an inexplicable, explosive event . . . and I had fallen with all the force of first love. I was innocent. I was imaginative. And perhaps I was a little insane. I actually believed that if I didn't make a fuss . . . didn't make any trouble . . . just loved him, and let him do as he liked . . . I thought—I'm embarrassed to say this—that he would fall in love with me, too . . . and leave his wife . . . and we would make love forever after because I had just found out I liked sex better than anything in life. Even art. But, as he said, he could promise me nothing, and I never saw him again . . . well, not for seventeen years."

Awareness had fallen on me like an axe.

"Until Venice."

"It's good to see you again, Aidan."

I had not the slightest recollection of her. Nothing. Blank. Gone. Impossible. She was unforgettable, but I had forgotten her. She had remembered me. Loved me? All these years? Or did she hate me now?

"Are you sure, Mira?"

"Birthmark," she replied. "Resembles a bird in flight. Right shoulder. There." She reached out her hand and touched the exact spot where the birthmark was hidden beneath the silk of my pajamas. There could be no mistake.

I was thrilled and horrified. The world suddenly seemed very wobbly in its ways. She had turned a teenage crush into love and remembered me for seventeen years, and, given the chance, saved my life. I had taken her virginity and wiped her out. It was unforgivable. I had always prided myself in the way I had held my lovers in my arms, in my mind—the perfectly preserved and polished memories. Had I been deceiving myself all those years? Was I simply vain and vile? Had I forgotten others? Had I merely used the women who wanted me and cast them aside? No. Surely this was an aberration. Surely I could be forgiven one lapse among so many matings? But to forget *her*? And I had hurt her, too. I didn't know what to say.

"You think you don't know what to say, but you do."

"I'm sorry."

"You're forgiven."

"By you, Mira. But how can I ever forgive myself?"

"This time you might let my feelings matter more than your own. Then you will find yourself, as I've said, forgiven."

My heart was racing again. I was frightened. I suddenly wanted to run away.

"Years ago, when you made love to me, and realized how young I was, and how alone, and that I had been a virgin, you were frightened, frightened that you had hurt me . . . with your needs, with your actions. You ran, and I thought you had run away from me . . . that I was repulsive to you in some way I couldn't imagine. But now I know that you ran away from your own fear. Your disappearance hurt me more than you will ever know. Please don't run away again, Aidan. Let us have, at the very least, a friendship, so it won't all be for nothing all over again. Let me have a chance to know you."

"It's I who should be asking you for another chance."

"But you're not."

"I . . . I am. But Mira, oh, Mira . . . I don't remember you."

"I've got that, Aidan. Actually, I got that seventeen years ago."

"I don't deserve another chance."

"I know, but you have it anyway."

"Did you recognize me . . . weeks ago . . . at Florian's?"

"Yes."

"Then I was the ghost you were reluctant to join."

"You are not a ghost."

"Soon."

"Will you be able to sleep?"

"Yes. No. I don't know. Don't go."

"I'll come back in the morning."

She stood up to leave then, and I was, once again, struck with her beauty. How had she looked at fifteen? A perfect child. A perfect angel. After me, a fallen angel. A lost child.

"Don't let me lose you again," she said, I said.

And in that harmonious moment, she disappeared.

I slept for eighteen hours and woke peacefully in the coolness of the morning. Everything was different. A flood of sunlight washed through the bedroom doorway from the front room. I could smell freshly brewed coffee.

She was here! My heart began leaping about like a frog in a jam jar.

Prone under the light sheet, I was erect. I felt young and strong and sure. Was it possible that after seventeen years she still loved me, or fancied that she did? Could any

Casanova-turned-swine-turned-hermit be so fortunate? I heard her footsteps approaching and shut my eyes, watching her through my eyelashes as she drifted about the room like a casual breeze. She was wearing a different dress of soft, pale turquoise spun with blue and white, like a foamy sea. The folds of her skirt swept around her as she moved. She looked in on me, then stood for a while in the doorway, facing away, looking out toward the canal, the sunlight lining her hair in silver. She spoke without turning.

"You've fallen in love with me, haven't you?"

"How did you know I was awake?"

"I often sat by my mother's bedside when she was ill. I learned all about sleep. And about waking. Would you like your coffee now?" She turned to look at me, and her face brought the sunlight in to me. "Don't get up. I'll bring it."

"Don't go. Let me look at you."

"Just to the kitchen."

"I love you."

"I thought so."

"Can you still find a little love left for me—after all these years, after what I did? Or will you have your revenge upon me now?"

She took a step closer to me. "What you did was show me how tender, how beautiful, how glorious it can be to make love. Yes, I can still find a little love left for you—after all these years, after what you did."

I was dying to touch her. "Will you come here to the bed with me?"

"No."

"Why not? . . . I mean, if there's love both ways."

"I have no cause for revenge, Aidan, but I have every reason to be wary."

"Yes, of course. But it will all be different now."

"You wear a wedding ring. That's not different."

"I . . ."

"Same wife?"

"Yes. No."

"You don't know?"

"I've only one wife. But when I met you—if it is as you remember it, seventeen years ago—I was not yet married."

"But you wore a ring. The same one, I'm sure."

"I wore it for protection."

"What do you mean?"

"It kept women . . . most women . . . from expecting more than I could offer them."

She looked appalled. "You weren't married? But you wore the ring? What was the matter with you?"

"You already know. Fear."

"Of what? Of me? Of girls like me? What could any of us have ever done to you?"

"Just what you did! Love me."

"What could be wrong with that?"

"I had a broken heart."

"Love can mend a broken heart."

"Not mine."

She was silent, sullen. I was silent, scared.

"Let me tell *you* a story." I was pleading.

"Your coffee shop story?"

"No. Another story. One you need to know. Or I need for you to know. I don't know which."

"Well, if there is to be no shop, let's at least have the coffee." She left the bedroom and I followed her into the kitchen.

"Let me introduce you to someone first." I was desperate

to be in her good graces again. I opened the door to the garden and there on the wall was the kitten. I told her all that I knew about him, and she, delighted, insisted on giving him a breakfast while I dressed. I took another shower. For the first time in my life I took a cold one. It didn't work. Standing naked and full of heat in the shower stall, I watched her from the high window as she carefully stepped up the ladder. She had slim, lovely legs that my eyes followed upward to the irritating hem of her skirt. I imagined the rest of her legs, up to their logical conclusion. She was unaware of my gaze, and that excited me further. At the top of the ladder she talked gently to the little beast while she fed him. The kitten didn't hiss or move away as he did with me. I was vaguely jealous. Of him? Of her? I turned on the hot water and pressed myself under it.

"What's his name?" We were back in the kitchen.

"He doesn't have one."

"Everyone needs a name."

"You give him one."

"How about Wally?"

I laughed. "And I suppose the cat on the roof is Rufus?"

"Is there a cat on the roof?"

"There must be. There are tomcats everywhere."

"Tell me your story, Aidan."

"All right. I can't."

"What?"

"I'm suddenly too anxious. I'm not used to talking about myself."

"Aidan, it's me, Mira. We've known each other for years, remember?" I loved her for letting in a little light where I felt so dark. I took a deep breath and plunged in.

"When I met you . . . the first time . . . I would have been

thirty-two. I wasn't married. I had no plans to marry because I was dying. Or so I had been told. All my life I had
been in poor health . . . a frail child . . . often jaundiced
. . . and later, to my adolescent shame, I had begun fainting
without warning. I was in my twenties when the diagnosis
finally came in. It was a liver dysfunction: hereditary, Semitic, incurable. The disease had skipped my parents' generation entirely, and my ancient grandparents, back in their
village in Lebanon, denied any knowledge of it, if they had
any. As a result of the illness my cholesterol production was
monumental, and my heart had begun giving way under the
strain almost from birth. At thirty-two I had lived a decade
beyond my prognosis. I had been tested almost to death by
then. There had been some new drugs—experimental—
and some unexplained remissions. The doctors were
amazed, and I was alive and angry at the lot of them and
at my lot in life. I never promised a lady more than a
one-night stand because I never knew if I had another night.
I'm sorry you got caught up in my anger and in my fear; it's
just that I learned to live day to day. And I didn't die. Then
an amazing thing happened. I fathered a child—Michael.
He came without celebration. The marriage came later.
He's fif—fifteen. Sonia, his mother, and I are still married,
but it's ending now . . . I'm afraid it's all ending now. I can
tell I am finally dying. I expect I will make it through the
summer, and with luck through the fall. I hope to have one
last Christmas with my son in New York."

She was looking away from me. I couldn't see her expression. "Mira, yesterday you gave me a reprieve, and today
you give me comfort, so perhaps in the tomorrow that is
Christmas you will be with me, too."

She had begun to cry softly. I pulled my chair closer to hers and put my arm around her.

"It's so very unfair, isn't it," she said, "the horrible things that happen to people? Look at you. Look at us. We met, and you were afraid to know me because you thought you were dying. Now we meet again, and I'm the one who's afraid. I didn't fully acknowledge it yesterday, didn't believe it. My mother had so many false alarms . . . and she always pulled through . . . and I saw you and I saved you and I felt we were invulnerable, against time . . . against all odds. But today it's different. I feel what you say to be true. You know you're going to die. And I don't think I can go on seeing you."

My blood ran cold at her words. I knew then that I shouldn't have told her. "Are you so afraid?"

"Do you think I could bear to lose you again?" There was genuine terror in her eyes, in her voice.

"Was it so awful, for you . . . before?" I wanted in the most macabre way to hear from her just how I had been loved, and how I had been mourned.

"Yes. Yes, it was terrible."

"Tell me."

"No. I think I'd better go now."

"Go? Where will you go, Mira?"

"Back to my hotel. I have a novel to write. You have work to do, too." She nodded in the direction of my work-table with its few scribbled sheets, its stack of unmarked paper.

"I'll go with you."

"No."

"Just to walk you there. Then, if you still want me to go, I will."

"All right." I had won another reprieve; however brief, it counted. Every moment with her counted.

As we walked I dared to take her arm. She didn't protest. She didn't respond. We traveled in silence and after a time, for it was murderously hot, we stopped to rest on a low bridge. A gondola, empty but for the gondolier, passed beneath us, the oar barely wrinkling the water. I was trying desperately to control my thoughts, which whirled away from me into the unhappy past then swam spasmodically into uncertain futures.

"What are you thinking about, Aidan?" I was unprepared for the question and for the kindness in her voice.

"My mother."

"Aidan. This isn't going to work out. Let me go now. Please." And she stepped away quickly, down off the bridge, and turned, abruptly out of sight, into a narrow *calle.* I could hear her footsteps echoing on the pavement. She was walking fast. The sudden turn of events had left me dizzy, but I went after her. She heard me coming and increased her pace. Was she trying to kill me? I ran.

Venice is a dreadful city in which to chase a woman: the alleys narrow just as the crowds increase; you suddenly empty out into a campo she has already crossed and there are a half-dozen ways she could have gone; byways that look like shortcuts abruptly end against a wall or a canal. She was heading with the speed of her youth and health toward the Rialto market, the busiest, darkest, most convoluted part of the city. I had long ago lost sight of her. It was hopeless. Out of breath, I sat down in the corner of a sweltering courtyard on what appeared to be a marble lion munching on a marble snake. From that vantage I watched the plain-faced local women carrying home their cabbages. I felt for the first time in my adult life that I might cry. I knew that the smart move would be to go to her hotel and wait. Even if she decided to leave the city, she would return there to collect her clothes and her novel—but I felt impelled to go on. I was trusting myself to the fate that had brought us back together again after so many years. I struggled to my feet and headed onward, holding my heart in my hands.

The marketplace was jammed with every kind of fish and foul thing: dead sea gulls hung upside down next to stalls full of cheap souvenirs, hideous Venetian glass vases, fake leather goods, smelly cheeses. Butchers vied with Japanese tour groups for the space to push along their rumbling carts loaded with raw red beef flanks and glistening maroon kidneys. Eels wriggled. Children skidded in puddles of un-known wetness and mangy cats crawled everywhere look-ing for anything. The only relief to my eyes were the brilliantly stacked and carefully tended piles of fruits and vegetables. At another time I would have been tempted to taste the gigantic peaches and fat purple plums. Now I looked only for Mira, but she was nowhere to be seen.

Discouraged, I entered the tiny Church of San Giacomo di Rialto, tucked away behind the market stalls, where I hoped to cool down and to rest again. The plaque mounted on the creaking door told me it had been founded in A.D. 421 and was believed to be the oldest church in Venice, which was humbling, in a creepy sort of way. I have had no religion since the death of my father, but the atmosphere of these ancient and awesome structures could comfort me nevertheless. As I stepped inside the church I was drowned in the most glorious sound of male voices: monks cloistered somewhere nearby sending up their praise to God. It was the sort of unexpected experience that was typical of the city: gifts, unasked for, suddenly delivered. I sat, spellbound, listening to the music. I seemed to be the only person in the church—and I would have prayed if I could. Then I noticed a remarkably ugly old woman who was peering out from behind the altar. At first I thought she was a crazy woman. She came out dragging a cumbersome Hoover behind her that looked almost as antique as the church. She must have decided that I was not a parishioner or a person of consequence, because without warning she pulled the plug on some unseen stereo, stopping the music in mid *Te-Deum.* She plugged in the machine and with an echoing roar began to clean the carpets. Our Lady of the Vacuum Sweepers. Perhaps God knew I was an atheist. She worked her way tediously down the center aisle, and I followed her as far as the front door, then left the church, putting myself back into the hands of fate.

Mira sat on the steps of the church.

"Mira."

She looked up and around at me, startled, then unmistakably happy.

"Aidan."

"You look for all the world like Eliza Doolittle, sitting here in the midst of this marketplace. Let me take you home and turn you into the happiest of women."

"Doesn't she leave him in the end?"

"That's not our story." I sat down next to her and held her close. She seemed to have gotten younger and smaller, as if the run through the city had been a run back through time. She clung to me like the lost child she once had been. I felt a surge of desire.

"Oh, Aidan, what will be our story? Let's not let it be short. Let's write it together—the world's longest, longest novel."

"You're not afraid anymore?"

"I'm scared to death, but it doesn't matter. I can't escape you. Now that I've found you again, I want to be with you again. I always have. I was just catching my breath. Then I was going back to you with all of my feelings. I'm so sorry I ran away."

"I ran away first—for much, much longer—but now you've had your turn, promise me you won't do it again."

"I won't. I promise."

"Why did you change your mind?"

"I saw . . . all this *stuff*"—she waved her hand in the direction of the market—"all these *things,* and I knew that things, any things, all things, were inconsequential. That they're all a kind of magician's trick—gaudy mirages and flamboyant gestures meant to distract our attention while what really matters eludes us." The words tumbled out of her. "Why do you think God does that? What were you doing in the church? Are you religious? I'm not. Do you mind? I want to know everything about you. I want to know if all the things that I ever imagined about you are true. Will you tell me everything . . . everything?"

"Let's do something mad, Mira."

"What? Why?"

"Come." I led her out of the dank marketplace into the sunlight and along the Fondamenta del Vin to the place where a dozen gondolas bobbed like a flock of black water birds. "Let's hire one to take us home."

"Aidan, they're ruinous. Are you rich?"

"No. Yes. Today I am rich."

My courage wobbled a bit as we stepped into the unsteady craft. I have reason to be worried in boats, but the joy of having her back, near me, next to me, overwhelmed all else. We slid smoothly along the Grand Canal in what I began to think of as one of our silences. We were strangers and yet completely at ease with one another. Surely if I tried, I would be able to recall this woman! But I could not. The particular night that had so overwhelmed her had left me without a ripple of remembrance.

I put my arm around Mira and thought of Sonia. I expected the familiar pain to assail me, or for guilt to creep upon me. Nothing. I felt nothing. I thought of Sonia naked. I thought of her nagging. I thought of her with Mallory. I thought of her with me. Nothing. Nothing. Nothing. The channels of feeling, so well charted, so often navigated, were blocked. My arm was around Mira's shoulders and my hand rested lightly on her upper arm. I saw the glint of the wedding ring that had hurt her so long ago, and again today. I reached over with my right hand to remove it, kissing her as I did so. It was a kiss that promised of passion. I held the ring in the palm of my hand. It was an old, old friend.

"It was a tradition in Venice for many centuries," I told her, "for the Doge to be rowed out into the lagoon once every year. From the prow of his opulent gondola he would throw a golden ring into the water. It symbolized the marriage of Venice to the sea."

She looked at me calmly, with curiosity.

"Watch." I hurled the wedding band far out into the canal. I had never made such a romantic gesture, never dreamed of one, and it was golden.

"Aidan!"

"And that," I declared, "symbolizes my marriage to a new life . . . to the woman who saved my life . . . to the woman who is my life. Mira."

She moved closer to me then, and I felt her tears through my shirt. Quiet tears, of happiness, this time.

I think the salt-hardened, old gondolier behind us was impressed, for he began to sing. He was good, and for the next half hour, as we drifted home, we were all in love with each other, and with the day, and with life.

The oarsman left us on the *fondamenta* directly in front of my apartment and floated away into our past with a friendly wave and a knowing smile. We went in through the garden entrance. The kitten was sleeping peacefully on the wall. I felt a shyness I had not experienced for many years. We were silent again, although this silence was not composed of comfort, but of slowly building tension.

Mira went into the bathroom, and I heard the sound of the shower. As I undressed I thought of the soft slide of the soap, the warm spray of the water over her body, and I was weak with anticipation. She emerged, luminous in the dim light, wrapped in a thick white towel, her hair damp, her body moist, and she came into my arms without hesitation, letting the towel drop away. I made love to her as I hoped I had once made love to her before—eagerly, tenderly—remembering, with each caress, what I had so long ago forgotten: how to worship with my body. She responded with tremors of pleasure to my every touch, moving to make us closer, opening to bring us together, and, when I entered her, arching to bring me deeper.

It was union and reunion and rejoicing.

For the next few days we emerged from each other's embraces only for matters of survival. Self-discovery and the discovery of Mira were, to me, one. I experienced the happiest days of my life. I frightened myself sometimes with the thought that this rapture was what I had been living for, and now that I knew it, I would die.

"Tell me another story." She spoke from the rumpled depth of the bed that had become our burrow. She wanted to know everything about me. On a humid afternoon I had told her all about Sonia, on which subject she was silent; and about my difficulties with Michael, in response to which she was interested and concerned, and apologetic that she had no experience with children. She was moved by my notion of the account of my life, written for him, to him, and she offered to help me in any way she could. Late one night she had questioned me about other women and had been, amazingly, amused at my promiscuity, particularly by my predilection for young females. She was, however, properly (or was it improperly?) sympathetic in regard to my years of impotency, admitting, in light of my energetic perform-ances with her, a hemisemidemiquaver of disbelief. In the cool, colorless light of dawn I had told her about my work in the theatre—the pleasure that actors seemed to take in pickling themselves in predicaments and then waiting for me to pluck them out just in time for the show. She thought that taking care of the real problems of real people so they were able to act out the fictional problems of fictional peo-ple was a delightful way to earn a living, setting me apart from the ordinary breed of bankers and businessmen. Over breakfast one morning I had told her about the butterflies, which delighted her—and she boldly proposed (for we had not yet left the confines of the apartment and garden) a field trip to the island of Torcello to go in search of new varieties. She seemed as insatiable for my history as she was for my body.

I propped myself up on one elbow and gazed at her, an activity I never tired of. Her body was a woman's body, but taut and lean, like a child's. And white. "Fish-belly white," she had called herself in a moment of self-devaluation. "Al-abaster," I had countered, pleasing her, for she seemed hungry for compliments to her physical appearance—not trusting her extraordinary beauty. Had my sudden arrival and departure from her life, so many years ago, damaged her, lowered her self-esteem in some unfathomable way? I refused to believe that I had ever held such power. But I worried about it. Her mind, she valued. And to the extent that she would let me know of it, I valued it, too. But she was reticent about her own life, persistent in the pursuit of my past, as if knowing all of my exploits would mean we had shared them.

"While you were asleep I looked you up in my dictionary."

"What do you mean?"

"Mira. I looked up your name. Do you know what it means in Italian?"

"I didn't know it meant anything in Italian."

"It means aim, end, object, purpose, sight—and I feel that all my life has been aimed at this meeting, that you are the end for which I have searched, the object of my desire, the purpose of my suffering, and the sight of you is all that I will ever ask of life."

She was clearly pleased at my effusiveness. "I wasn't wrong to love you."

"You've known me now for almost a week. Am I anything close to what you imagined?"

"Every now and then, over the years, I would tell someone about you," she admitted. "It was always an appalling mistake. I was told that I never loved you at all, that it wasn't possible to love someone after only one night, that I loved a fantasy. A psychiatrist once suggested that I loved a part of myself and then projected it onto you, that you were a defense against a real relationship. A friend of mine who writes poetry took the position that it couldn't be love because it wasn't mutual. Other speculations included the possibility I wasn't capable of love at all, only longing, that I really hated you and covered up the hatred with an illusion of love, that it was merely a sexual obsession, that passion was an illness, that I was unbalanced and had simply imagined the whole thing!''

She had been angrily counting off the objections on her fingers. Now she relaxed her hands and held my own in hers.

"The *that* that I began to realize is that most people are terrorized by the idea of romantic love. They are determined to prove—like ghosts—that it just doesn't exist. I think it's because they have all—most of them, anyhow—settled for some diluted, polluted version of love. They've chosen for comfort or security or sex, or worse, they've just given up on love altogether and become cynical and bitter. They're all wrong. Every one of them is wrong. I don't know about ghosts, but love lives. I loved you and I love you and I didn't make you up. You're everything I knew you to be.''

"But, Mira, seventeen years . . .''

She dropped my hands. "You, too, Aidan? You won't believe that I loved you?''

There was defiance and a little, hidden howl of pain in her question. I thought of the previous days and nights with her.

"I believe that you loved me. But how did you do it for so long?''

"I was living a poem.''

I took her into my arms. "You are a living, breathing poem, and I am going to learn every line of you. By heart.''

"First, the story.''

"Mira. Mira, my aim, end, object, purpose, sight . . ."

"All right," she relented, "second, the story." And then she drew me gracefully inside the body of her verse.

When we awoke again, it was late in the day and the harrowing heat of the previous week seemed to have broken. We decided to venture out for a walk along the Zattere, where the breeze would lick the waves against the stones and the evening light would fade from gold to rose to pink against the ancient houses.

She slipped back into the turquoise-blue sundress, and it was shocking to see her covered, however lovely. We hadn't been dressed for days. And then it was wonderful to be outside with her.

"My legs feel quite weak," I told her. "They seem to have forgotten that their job is to walk me about; they're under the misimpression that they're supposed to be wound around you."

"Tell your lean long limbs that they can't always be on holiday. I suppose you and I should get back to work as well. Neither of us has written much in the past week."

"I, at least, have been getting some practice putting my life into a narrative form. Don't you think it's time for you to tell me a bit more of yourself?"

"You still owe me a story."

"True enough, but it was a delicious delay, wasn't it?"

"Mmm . . . Look over there across the water."

"Yes?" The island of La Giudecca appeared as it always did, long and low and hot and tired.

"Did you know that Michelangelo once retreated to Giudecca to live in solitude?"

"So my idea was not original. I wonder if he was more successful at it than I have been."

"And right here"—she indicated an unprepossessing building on our left—"is the Pensione Calcina, where Ruskin lived while he wrote *The Stones of Venice.* Do you think that Shakespeare was here, too? Nobody knows, I know, but there's *Othello* and *The Merchant of Venice.* They are such wonderful stories, wouldn't it be sad if he wrote them out of longing—because he couldn't actually travel here?"

"Certainly sad for Shakespeare. Not for posterity."

"Posterity is just a lot of other, younger people that you will never get to know. Most writers that I've met don't care much about other people, but they care very much about posterity. No, that's unfair. They don't know *how* to care, except by writing—in a way that works out for everyone."

"Now that is a sad thought." I thought of Michael.

"I know I don't qualify as posterity," she said, "although I am younger and you don't know me very well yet, but will you tell me your story, nevertheless?"

"I'm afraid I'm intimidated by all this talk of Ruskin and Shakespeare. Besides, I've told you most everything there is to tell."

"The last time we were out together, just before I ran away from you, we were standing on a little bridge near the Ca' Rezzonico. Do you remember?"

"Yes, and it makes me nervous just to think of it."

"Don't be." And she placed her hand over my heart. "All is well with us." I was mollified. "Anyhow, I asked you what you were thinking about, and you said your mother. You haven't told me about your mother." I noticed that the sky was darkening.

"It's difficult to tell you the story of my mother without the story of my father. They were always, always, together."

"Then tell me about both of them." I was momentarily distracted by a swooping and circling of sea gulls, calling after one another in the nearby sky. "Aidan?"

"I never talk about my father."

"Was he cruel?"

"I'm serious, Mira. I never talk about him. To anyone." There was a rough edge in my voice. She appeared stunned by the unexpected rebuff. Hurt. I couldn't bear it. "I can't, I . . . it's not you . . . it's . . . I just can't."

She saw that I was the one hurting now, and she stopped walking abruptly, bringing me around by the arm to face her. She looked into my eyes in the way she so often did—searching, trying to know me. "It's all right, Aidan." But it wasn't. Not with me. I wanted to tell her everything. I wanted to give her anything, everything, she wanted. I wanted to cross treacherous seas for her, battle armies for her—and I couldn't open my mouth. We walked along in silence for a long, long way. Our direction was out toward the tip of Dorsoduro, the sunset behind us, and, as we passed the small boating school with the dozen, intently rowing children bobbing about in their unruly skiffs, I made a decision.

"I want to tell you. It's right and good that I tell you."

"Are you sure?"

"I'm sure, but not here."

"Home?"

"No. The wind's come up. Let's walk around to the protected side of the island, to the Salute. We can sit on the steps there, where we can see San Marco. That will steady my nerves and keep me in the present. We can watch the colors change on the palazzos while I talk, and then we can walk home together in the dark." It was a plan of sorts, and

I needed to bring some sort of order to my mind. I was sweaty, and I knew it was too cool for the weather to be the cause. And I could hear my heartbeat.

Soon enough we were seated on the steps of the massive domed church that had always looked to me like a great overgrown misplaced badly decorated wedding cake. Salute: it meant health, safety, salvation. It seemed like the right place to talk. Mira sat close by me, holding my hand. The hand no longer restrained by a wedding band.

"When I was a little boy, I was very close to my parents. They were extraordinary people. Even to me, given my American upbringing, they seemed exotic. They had been born in neighboring villages near Beirut. Little more than peasants, but gifted with unusual intelligence. They had met by the age of six, were in love by twelve, and married at eighteen. They both worked hard, especially my mother, to achieve a decent education, and then, taking only what they could carry in their minds and in their hands, they left Lebanon forever.

"They lived, first, in Europe . . . Nice and then Paris, working more, learning more, and then, when they had saved the fare, they sailed for the United States. There was Bedouin in my father's blood. He kept moving them around until they found themselves in Texas, which was hot and flat and dry enough for him. It was there that they put down their tenuous roots. Small, dark people, with pronounced Semitic features, they knew they could never assimilate, but they were convinced that hardworking, honest, clean people could make a life for themselves anywhere. And they did. By the time I was born, my father had turned the ground floor of our house into a pleasant little restaurant in which he served all the standard Texan fare, but had slowly added a selection of Middle Eastern dishes to the menu, developing a reputation for the unique and the delicious. My mother helped him and they were happy. I always assumed my life, my marriage, would be as theirs.

"I was a wanted child, the only son of an only son. (And now Michael follows in that tradition.) My earliest memories are all set in the warm, brick kitchen of the restaurant. I would sit contentedly at the end of the scrubbed and battered worktable, watching, while my mother organized the help, prepared the vegetables, and energetically scoured pots and pans, often singing the strange, arrhythmic melodies of her homeland, or reading to my father while he baked and stewed and broiled.

"I was given massive amounts of attention, particularly in regard to my studies. Like many immigrants, they wanted me to become an academic or, failing that, to choose some traditional, respectable, financially sound career. For my part, I enjoyed learning and, unlike the other schoolchildren, I never resented the homework assignments, because I knew those times of evening study, backstage, in the restaurant kitchen, while my father cooked and my mother cleaned, were the best of all times with my parents. Although I was unsure what course I would follow with my studies, I did know that when I was grown, I wanted to be like my father. He was a man who knew who he was. And I knew that someday when I had a child, I wanted to be as he was to me: loving, interested, concerned, good. He was simply good. My mother seemed almost to be part of him, his right hand, his helpmate, and, I knew, his lover, for they were sensual people . . . always aware of flavors, colors, textures, scents, always sharpening my awareness of the world around me.

"The only gray clouds of my youth were the, then, unexplained bouts of illness, which left me delicate and dreamy, and my parents cramped with concern. We persevered, and as the day of my graduation from high school approached, excitement was at an all-time high. They seemed never to stop cooking and singing and smiling in my direction. There was to be a great party at the restaurant, of course, but then after the neighbors and my schoolmates had left, we would clean up and close up and go off together on a short camping vacation in the mountains. My parents had never seen the mountains, and it was decided that we would just keep driving west until we found them.

"You may wonder why I would make such a choice at that age . . . the age of teammates and girlfriends . . . but I had no one as important to me as my parents. My frail health had kept me from athletics, which didn't interest me much anyway, and I had not yet discovered girls. I was, frankly, overprotected and immature, and seriously worried about attending college in the fall. I was still uncertain as to the direction my life should take. Although I had graduated with honors and had been accepted at Columbia, the school of my choice, New York City seemed overwhelming and too far away from my father, although he was proud as a fighting cock about it all.

"We camped in a state park on a tributary of the Rio Grande. My parents were enchanted with the change of scenery, and they surprised me with their stamina as we pitched a tent on the forest floor and hiked over the rugged terrain. It was I who was worrisome, so often needing to rest, once or twice fainting dead away. It wasn't long before my father developed the idea of a boat trip, which he believed would be less strenuous and give us some time to talk quietly together. My mother wasn't for it, said she might get seasick, and decided that she would rather stay at the camp for the day. We put up a mild protest but she was adamant, began packing lunches for the two of us and being generally cheerful about our manly adventure. We rented a rugged little canoe from the ranger station and headed out on a placid stretch of the river while there was still coolness to the morning. I will always remember my mother, standing on the riverbank, strangely alone, waving good-bye until we were well into the current and she was only a tiny, colorful spot in the midst of the greenery."

The sky over Venice had begun to pulse with flashes of heat lightning, and I could hear faraway thunder coming down from the mountains. I had begun to cry, and Mira was quick to comfort me. "Aidan, do you want to stop now? Or should we walk a bit?" I realized in that moment that it was my mother, my-mother-up-to-the-day-I-was-describing, of whom Mira most reminded me—always caring, always (as they say nowadays) supportive.

"No, I'm all right. It feels good to cry, right to cry." And I plunged back into my story, letting the tears come and go as they chose.

"My father and I had been out for a couple of hours, developing a harmonious alternation with our oars, talking of the possible majors for me at Columbia and the careers they would lead to. My father was enthusiastic about pre-law or pre-med, and I was steadily working up the nerve to mention entomology or dramatic art, both of which were sure to puzzle and concern him.

"We began to scan the riverbank for a likely place to beach the canoe and enjoy the lunches that mother had prepared for us when we noticed the current had become suddenly stronger. We began to have trouble controlling the craft. We must have gone unwittingly down some wrong fork in the river and taken ourselves off the course so carefully mapped out by the rangers, for we were soon in a nightmare of rapids. We were both very frightened, and I remember thinking how glad I was that mother had not been persuaded to come along. As we lost all control and were being thrown helplessly down the river, barely missing the sharp, black rocks that loomed all around us, my father turned and shouted back to me—words I will never forget: 'Aidan, if we capsize, I'll try to hold onto the boat and let it carry me. I can't swim.' Those were his last words. Almost immediately we overturned, and when I surfaced in the roaring, raging water I grasped for him and for the boat, but everything hurtled away from me in the swirling current . . . forever.''

Huddled on the hot, dry steps of the Salute, with the storm still distant but approaching fast, I was soaked through, as if I had just emerged from the icy river of the past. I was shaking. Mira held me close.

"I don't remember much about the hours that followed. I know I scrambled along in the direction of the current for a while, screaming his name, until I was cut off by a sheer cliff face. And then I sat on the edge of the river, too cold and numb with shock to cry. And then somehow I made my way back to the camp. My mother had heard the sound of someone coming through the underbrush and had come out of the tent to see who it was. I didn't have to tell her what had happened. She took one look at me and knew. And I knew she blamed me.''

"Aidan, no! You must be mistaken. She couldn't have. It's nothing like how you've described her.''

"She did. And I did. Why hadn't I asked him if he could swim? Why hadn't I asked her? We were desert people! Why would I have assumed that he could swim? I had had lessons at school and at the YMCA on Saturdays, but my parents had had no such advantages. It was the thoughtlessness of youth, the taking-things-for-grantedness of a spoiled son. He had rented the canoe with me in his mind, without worrying about himself. And I had failed to worry as well. A deadly sin of omission."

"She could have told you, or stopped him . . ."

"No. My mother would never have crossed my father."

"Would you have?"

"I think so. I was inexperienced with boats, and I knew they could be dangerous, especially in unknown waters . . . I think so . . . well . . . it's water over the dam, isn't it?" I said, ruthlessly, mirthlessly. And then went on.

"My mother changed on that day in a way I couldn't have imagined. You would expect a change, of course, after such a closely shared life, after such a dramatic, tragic loss. All the song went out of her. But the thing I couldn't understand, the thing I couldn't believe, was that she simply stopped loving me. I had been her cherished son for seventeen years, but it was as if she had forgotten me. I could have been the newspaper boy or the grocer's son. I wasn't hers anymore.

"She stood on the bank of the river that evening, at the place where, earlier in the day, she had last seen my father and me together. She was staring out at the water, or into the water, while I told her what had happened. She listened to the details, and, in those few minutes, she became a stranger, remote and cold. Expressionless, she called the rangers, and, two days later, they recovered his body, so battered I could barely identify him. Half of his face was gone.

"After the funeral I decided to forgo college in the fall and stay with my mother and run the restaurant for her, though she showed no enthusiasm for the idea. We were both so grief-stricken we couldn't talk to one another, and the worst was the feeling that even if I could, it would not be a comfort to her. I used to follow her around silently . . . just not getting it. How could a mother forget her son? Then one evening, about a month after the funeral, she looked up from her needlework and said to me, 'Aidan, he will come for me very soon. And for you, too, but not for a very long time.' A week later she was dead. Pneumonia . . . I watched while she drowned in herself and joined him.''

Now it was Mira who shivered.

"My life went on, of course, as I've told you: college and girls, illness and diagnosis and treatments, work and women—you, my love, among them—and, finally, Sonia and Michael. But I could never be to Michael as my father had been to me. I *knew* I was going to die . . . I thought in some misdirected way that it was better if he didn't become too attached to me. Now I know better. There. I've finally said it all.''

I was wrung out. "Take me home, Mira. I need to sleep, if I can." I no longer needed to cry. The sky had relieved me of the responsibility. The first huge, hot raindrops had begun to fall upon us. We stood up to begin our return.

"What was his name?"

I looked at her blankly.

"Your father's name. What was it?"

"Michael. My grandmother named her son for a saint. His name was Michael."

And we walked home in the dark as I had planned, and in the storm for which I had not planned.

SIX

Torcello

The storm that rumbled and raged all through the night brought a freshness to the morning. Wally appeared from a secret haunt, high and dry on the wall, with a pure, blue backdrop of sky behind him, and the flowers in the garden glistened like a chest of Murano glass beads, bright with every gaudy color.

I awaited absolution, but it came not. If we are all, every one of us, only the shrapnel of some big bang, the debris of some universal thump in the remoteness of time—meaningless, inconsequential, wending our predetermined way through some infinite, expanding space—still, there is a way to treat our fellow beings, and when our efforts miscarry, we suffer. We feel the misery of guilt and regret, and nothing, no thing, no being—priest or prayer, mistress or mystic—can absolve us.

Nevertheless, I felt relieved to have told her, lightened, and eager now to put my confession into the context of my novel. Michael had a right to know the story of his grandparents, a right to come to his own terms with the failings of his father. Mira was encouraging, setting about her own work with an admirable, enviable diligence. She wrote in longhand, and I found a historical delight in watching her, sitting at the table by the window, pen in hand, writing like Austen or Woolf. I, with less grace, pounded noisily away at a portable typewriter. It was a new and companionable way for us to be together.

"Isn't it time that we checked you out of the Pausania?" I asked her. "You're practically living here with me. You call it home."

"No."

I was brought up short by the brevity of her reply.

"Isn't it time, then, that you told me about it?"

"About what?" I could tell she was playing for time.

"Your being in Venice. Your hotel. Your benefactor."

"No."

"I see."

"What do you see?"

"Your benefactor, as you call him, is a lover. Someone wealthy and wise—and busy—who has sent you away to write your novel until it's convenient for him to call for you. It would look fishy if you suddenly flew the coop."

"You're very imaginative, Aidan. You should put your imagination into your book. But beware of mixed metaphors." She said this lightly, with the hint of a smile, but she offered no alternative explanation. I felt a flush of warmth around my neck and face. I was angry. I was surprised to be angry, and, after a moment of consideration, I decided that I had a right to be angry. I fought it down, nevertheless.

"Mira. Please tell me more about yourself."

She put down her pen and studied me for a few moments. I could not fathom what she was feeling.

"What would you like to know?"

"Everything. Anything."

"You told me about your childhood. Perhaps I should start with mine?" Still playing for time, but I was eager now for news, from whatever era she chose.

"Yes. Tell me about your childhood."

"It was not at all secure, like yours."

"Because your father died?"

"Because my father died." And suddenly I didn't want to know. I wanted to keep her as I had her, unsullied by a past in which I had no part, a past I could not alter or alleviate. And I didn't want to hear again the part I *had* played, for I knew my thoughtless behavior was woven into the pattern of her life. In the short, intense time we had shared together in Venice, we had become of one fabric, Mira and I, and I feared that a tug on a single thread could undo us both. But she had, finally, on this perfect morning, begun to tell me her story.

"Unlike you, I barely knew my father. There are a few warm embers of memory . . . of strong arms, a bearded face, a traditional blue collar, and, oddly, a bowl of goldfish that he won for me pitching pennies at a spring fair. Then he was killed. I was three at the time. I remember a tremendous explosion that seemed very nearby, although it was all the way across the town, and a brilliant flash of light. I thought he had run away and forgotten me on that scary morning, for he never came home again. When I was older and could understand such events, it was explained to me that he had been on his way to the factory and was waiting at the local railway crossing for a train to pass when a tank car full of jet fuel had exploded. It took out a lumberyard near the tracks, two houses, and my father in his beat-up old pickup truck. So when I think of him, it is mostly the sound of an explosion and a flash of light that I see. Other children, growing up in the fifties, were afraid of the atomic bomb— with good reason, I suppose, being subjected as we were to the postwar air-raid drills once a week, crouching under our school desks until the all-clear siren sounded. Stupid thing to do to children . . . Anyhow, I wasn't afraid, because, in my own life, the bomb had already dropped.

"My mother remarried fairly soon, and the father I remember is Harry. He was fat and he was mean. Not cruel . . . hitting or anything like that . . . but mean in the sense of greedy, tight, ungiving. He tried to keep my mother to himself, along with anything else that was worth having in our home, music or books or desserts. Everything was hands-off. When the goldfish went belly-up, I wasn't allowed to have a dog or a cat because of the expense, and my clothes were generally a disaster area."

She was framed by the window as she spoke; the sunlight coming in from behind her enflamed her hair and outlined her perfect form, more beautiful than any Renoir. She wore a lovely yellow sundress that she had retrieved from her hotel at dawn. It was hard for me to imagine her deprived, or poorly turned out. It was hard to imagine that anyone would want to deny her anything, and I thought: dear old Harry, may you rot in Hell. I hadn't long to wait.

"Harry had a brain hemorrhage when I was ten that killed him. Mother explained it as best she could, stumbling over the word aneurism. I got it right away, though. His brain had blown up. I thought of myself as the girl with the exploding fathers. I didn't miss him. I had mother to myself, although she came with her own price tag. The years had taken their toll on mother, and she had her first heart attack right after Harry died. I decided to become indispensable to her in the hope of heading off another father, and I succeeded. We were very close, and if there are any years to be called happy in my youth, they are the five years in which I nursed her. Except for the house, which was secure and comfortable, we were genuinely poor. Whatever meager savings my real father had left us, Harry had eaten up.

"Fortunately the things I cared about were all within reach . . . watercolors are cheap . . . books, I got from the lending library . . . time to read them . . . someone to read them to . . . mother had never brought herself very far scholastically, but in those years she got an education along with me and at the end could quote Shakespeare and Yeats. I don't know where I got my artistic inclinations. All my family were working-class people with no pretensions, and no strivings for anything grander. Perhaps I was a throwback to some long-forgotten poet in the old country. They were all of European extraction—Italians, Germans, Poles—so I suppose anything is possible.

"When the lighting demolished my mother, I felt as if I had been struck down myself. I just wanted to get out of that deadly town, and I did, and I've never regretted it."

She stopped as if to catch her breath, looked up, out of herself for an instant, and seemed surprised to see me there. She smiled.

"Aidan, let's go somewhere today. Let's take that trip to Torcello. There's still most of the afternoon and evening light left to us."

The abrupt collapse of the story at such a juncture left me uneasy. I felt I should comfort her, but she showed no outward sign of distress. Her desire to seize the day caught hold of me, too, and we set about putting bread and cheese and wine in a basket. My mind, as unruly as a butterfly, began to think of them, and not of her, which I believe was her intention.

We considered taking a water taxi, but decided instead on the slow-moving vaporetto, and at the Fondamenta Nuove we gazed out across a lagoon as smooth as glass, with air as clear. We sailed sluggishly past San Michele, the cemetery island with its high walls enclosing rows of tombstones and groves of slender cypresses with their roots down in the dead and their branches pushing upward toward heaven. After a change of boats in Murano, the island of the glass blowers, we churned our way past Mazzorbo, a suburban island where they made babies, and Burano, where they made lace, arriving in Torcello, where I hoped to make love. The day's heat had just begun to peak, so we meandered slowly, hotly, along the bank of the narrow canal that entered into the island, making our way through overgrown pastures, vegetable gardens, and past the few dilapidated houses, arriving in time on the grassy campo in front of the ancient basilica. We paid a respectful visit inside, to the impressive mosaics: the monumental Last Judgment, with its sinners reduced to body parts in the depths of a Byzantine Hell (just what I hoped for Harry) and, on the wall opposite, a sorrowful Madonna weeping Greekly under dire Latin warnings about the perilous sea. It was the island where Venice had begun—and had been abandoned centuries before for the greener waters of the inland lagoon.

But on this afternoon we had not come for art or history, and we soon made our way out behind the cathedral to the fields, where we spread our lunch and ourselves among the wildflowers and took the splendor of the day into our lovemaking.

There were six varieties of Italian butterflies to be seen that afternoon, four I had already spotted in my garden and two new ones, along with a host of raggle-taggle gypsy moths, some industrious bees intent on increasing the flower population, and flocks of enormous green grasshoppers with the beady eyes of voyeurs. I had never shared this private pleasure with anyone before, and lying next to Mira with the tiny wings all around us was marvelous. My heart curled up warmly in my chest and purred like a contented Venetian cat.

"When I was a boy, I used to wonder how people could catch butterflies, collect them—euphemism for murder them. It made me angry that the people who killed them professed to do it out of a love for them. I gave up the idea of entomology because I didn't want to associate with such people, although I suppose in all fairness they do some good—yelping if a species is threatened and curing butterfly plagues. Perhaps I was simply not made for scholarship. My love was ethereal. I wanted to be the Christ of the Butterflies."

"What do you mean?"

"Well, I had this idea that when I died, the souls of all the butterflies, pinned everywhere behind the dusty glass of everyone's horrid collections, would be freed, and that they would soar to heaven and form a glorious canopy of butterfly wings, like living stained glass, above the world. And it would be so beautiful, so breathtaking, that no one would ever harm one again."

"The Christ of the Butterflies," she murmured, fondly brushing my hair back from my forehead.

I moved down the length of her and over, so that my cheek rested on the softness of her inner thigh. From this perspective I could move my eyes up from her secret caverns, through the enchanted forest of her pubic hair, across the rolling plain of her belly, to the distant hills of her breasts, which hid from me the valley of her neck, but allowed me a view of the splendid architecture of her features. I could not imagine wanting to live in any other place. I let my mind wander about in and out of this magical landscape, in and out of the past and present, with, for once, no thought for the future.

"What are you thinking about?" she asked me.

"The last time I answered that question, you ran all the way to the Rialto."

"I am rooted to this spot."

"I was recalling the story you told me this morning, wondering if the shrinks are right, and if you have refound in me, not only me, but the father that you lost so suddenly and so painfully in your childhood."

"And you have refound your mother in me?"

"Mmm . . . so they would tell us."

"And who did you refind in all those other women?"

"No one. I was searching."

"And in Sonia?"

"Sonia found me."

"That's a dodge, Aidan."

"You should know. You've been dodging my questions for days." I moved up to lie next to her again, so that she could see by my expression that I was not angry.

"I'm afraid of your questions."

"Of my questions, or of your answers?"

"The effect of my answers. I'm afraid you won't love me anymore."

"That, truly, is out of the question." But her countenance was still troubled.

"People always give reassurances when they want to know about you," said Mira. "They say that you're wonderful and that nothing you could tell them about yourself could possibly change the way they feel, but then you tell them, and it does."

"You're speaking from experience."

"More experience than you know."

"Then tell me."

"I went on the streets."

My heart dropped. Nothing in her voice or her manner could have prepared me for this. Nothing of what I knew of her could have done so. She was very close to me, and I could sense that she wanted to touch me, to reassure herself that I was still there, still Aidan, still loving—but she didn't move. She was waiting through the long silence that was not a silence, for my mind was humming, and the insects were humming. I reached across the space between us with a gentle hand.

"When?"

"After you."

"Why?"

"I, too, was searching."

"For how long?"

"Long enough."

"And art and poetry?"

"They were there when I got back."

"And love?"

"No."

"Mira . . . I am so sorry."

"Aidan. Don't."

"I love you."

"Do you still want me?" Her chin was held high, prepared for the worst.

"Pay attention." And I took her again, passionately, profoundly, hoping that my touch, stronger than any words, would assure her of my love.

We had reason to be silent then, each thinking of the other, of the unhappy lives we had led, one without the other.

It was time to go. We stopped for a drink at the once sleepy *locanda* where Hemingway had lived and written his Venetian novel, then made our way home in the dusk-turning-to-dark, over the gray-waters-turning-to-black.

Home, safe, we sat in the garden without light, listening to the sounds of the neighborhood families as they ate their evening meals. Music floated out from behind half-closed shutters, dishes rattled, children shouted, and there were arguments and eruptions of laughter.

"We are not ordinary people, Mira."

"Then we must do extraordinary things with our lives to prove it."

"Or to justify it."

"We must take more time for the writing."

"Time."

I had promised her not to speak of my death, but the mention of time always led me to that deep hole in the ground, like a stupid, disobedient puppy. How much time did I have? I had felt a surge of renewed vitality when Mira arrived in my life, but I knew my body in ways no healthy person could ever imagine, and under this glorious Indian summer, I could still feel the chill approach of winter. Mira was right to press me about the writing. I felt an immediacy about it, too. But I also wanted to make plans with her, arrange a return to the States together . . . God!—a divorce before death. Who would have thought it? Sonia would want to make a big to-do, but her father would insist, politically, on brevity and discretion. For the first time, and I feared the last time, I felt some fondness for my father-in-law and his aching, arching conservatism. And Michael must be told and meet Mira. That wouldn't be easy. And in time, if there were enough time, there should be another marriage.

Mira's confession on Torcello had stunned me, but it had not evoked the recoil she feared. Instead I wanted to protect her. I didn't tell her so. I was afraid she would feel insulted. For whatever mistakes she had made in her youth, whatever the resultant horrors she had suffered, she had matured into a woman of intelligence, a woman of culture, a woman who took pride in the appearance of independence and in her ability to care for and protect herself. In that respect she would have to be wooed and won. One question remained unanswered.

"Your benefactor?" I could not see her face in the night.

"All right, Aidan. If you insist. There is a man."

I was glad she could not see my face, either, because in that moment, and just for that moment, I *wanted* to die.

"His name is Robert Myers. He's an investment banker. I . . . I knew . . . him in my twenties. . . . It's been years since we . . . but he has always taken an interest in me. Maybe he loved me. I don't know. He helped me put my life back together after . . . I was burned out. I don't know where I would have ended up without his intervention. I wasn't on drugs, so I suppose there was always hope. I had always managed to work for myself. I had saved a little money. He invested it for me, and I was, for once, fortunate. In time I was able to restart myself in school, and he paid for me to see a psychiatrist, but I don't think that did much. I think it was the relationship with Robert—his consistency, his givingness. He still looks after my money and keeps in touch with me, but our lives are very different, very separate. He is not my lover. He did not send me here. I stay in the hotel because it makes me feel whole. It makes me feel that I can make a home for myself, a safe, secure home anywhere in the world. It reminds me that although my life is entwined with the lives of men—my father, stepfather, lovers, teachers, now you—I am not dependent on them anymore and never will be again. I love you, Aidan, but I am my own woman, and I am my own benefactor."

"And mine."

This time she reached out and touched me, pulling me close for a black, sweet, licorice kiss, this woman of the night.

"I can feel your question in the silence, but I don't know what it is."

"You are so good to me, Mira. You are so good-tempered in general. What do you do with your anger, with your rage against all that has happened to you?"

"I have had a changing relationship with my anger. When I was on the streets, clearly I was taking it all out on myself, though I thought I was taking it out on men. Robert helped me understand that. When I was in therapy, I went into an appalling depression, but I worked my way out of that in time. Now my anger goes into my work. My stories are often angry bursts of bitterness. People seem to think they're humorous. Black humor. And, I know this sounds defensive, but often I'm not angry at all . . . about any of it. My life just was what it was, not much worse than anyone else's life and a good deal better than most. More questions?"

"Only one. I was wondering about his name."

"Robert Myers?"

"No. I mean your father, your real father. What was his name?"

"My dear Aidan, his name was Daniel. He was a Dan."

And we laughed a dark little laugh, there in the dark, then went inside to sleep. We knew that all was well with us, that revelation brought us closer together; it did not take us farther apart—and we slept wrapped up in each other, protected by the lions and the dragons of the bed.

In the morning she was gone.

SEVEN

Isola
San
Michele

Once before, she had been missing in the morning when I awoke. She had gone for a long soak in her bathtub at the hotel, which she said she preferred to my tiny shower stall, then in fresh clothing she had returned in time for breakfast. So at first I was not alarmed. The shutters had been opened, letting in another white-hot day, and coffee was brewing. Wally, who was getting positively rotund, had clearly been fed and sat on the wall washing his face, his blind eye turned my way in a blatant attempt to ignore me.

I went to work right away, hoping to have something to show her when she returned. It was going very well, the words coming in correctly tied knots, and I was surprised, when, in what seemed mere minutes, I looked up to see that it was almost midday. There was no sign of her. I wished that she had left a note. I dislike uncertainty. The arrival of noon ignited a small fuse of worry. I leaned back in my chair and tried to assess the situation.

The sun, the wine, and the emotion of the previous day had exhausted me, and I had slept soundly. I hadn't heard her stir, but dead to the world as I was, I wouldn't have noticed. Perhaps she had had a difficult night. It couldn't have been easy for her to come out with the announcement about her early life—not to me, not to anybody. Perhaps I had taken the news too calmly, appeared too complacent in the face of her history, and she had felt it as a withdrawal— but I remembered the way we had touched on Torcello *after* her confession, and there was no way she could have felt unloved. Unless, of course, sex had become an untrustworthy measure of feeling for her altogether. That would make sense after what she had been through. But surely it was *because* of her experience that she could feel the difference between our sexuality and all the rest. We didn't just have sex, we expressed love, made more of it, gave that to each other as well. It couldn't be different for her—could it? Ours was a collaboration of hearts, a confluence of spirit.

By the last chime of the noon bells of the nearby Carmini, my confidence was beginning to sink. It hadn't taken long. I hated my fear. It felt old and tough and unmanageable, and I began to prepare a lunch for us in the face of it—an extravagant salad, grilled pork chops in nutmeg (a recipe of my father's), and baked potatoes with butter and cheese—

to no avail. By the half-hour I could wait no longer and was on my way hurriedly down the *fondamenta,* heading in the direction of her hotel. I had packed the lunch in foil and taken it along to cover my distrust. I would suggest another excursion, perhaps to the Lido to see the old Hôtel des Bains, where Thomas Mann had set *Death in Venice* . . . Mira would like that idea.

She did not answer the room phone, but she hadn't checked out. I tried to persuade the man behind the desk to let me see her room, and he listened with an air that managed to suggest that in his capacity as concierge he saw and understood everything, but from beneath a permanently raised eyebrow. At last he handed the keys to a sullen young woman—his wife? his daughter?—who casually led the way with an air that managed to suggest that in her capacity as bellhop she had seen everyone and that I didn't actually exist. As I followed her bountiful bottom up a crooked marble staircase, I realized that Mira had brought me back to a state of being wherein I could again appreciate the female form, though my feelings were entirely centered on the room to which we made our winding way, in the hope that Mira might be secluded safely somewhere within it.

Her bed was made, the tub was dry—there was no sign of her. I felt vaguely dishonest, there, among her personal belongings—a stranger—and something about the empty bedroom made my heart ache. I thought of her in the bed: alone, with another man, with many other men. I backed out of the room, still hurting, and the disenchanted woman closed the door behind me with a thud. I was glad to go home.

Back in the empty apartment I was restless and depressed

and I decided, belatedly, to straighten up the place a bit, to make the bed. It was then that I picked up the pillows to fluff them out and saw the note.

> Aidan,
>   Please don't be upset with me, but yesterday took its toll on my nerves, and I need a little time to myself . . . just to meander around for a while . . . try to think where I am to go in my novel. I know where I'm to go in life . . . with you . . . so don't worry. Back by suppertime. Where I come from that means about six. I love you.
>   Mira

I felt the perfect fool. Then, of course, I realized that I was irritated. I wished she had talked her plan over with me first, shared her distress with me.

I ate her lunch as well as mine, and I drank too much wine. Afterward it was not surprising to find that the muse had left me in disgust, so I decided for once to have an Italian afternoon—asleep. Truth was, I missed Mira terribly, and my recently acquired ability to be peacefully alone with myself was no more.

Sleep, in the overheated afternoon, was dreamless and unrestful. I awoke exactly at six. No Mira.

The evening wore on with no sign of her. I fed Wally. I telephoned the hotel a couple of times. I tried to eat, tried to work, tried to read. Finally, with the light failing, I went in search of her, but, of course, I had no idea where to look and ended up wandering miserably into the dark. I hurried home then, certain to find her there, pensive, with her novel on her knees, but the apartment was as vacant as Christ's tomb. I wondered if I should call the Venetian police—show them the note, show them my watch—but what could they do? They could check the hospital, I supposed, but I could do that myself. Toward midnight I did. A sleepy night nurse, made cross by my broken Italian, assured me in a scorching, sarcastic voice that there was no such *bella bella* woman under their care. I was glad of that.

Perhaps she had decided to leave me after all. Perhaps she had left the note carefully behind in order to slow down the likelihood of pursuit. She could send for her belongings at the hotel. She had taken the novel. It was the most likely explanation. I was sure it was something I had done, and I tried and retried my memory, looking for a clue. Perhaps she had taken my response to her revelation in the wrong way—thought I saw her now only as a sexual object—but I had to believe my own body. She had been *with* me in the lovemaking. Of course, with her experience, she might have been able to make it appear so . . . even if . . .

The night wore on. A nightmare night of darkest despair. In the dead of it I finally slept. I slipped into the strangest of dreams. In it, I entered the Church of St. Thomas Aquinas, where, as I was about to put my notes into the vestry box, I saw a note from my father to me saying, *Welcome to Venice*—and then the bells began to toll and I was afraid because I knew there was no such church in Venice and that my father was dead.

I awoke to the ring of the telephone. It was such an unaccustomed sound that my head, still surfacing from sleep, could not at first make it out. When I realized it was the phone, my mind flailed around in unlikely possibilities: Michael calling just to say hello, Nell phoning from the office with a problem worthy of my attention at last, Sonia calling to say she had heard about the affair . . . Mira . . . Mira! I bolted from the bed, glancing at my watch as I went. It was seven in the morning.

"Signore Say. . . . eed?" An unfamiliar male voice. It was a crackling connection and I was sure the call was from far far away.

"Si."

"Parle Italiano?"

"Poco . . . poco . . . parlo Inglese."

"Then I will speak in the English."

"Thank you. Who is calling?"

"My name is Fratello Sebastiano . . . Brother Sebastiano . . . Could you, with pleasure, come to the Island of San Michele?"

"The cemetery?"

"Yes . . . yes . . . there is here a young woman who says you will come. I would to bring her myself but for me it is difficult to leave the island. You come?"

"Mira? Mira is at the cemetery?"

"Yes. She is here. You come?"

"I come." And before I could ask him anything more, we were disconnected.

I dressed hurriedly and dove into the first waiting taxi that I saw, stunning the driver with the combination of my destination and my haste. We careened through the waters to the distant island without conversation. The spray of cold water that was sent back to me as the motorboat hit the mild little lumps of wave drove away the horrors of the night. I was going to Mira. Whatever had happened, she was alive—in the unlikeliest of places, but alive. Either she hadn't left me or she had and had changed her mind—both explanations meant there was hope for us yet in the ever-shifting waters of our world.

As the boat sped toward the high brick walls of the island, I was reminded that, in my hurry to get to Mira, I had not given Wally his breakfast, and I imagined him pacing back and forth, irritably, hungrily—before I recognized the feelings as my own. What sort of fix had Mira gotten herself into? What was I doing in such a place at such an hour? A line of boats festooned with black ribbons and white flowers blocked access to the pier, and we bobbed unpleasantly about as a coffin was hoisted off the largest of the craft. Weeping women followed, and were helped ashore by a kindly looking young priest, also in black and white, and I thought he might be Brother Sebastiano, a sort of greeter at the shore of this most ungodly of godly places. But as my taxi finally found space to pull up and tie up, I saw that the priest had gone with the mourners through the gate and into the cemetery proper. There was no one left on the pier but the man in the kiosk selling vaporetto tickets. I asked the driver to wait and jumped ashore, feeling disoriented and a little seasick.

I followed in the steps of the early morning funeral procession, for there was only one gate through which to enter, and I found myself in the courtyard of the dank and dreary church that served this perished parish. San Michele in Isola. I knew from the guidebooks that it was believed to be the earliest Renaissance church in Venice, built before Columbus sailed for America—or wherever he was meaning to sail to. I wondered why, as a species, humans were so fascinated with the oldest, the newest, the biggest, the smallest of everything. Certainly this island must hold the record for the shortest cemetery stays: twelve years and then, if your family doesn't pay the rent, you're out on a bone heap with the rest of the hoi polloi—unless you're famous like Igor Stravinsky or Baron Corvo, who rest in perpetuity.

I wondered why, as a human, my mind was chattering away with this useless information. Perhaps to keep my feelings at bay. I began to search around for someone who could give me direction—the mourners having gone off, lost behind the monuments. There was no one in the church. Behind it, the cloister, also deserted, showed signs of neglect. The courtyard stones were shot through with weeds. I heard the sound of slapping footsteps. A portly Jesuit friar wearing a brown cassock tied with a rope approached me on sandaled feet. He had a kindly, weathered face as brown as his robes.

"Mister Say-eed?"

"Father . . . Brother Sebastiano?"

"Yes. Come this way with pleasure."

"What has happened?" But he made no reply. Sauntering gracefully, he led me along the columned passage that skirted the courtyard into a plain little office with a battered desk, a telephone, a bench running along the far wall, and on it, a woman.

"Mira."

She looked up but she didn't speak.

"Mira?" She seemed to be folded into herself, looking old and cold and dazed. I had seen that look before and a bolt of terror ran through me.

It was Brother Sebastiano who spoke. "She was locked into the cemetery yesterday afternoon. It has not happened to us before. We do not lock the walls inside of here." He indicated the domain beyond the cloister. "But we have a new brother, and he pulled shut the gate on his way into the dinner, thinking it was right. He did not see this woman, and it was after four."

"I didn't know the cemetery shut at four." Mira spoke without moving.

Appalled, I realized that something had held me at the doorway. I had not gone to her or offered comfort. Was it something in the look of her? Or was it the presence of the Jesuit? Or had the remains of the night I had just spent, alone and full of the certain and complete loss of her, juxtaposed themselves against the reality of her presence? I shook myself loose from my paralysis and went to her, putting my arm around her shoulders. She was like stone at first, as though transformed into a monument to herself, then suddenly she shuddered and melted into the Mira I knew, soft and warm and responsive.

"Perhaps, now, you take her home?" He was friendly and polite, but obviously eager to be clear of the situation. Doubtless he didn't know what to do with a woman. He lived in a man's world, a world of the dead. I had recently had near misses with both, and I clutched Mira to me like a life preserver as we took our leave. I heard the door to the office sigh with relief as it shut behind us.

Outside I began to lead her toward the pier and the waiting taxi, but she balked.

"I need to show you where I was."

"Mira, come along. The sooner you are well away from this place, the better."

"No. I want you to see. I want to see for myself, in the daylight, with you, or it will haunt me."

There was not much of my Texas heritage that remained with me, but I had been taught that if you fall off a horse, the first thing you should do is get back on. Perhaps it was in this spirit that Mira needed to go back to the place from whence she had just been released.

"All right. If you think it will be healing."

"I do." And she led me past the high rows of vaults that looked like marble filing cabinets—with a Venetian in each drawer, their pictures on the front to avoid confusion—and then through the neat, green fields of simple white crosses over graves full of nuns and priests, to a red brick wall with a rusted iron gate, now pulled partially open. We stepped inside, just a few feet, for she would venture no farther. This was the Protestant section of the graveyard, and by contrast to the neatly kept Catholic plots, this one was completely neglected and dilapidated. The crumbling tombstones stood awry; ivy and weeds were dancing together in death. Dry, dead leaves crunched under foot, and everywhere—where all should be still—there were the rustlings and dartings of living creatures.

"The lizards," she said. There were thousands of them. They scuttled everywhere. "After I realized the gate had been locked, I yelled for a while, but when no one came, I sat on that grave over there. The large one. It is the grave of a woman and her daughter who died together at the turn of the century. It doesn't say how." Mira told me all this, spouting information like a bored tour guide, without observable emotion. "I sat there on top of them and I thought about my life. I have had a difficult life, but I realized that I didn't want to be anyone but myself, not anyone I knew or had ever known, and I didn't want to be dead. There were, maybe, times in the past when I wanted to die—never enough to try to kill myself, but to wish for a passive death, a slipping-away-into-the-night death, but not now. I have found you, and the chance that I would find among all the humans on the earth the one I was meant to find is miraculous. I've done it twice. I found you once, and even if that was the only night I ever spent with you, it's more than most people have in a lifetime—more than any of those poor dead nuns neatly laid in rows out there ever had, unless they really did find it with Christ, which I doubt. And then I found you again and you *love* me—a reformed whore. I wanted so much to come home to you, stay with you, be with you forever. I was sure someone would come before nightfall. But no one did."

"My poor Mira."

"All night I heard the horrible lizards. I thought there were rats in here, too, and I was afraid they would attack me. And I know it's hard to believe, but it was cold. Oh, not at first—the tombstone held the heat from the sun—but then it grew colder and colder, much colder than the night, which was an unimaginable black . . . and I realized why we are so hateful of the dark. It's because it makes us utterly alone in a way we can't control. And there was a terrible, chill wind that blew up . . . up, like steam or smoke, from the graves: the wind of San Michele. But worst of all was that, as frightened as I was for me, I was more frightened for you. I could kind of talk myself out of my own terrors—remind myself that lizards are just lizards, not rats, and that I wouldn't freeze in Italy in summer, and that the dark is just light turned inside out, and that dead people couldn't hurt me—but I couldn't talk myself out of my fear for you, all alone in the apartment, not knowing what had become

of me. I knew you would be worried to death . . . worried
. . . and a terrible fantasy took hold of me. I remembered
what you had told me your mother had said . . . just before
she died . . . about how your father would come for you
. . . and I was afraid it was *that* night that he would come,
and I wouldn't be with you . . . and then it seemed that the
dead can hurt us after all, that they remember us and think
of us and resent us . . . and here I was surrounded with the
dead and they seemed to want me, welcome me. Oh, Aidan,
it was dreadful."

I remembered my dream of the previous awful night.
Welcome to Venice.

"And then I was afraid they had shut up this part of the
cemetery for good—you see how filthy and awful it looks—
and they would never come back and I would never get out
. . . and I would never see you again."

"Enough," I declared. "Let's get you out of here."

This time she did not object, and we hurried from the
ground and the stone to the comfort of the water. Safe
inside the taxi, I put her on my lap and asked the driver to
return slowly, letting the waves rock us gently, and I felt
like a grandfather soothing a young child.

"Mira, what were you doing in that place in the first
place?" I tried to ask this without a hint of censure.

"I wanted to see the grave of Ezra Pound."

"Why?"

"He was generous to James Joyce."

"Yes, of course."

"And he was an impressive writer himself."

"You live among these writers, don't you? These dead
men who told tales."

"Women, too. Did you know that George Eliot's husband tried to drown himself on their honeymoon by jumping into the Grand Canal?"

"No."

"He survived. But then she got sick and died. Isn't that sad?"

"Very sad." She seemed to be talking herself into a sleep, and very soon she was quiet against my chest. I was sorry to wake her when we pulled up in front of the apartment, but she let herself be led without protest, and was soon asleep again, curled in the center of the bed.

I went out into the garden to feed Wally, who tried to appear nonchalant about my late arrival but couldn't manage the pretense. I brought my typewriter outside, where the sound would not disturb her, but I was unable to concentrate. I was awash in guilt. I had failed utterly in my wish to protect her. She had had a horrific experience, and all the while I had only thought of myself, pitied myself. Of course I had worried for her, but Venice is a safe city and she was a competent woman, so, in my heart of hearts, I hadn't really believed she was in any danger. I supposed, in truth, she hadn't been in the way of physical harm, but she had been in distress while I was poor-me-ing it all night long. Perhaps it was I who was incapable of love. But when I thought of her, it felt like love.

She slept the whole day and the night, often thrashing around, once awakening with a scream.

"I had the most awful dream, Aidan. I was in the cemetery again and they were burying the mother and her daughter . . . but it was a false grave . . . a hole that went right through the island . . . down into the water . . . and they just dropped them into it . . . and then I was the daughter somehow and the fishes were eating my eyes and—"

"Ssh . . . it's all right now. You're safe here with me now, warm and dry." But was she safe? Was I not prone to the sins of omission—not loving enough, not thoughtful enough, not careful enough? Didn't my loved ones always pay the price? Father. Mother. Sonia. Michael. Mira. Even hungry little Wally.

I felt I should be beaten to death with my own heart.

EIGHT

Scuola Grande di San Rocco

The morning came at last, covered though it was in sheets of rain. Mira awoke with a Wally-size appetite, and over mounds of scrambled eggs and piles of cinnamon toast I talked to her. I had been up most of the night preparing the lecture that I planned to give her. I had never done anything like this in my life. It was heartfelt.

"Mira, the day before yesterday you did what you are used to doing. You decided how your day should be spent and you set out to spend it. But things went wrong and you had a ghastly time of it. So did I."

"I'm sorry."

"No matter. Here is what matters. We love each other now, and that changes how we must live. You're used to going your own way. So am I. I came to Venice to become even more independent, but that's not how things have turned out, and I'm glad. We have to think of each other now—always—against our habits of self-absorption. You must tell me if you're upset. Maybe I'll have a better idea of what to do about it than go roving around cemeteries looking for Ezra Pound's name on a stone. Maybe I won't. My idea was the beach and the Hôtel des Bains and a look around the Lido for poor old fictitious gay dead Aschenbach, but nevertheless, we must face our problems together. We are a couple now."

"What about my work?"

Her question was the last answer I had expected.

"What do you mean?"

"Well, if it's a choice between what's best for the writing or what's best for us, what would you have me do?"

"I still don't know what you mean."

"Sometimes everything must stand aside for the work. I've learned that, if I've learned nothing else about life. Yesterday . . . the day before yesterday . . . I was lost in the novel. I didn't know where my characters were going next. I know from experience that at times like that it is best for me to walk . . . just go . . . and let my mind run. As awful as it was on San Michele, it was necessary that I go. The night I spent there will show up in the work, sooner or later."

This was a new concept for me. After my carefully obsessed speech, I was stung.

"And what about me?"

"You will show up in the work, too." And she smiled complacently.

"I mean, what about the way I *felt,* while you were out having your adventure-in-the-name-of-art, and how I've *felt* since you've been found? It hasn't been easy for me."

"Whatever you feel should go into your work," she declared. She was patronizing me. She went on. "That way nothing is lost. Then everything that we suffer takes on value."

"I don't need the work to give value to my life. *You* give value to my life!" I couldn't keep my anger safe behind a dam of composure.

She looked at me coolly. "Maybe you can find value in me . . . meaning in my existence. Maybe that is your gift. But I can't. I've never been able to find any meaning in my existence at all, unless I make something of it. That is what I am trying to do with my writing. The meaning of my life is in my work."

"That has to change!" It was out before I could stop it. I tried to cover it. "We both have to change. We've never been here before."

Now she was angry. "Haven't we?"

We were silent for a while, both of us tasting the newness of argument. Neither of us liking it. "Look, Aidan, you've been able to make a life for yourself in spite of your tragedies. You have a wife, a child, a home with a family in it. You've had other love affairs, too, and you can probably name all ten hundred of them. And you've got your work in the theatre, and now your writing. That's something."

"None of it means anything next to you."

"All of it means something, whether it is next to me or not."

"I'd throw it all into a canal at high tide for you. You know that."

"Michael?"

"Not Michael."

"Not Michael, and not bloody much else, either, if push comes to shove at the edge of a canal. I'm not counting on you, Aidan, no matter what you say. Your actions, over time, whatever they may be, will speak much stronger to me than any of your words—like your actions on Torcello."

I felt a surge of relief to know that she had understood me and had really been with me, there. "What do you want me to do?"

"Write."

"Write?"

"Yes. Write something that means something—for Michael. Don't die until you do. Don't die, Aidan. Don't die." Her anger had dissolved into the anxiety that haunted us both.

"I'm doing my best to live, Mira. But you must try to help me. Think of my feelings in relation to what you do. I don't think your work has to suffer. Just let me share in it with you. Don't go wandering off without me."

"I'll try. But I can't let myself live for you, not again. In your absence I learned to write for you—then I learned to write for others. Then I learned to live for the writing. I learned that if I wrote well enough—if I could make *literature* of my life—then the pain of living it was transformed, and I couldn't be hurt by it anymore. Not in the same way. I can't let that go, even if it makes me a little less than human."

"I have never known anyone more human, or more desirable, even with egg on her face that should be on my face." I leaned over and licked her on the chin where a bit of egg had clung. "I'm sorry for wanting to be the center of your life. I know I haven't yet earned that right. But I never thought that work—any work—could matter as much as love, as a person."

"It has to. Otherwise, you're—"

"Dead."

"I'm sorry."

"I'm sorry that people, myself chief among them, have let you down so badly. I wonder if there is a false idea in your argument somewhere."

"What do you mean?"

"I follow your logic, but isn't it possible that what is beneficial for us is beneficial to the writing as well?"

"That would be a whole new world."

"Didn't it work for the Brownings?"

"Let's try. It's a dreary day. We could just stay in, and sit close, and write." The idea of working together made her whole face light up.

"Yes, but first could we . . .?" I leaned over again. This time to lick her breast as lightly as a butterfly licks a flower. "You once said you liked sex better than art." The idea of playing together made my whole body light up.

"Let's open the shutters so we can hear the sound of the rain on the water while we make love. We'll pretend it's the sound of Aidan throwing everything into the canal for me."

It was a lovely morning inside.

248

Later, I was able to write well again, and Mira professed to be working well, too, though she wouldn't let me read what she was writing. "When it's done, when it's good," she promised.

In the evening the rain finally stopped and it seemed the right time for a walk. We felt we had earned it.

"What ghostly haunt shall we visit?" I chided her. "San Lazzaro Degli Armeni, where Byron hung around in the winter writing poetry and learning Armenian, or Ca' Rezzonico, where Browning died, or maybe the Doge's Palace, where Casanova escaped from the dungeons and lived to tell the tale?"

"Let's go to San Rocco. Have you been there?" she asked.

"No. I've missed it somehow on every visit. I've never quite been able to find it."

"It's massive, and it's near here, right behind the Frari." She got out the map. "I can find it. Let's go."

"But first tell me which illustrious writer made love or made pizza there?"

"No writer I know of. This is for the visuals. It's Tintoretto till you go blind. Come to think of it, I think Tintoretto went blind."

It was so good to be happy again.

She was right. The scuola was massive, as were the Tintorettos covering the walls and, upstairs, the ceilings as well. Every miracle and massacre in the Bible.

"These old Venetians seemed to have taken their religion seriously."

"I wonder what that would be like."

I wanted to keep the conversation light, even in the face of such dark magnificence, because a new feeling had come upon me, one, in spite of my morning's speech, that I was not yet ready to share with her. I had often been pleasantly out of breath with Mira, and expected that I would be so when we climbed the wide, marble staircase to the second floor, but it was as we stood, resting on the first-floor landing, flanked by two gruesome depictions of the plague, mortal enemy of the Venetians for so many centuries, that something changed in my heart.

It was a slight twinge, difficult to describe—a sizzling or crackling, not painful, but it carried with it a powerful message. The visual image was that of an electrical charge, a short circuit in the wiring of an old house that had just started a small, imperceptible fire within its walls. It was a matter of time, a very short time, before the whole building would explode into flame, taking the sole occupant with it. I was going to die very soon.

I needed a few minutes to accept this inner knowledge. I didn't know yet if I would tell her or not. We continued our way around the room, admiring the Angeli paintings— *The Baptism of Christ,* the *Agony in the Garden,* the *Ascension*—without much comment.

"Tintoretto's masterpiece is in the Sala dell' Albergo, just off this room," she announced. "Are you ready for it?"

"No time like the present," I replied, meaning it. But I wasn't ready. It was not something you can be ready for. An immense canvas that covered the entire wall of the sizable room confronted us as we entered. A vast *Crucifixion.*

"I'm never prepared for it either," she said, noticing, even in the dim light, how pale I had become, "although I have seen it many times."

"Let's sit down."

And we sat on the wooden bench that ran the length of

the room, opposite the painting. It was a long time before I could begin to grasp the enormity of what was confronting me. The Christ on this cross hung, young and strong and serene—indomitable—above a toiling mass of humanity. He was so lifelike that I expected him to shake his head in dismay, in sadness, at all that he saw below him: the beggars gambling for his clothes, his mother and Mary Magdalene and the disciples suffering at his feet, the workmen bent with the labor of hoisting the thieves onto their crosses and up into position, the horrified onlookers, the soldiers eager with spears and sponges. If this Christ spoke, he would say, "Don't you know how foolish you all look, how desperate, how unhappy—don't you have something better to do with your lives?" But, of course, he had said that, with more compassion, with more faith, and Tintoretto had captured the exact moment when the plea was forming in his mind: "Father, forgive them, they know not what they do."

"Each time I see it," Mira was saying, "he seems to speak to me of something different. Sometimes it's peace, and sometimes strength, and sometimes I am caught by his suffering and I think, oh God, if I was only a Catholic, or even a decent Christian, I could offer up my suffering to him and he would say, 'Mira, this is for me to do.' (He was forgiving of whores.) I sit here and I wonder what Jacopo Tintoretto could have been suffering in *his* life to be able to paint this scene?"

"Mira. I need to talk to you." My voice was solemn, and she heard my tone and turned from the painting to me with concern.

"What is it? Has the painting upset you? I'm sorry I was going on that way."

"It's not the painting. The painting is helpful. Mira, the

story I told you about my father . . . I've never told anyone that story before. I never loved anyone enough to feel safe enough to tell it. When Michael asked about his grandparents, I brushed him off . . . told him they died in an accident . . . avoided his questions. That wasn't right. And raising him from a distance wasn't right, either, so . . . well . . . when something happens to me, will you tell him for me . . . I mean if I don't have time to finish my writing."

"If you want me to."

"I do. It might be difficult for you, with Sonia and all. I don't, as I've told you, have a good relationship with the boy. He might be hostile to a friend of mine, might not want to see you or listen to you."

"I'll manage."

"How will you go about it?"

"I'll find a way. The right way. It would depend on circumstances we can't even glimpse as yet."

"Thank you, Mira. It means so very much to me." I took her hand and squeezed it, and fought back some tears that were welling up from deep inside me.

"Now, what is this all about? What has happened to you here to make you so morbid?"

"The painting, I suppose." It was a believable explanation, and she accepted it.

"Shall we go, then?"

"Yes." And we turned away from the *Crucifixion* and left.

We walked along on streets still wet from rain, drying now in the dying rays of the sun, actually golden, as it splashed along the pavement. Home, I sat her down near me on the velvet couch for a talk.

"You have twice in two days called yourself a whore, Mira. Must you do that?"

"You sound as if it hurts you."

"I love you. It hurts me to hear you devalue yourself. And I feel so responsible for what happened to you."

"You're not responsible. No one is responsible for the life of another person. We can affect people, we can influence them, teach them, guide them; but we are not responsible for the choices they make. Surely you know that from your own life."

"But you were only a child."

"I was an old child—and now I'm an old whore. It's not a devaluation, just a description, a truth."

"But you haven't done . . . that . . . in a long time. Why describe yourself as you were in the past?"

"I guess my past is part of my present. I'm not ashamed of it. I did what I had to do. Now I have to do other things."

"What was it like?"

"Everyone wants to know that!"

I savored the rebuke. "I'm sorry."

"Oh, don't be. It's natural to be curious. I was curious, too. It was, essentially, dull. I wanted romance, and I got sex. I wanted great sex, and I got routine. I wanted adventure and I got abuse. Even the money I made was meaningless without a pimp or a habit. It was just a way to survive. I was too good for the street, too smart and too resilient and too pretty. It wasn't long before I had regular clients, then one who kept me for a few months, then another, and another. Then Robert."

"Did you love him?"

"No. I loved you."

"I wish I had known."

"Do you?"

"There was no way to find you. I only knew your first

name, and I wasn't at all sure you had been truthful about that."

"Why didn't you come back to the hotel?"

"Why? You wouldn't have been there."

"Of course I would have. I lived there."

"You *lived* there? In that weird place? Sorry. I thought you just took me there for the night. The place was heaving with whores."

"Actresses."

"Whatever. You lived there and I never knew it?"

"All these years."

"And I never saw you? I worked those streets."

She was silent, and we were sad. "There's another question you will want to ask me sooner or later, Aidan. The answer is: sometimes. Sometimes I enjoyed it. Mostly not. And sometimes I hated it. Okay?"

"Okay? Okay, what?"

"Okay, do you know enough? Can we let it go now?" The memories, in spite of her appearance of self-acceptance, had upset her.

"I will let it go . . . into the past . . . forever . . . if you will."

"All right."

"And the names you call yourself, too."

"All right."

She got up abruptly and went to the windows; she closed the shutters against the gloom. "Aidan, I can't let it go."

"Why not, Mira?"

"There is something I haven't told you. Something you have a right to know."

"Tell me." She was agitated. I tried to steady her with my eyes.

"There was a child."

"A child. When. Not ours? *Ours?*" Now it was she who steadied me.

"Yes. Then. Ours. There could, at that time in my life, have been no mistake."

"A boy or a girl?"

"A boy."

"A son. My God. What happened? Where is he?"

"I couldn't bring myself to get an abortion. It was yours, after all. I had no home or any way to support a child. I decided to have it and give it up for adoption. I knew if I couldn't bear to part with the baby, I had a full month to change my mind and figure something out before the final papers were signed. Everything went as planned. It was an easy pregnancy and a normal delivery. He was healthy. Handsome. I thought he looked like you. Giving him up was the hardest thing I have ever done." She began to weep.

"Mira . . ."

"There's more," she said, trying to hold back the tears. "You better hear it all. I hated myself after the baby was gone. Alone in my shabby room, I heard voices, actual voices, in my head, telling me how bad I was, how I didn't deserve to live. I couldn't stand it. After three weeks I called the adoption agency and told them I wanted the baby back. They hemmed and hawed and I knew they were very put out with me, but they made an appointment for me to come in and get my . . . our . . . son. But when I got to the agency they told me the baby had died. Crib death. They showed me the death certificate. He didn't even have a name. Just Baby Boy and my last name. I was devastated.

I hadn't been there when my baby . . . our baby . . . needed me."

"Mira, let me hold you. I'm so sorry. You've suffered so much because of me. I can't believe it."

She stayed across the room from me.

"I can't believe it either."

"What?"

"After the initial shock wore off, I found that I didn't believe that the baby had died, but I had no way, no power, to challenge them. I was always sure he was alive somewhere; that they had placed him in a home that they thought more fitting. It never made sense to me. I could remember the look of that child. Could I ever forget him? Why would such a healthy child just stop living? Now that I've met you again, now that I know about your illness, I've had doubts for the first time. Perhaps he did die as an infant. But I think I would know it; I would feel it somewhere inside myself, if he was dead."

"So you believe he's alive?"

"Yes. He would be sixteen now, about the same age as your Michael. Oh, Aidan. How could you? Had you met Sonia yet? Were you cheating on her already? Or was it the next day, the day after me, that you found her?"

"Mira, dear Mira. I don't know. There were a lot of women when I was young . . ." My voice trailed away.

"And you were right there all the time. While I was pregnant. If I had only known to come to you, why, you might even have married *me*."

Now she was crying full out. I wanted to die right then. "You have lived with so many losses, so many years."

"Now it is your loss, too." And she came into my arms at last. I wanted to live then, and hold her forever.

"Now it is our loss, our shared loss. Our son. Lost." How had she been able to stand this alone? It was more than I could begin to take in. "You've told me everything now? Everything?"

"Everything."

"I know that such a wound as this can never be healed. I don't expect you to ever forgive me. I know that it will never be possible for me to make it up to you. But now that you've told me, my dearest Mira, now that we love each other, you must try to let me do the impossible."

She nodded against my chest.

"All right," she whispered. "I will be all right."

"We will be all right. In time."

"Yes."

"I will live only for you, my love."

Could I will more life for her, for love? I prayed then. Prayed that I could. But within the walls of my heart, the fire was burning hotter.

NINE

❧

Fondaco
dei
Turchi

"Why did you choose Venice? You could have gone any-where in the world to write your novel."

She looked up from her writing at my question. I had learned that it was all right to interrupt her while she was working. She had the uncanny ability to return to the place at which she had been distracted, without difficulty. It was as if she could just pick up her thoughts and put them down somewhere else while she dealt with me, then reach over and take them back when she was free to do so. She always put me first, but the writing never ceased, and I had the distinct feeling that I was in it—that my demands on her time and attention were simply turned into it, like a fresh ingredient added to an already simmering soup, making it richer.

"I liked the idea of a city without streets."

She never forgot her past, in spite of her promises. References turned up in unlikely places at unexpected moments. Inwardly, I would flinch.

"Of course the first time I came here," she continued, "I realized that there were streets after all, thousands of streets: the Street of the Monkey, the Street of the Swords, the Alley of the Curly-Headed Woman, and my favorite, the Filled-in-Canal-of-Thoughts. But they are all safe streets. I can prowl without being prowled. I like the quiet of it and the surprises of it and the age of it, and most of all I like the artistic history of this city. Painters come here for the light, writers for the eccentricity and for the quiet. It inspires me. Why did you choose Venice?"

"I belong here. I look just like Paolo Veronese."

She looked at me then as though she had never seen me before, like someone sizing up a stranger, or a sculptor considering a model. "You're right," she agreed, looking happily astonished. "You do." And she went back to her writing without missing a beat.

Since the afternoon at the Scuola Grande di San Rocco, we had enjoyed several weeks of tranquility. I could feel the fire burning quietly in the privacy of my chest. I had always been afraid to perish in a foreign country, but now it appeared inevitable, so I had set about surreptitiously making plans and arrangements with lawyers and accountants by telephone. I had provided for Mira in a way that was sure to be challenged, and I had checked and double-checked the legalities to be sure that her rights, which she wouldn't want and wouldn't fight for, would be protected nevertheless. I felt that Michael and Sonia had also been fairly treated in the new will, and letters, sealed until after my demise, had been filed. Small bequests to various women had been arranged in earlier wills, and I indicated they should just be carried over without review into this last version. I didn't want to think about them in light of Mira.

I had called the Centro Internazionale Adozione Gatti Badoer, a small but active organization that exists to care for Venetian cats. They had agreed to watch over Wally, to see that he was well-fed and healthy, with an eye toward possible adoption, and I had sent them a large donation with a promise of additional funds, via Mira, if the job was done properly.

The one matter left unattended was the matter of the body. My body. I had always supposed I would rest by my father and mother. That the family, reunited, would mull over what had gone wrong that day on the river, as we lay next to each other, talking late into eternity. Now, it appeared, a return to Texas was unlikely. For one thing, I didn't like the idea of being shipped home like a parcel. And for another, I didn't want Mira to have to deal with the wrapping and the stamping. I entertained the idea of being buried on San Michele. I could do worse than Ezra Pound for company, but I was afraid that Mira would be anxious and unhappy about revisiting the island. I would be put in the Protestant section, an unattended grave among the lizards. No. The only solution that held any appeal was a cremation, with instructions to sprinkle my ashes over the waters of the lagoon near Torcello, where they would flutter for a while in the breeze, like butterflies, then float upon the water, then sink slowly into the depths—into those calm, green waters, the color of Mira's eyes. If I could make those arrangements, given my poor Italian and the peculiarity of situation, I would have everything in order. Although it seemed right to me—first the flame and then the water—I put it off. Perhaps because, once accomplished, I would have nothing left to do but await the explosion.

I could not bring myself to reveal the gravity of my condition to Mira. She was clearly making every effort to share her inner life with me as I had asked her to do, so my guilt in this ruse was great. I consoled myself with the thought that she didn't want me to talk about dying. And I didn't want to talk of it either. Life, in those weeks, was like a ripe, peeled peach, sweet and slippery and there for the savoring.

"I'm thinking of a walk." It was her turn to interrupt.

"Not surprising after that litany of street names."

"Seriously. I need to get out."

"Is something troubling you?"

"Only in the novel. I'm stuck again. The ideas aren't coming."

"You look hard at it."

"But it isn't very good. I thought I would walk over to the Museum of Natural History in the Fondaco dei Turchi."

"Whatever for?"

"I've never been there."

"And . . . ?"

"And I just happened to come across some drawings of the capitals in Ruskin's *The Stones of Venice* . . . and I—"

"Enough said." And I laughed with pleasure.

261

"Do you want to go with me?"

"No."

"You said that without much thought."

"I don't like natural history museums. They are full of dead animals."

"And dead butterflies."

"Inevitably."

"Well then, I'll go and have an adventure and bring home a story for you."

"Don't get locked in."

"I shall hammer my way out with a dinosaur bone if necessary."

And with a wave she was off down the *fondamenta*. I leaned from the window and watched her retreating figure, a jumble of color in the afternoon light.

"Wait!" I shouted after her. "Mira, wait!" She heard my call and turned. I ran after her. Even this short distance left me breathless. "It's hard for me to see you go."

"Only for an hour." I took her hand and kissed it.

"Only for an hour, then." I walked mournfully back to the apartment. An hour could be a lifetime now.

In the garden Wally was nowhere to be seen. I called to him, but the wild thing would not grace me with an appearance. It happened sometimes. He still would not let me near him, but he seemed appreciative of his dinners and was always there for meals on time. I was restless, but I didn't want to sleep. Sleep now seemed a waste of precious hours—and my dreams were horrific: waterfalls of steaming blood, vultures with ember eyes, broiling landscapes of caking mud that split into pits full of screaming babies. It was better to remain conscious.

I tried to write, but now, in retrospect, my life seemed

like a long, empty wait for Mira. God, how I loved that woman! She had only been gone ten minutes. Why did I love her? Why did anyone love anyone? What was love anyway? I loved her, of course, because she loved me. It's hard to resist, being loved. She was beautiful. That helped. Smart. That, too. But it was something else—something else that she did, or was, or had . . .

I hadn't stopped loving Sonia. I had just been released from her. I had once loved Sonia with the intensity with which I now loved Mira, and for much, much longer—and I had never understood that, either. I wondered what the world would be like when they figured it out—love. The scientists would do it. A balding man in a white lab coat and wire-rim glasses would isolate this chemical or that gene and we would all be able to go buy it, on prescription, approved by the U.S. Food and Drug Administration: snake-oil love, good for what ails you . . .

Except death.

Everything fails before death. I couldn't decide if it was right to die in her arms or not. I wanted to feel her close around me—I could think of no better way to ease myself through the iron gates of fear. But how would it be for her? Would the experience of losing me again, of being unable to keep me from going, have the same deleterious effect upon her as it had the first time? Or had we, in this brief summer, woven enough love, enough laughter, enough trust and treasure into our lives, to sustain her this time? Time.

Why did I love her? I loved her because she had remembered me. For seventeen years, and more, still she had remembered me.

I sat down on the velvet couch and cried then . . . a canal

of tears. *"Streets full of water. Please advise,"* Robert Benchley had cabled home on arrival in Venice. I wept streets full of water.

I was able to sleep then, a peaceful sleep, waking to her hot, afternoon kisses, and life was good again.

We made love lazily, long into the evening, then lay on the couch, crowded comfortably together, considering dinner in a desultory way. "Let's go out somewhere special tonight," she suggested.

"You *are* restless today, Mira. What's got into you besides me?"

"I'm nearing the end of the book."

"Really? I had no idea. What will happen then?"

"I don't know. Home, I guess." She had a way of coming out with short, simple words that changed everything in the world by the end of her sentence.

"What do you mean?"

"Well, if it's good—and I think it is good—you'll have to say what you think, too. Then I suppose I should go back to New York and talk with my agent and try to get the bloody thing started round to publishers. Also, I need to return to some steady work before long, paid work."

"This is just the kind of plan we should talk over together, isn't it? I mean, what will become of *us* if you go off?"

"Aidan, I am trying to share my mind with you." She was exasperated. "It seems I never do it fast enough to suit you. Of course, I don't want to go back without you, but there is no point in writing the book if it doesn't get published— and I am running low on funds, and I thought we should decide about it together."

"When were you thinking of going?" I was grim with the guilt of my illness.

"Soon. By the end of the month. Maybe it's the old habit of school, but I feel that life starts up in September. It seems like a good time to get back into the swing of things."

"This isn't life?"

"You're hurt, aren't you? Yes. This is life."

"But it doesn't swing."

"Why do you have to take everything I say so literally?"

"You're a woman of carefully chosen words. Why shouldn't I take what you say seriously?"

"We're fighting, and I don't know what it's about. Is there something you're not saying, Aidan?"

"I don't want to go back yet," I said calmly. I needed to scream: *I can't go back . . . I will never go back . . . I may not live through the night, let alone the end of the month!*

"What would you have us do? Live in Venice? Never go home? We have lives there. Sooner or later we have to go back, if only to face them."

No. Never. I will never see Sonia or Michael again, or the hotel, or the office or Nell. I will never sit in the coffee shop and muse about the time I lived in Venice. I will never sleep in my apartment again, in my own brass bed.

"Could we talk about this over dinner?"

"Sure." I could see she had become wary. "Aidan, are you all right?"

"Just worried about Wally. He wasn't on the wall after you left."

"Let's go check on him now."

But he wasn't back. I began to worry in earnest.

"What if something has happened to him?" I asked, voicing my concern.

"What could happen? He's a champ—knows his way around these back gardens with his eye shut."

"That's just it. I worry about him getting in a fight . . . losing the other eye . . . not being able to get home . . ."

"Aidan, what are you doing to yourself? Why do you conjure up these cruel fantasies? Come in and let me make you a dinner here at home. Have a drink while I work, and I'll tell you about my adventure today. Wally will be back by dessert."

I tried to turn my attention to what she was saying, but I was plummeting into a black pit of fear. Maybe I should tell her how close he was—Death, Death with his mangled face, waiting with crackling hot fingers to embrace my heart.

"It was the most impoverished, bedraggled collection I have ever seen," she was saying. "Exhibits all in the strangest order, a whole library of lagoon fish next to some African spears. In one glass case there was the embalmed body of some prehistoric Venetian that the mud gave up, and on the lower shelf was a crocodile. Top shelf, man; bottom shelf, croc. The curator must be mad."

That's one way to take care of a body. "What else?"

"Well, there was a prehistoric boat, too. A long, narrow, black boat. It had been hollowed out from a tree, sort of like a canoe, but really you could see the lines of a gondola in it . . ."

He was very close, and laughing.

"Were there any butterflies?"

"Do you really want to know?"

"Yes."

"Yes. They had a forlorn beauty about them."

"Good."

"Good?" She was slightly shocked.

"Nearby souls."

"Aidan, what has come over you? It can't just be Wally."

"Tell me what your life is like—back in the States."

"Why do you want to know that now?" I had confused her. Put her off the scent.

"If we're going to go back . . ."

She put down a salad, made earlier, and some cold roast beef. There was fresh bread and gorgonzola cheese, and an assortment of ripe fruit. I wasn't very hungry, but I pretended to be. She was watching me closely now.

I suppose it seems strange that I hadn't asked her about her current life before, but, in truth, I didn't want to know. I had kept her here, like a zoological specimen—live, but under glass. Mine, entirely mine. I braced myself for the worst . . .

"It's a simple life. I have an apartment on West Eighty-seventh Street—top floor, with the roof to sit out on in the back. It suits me up there. I don't like the sound of people overhead. I have a cat. Her name is Maggie. She is gray, lighter than Wally, and she has two eyes. My friend, Carol, is keeping her for the summer. I miss Maggie. I have a lot of friends. They often come by in the evenings, and we talk late into the night. I write there and meditate, and I paint there—only I enjoy painting more when there are other people around, so usually I enroll in some class or other in the fall and stick with it until about Christmas. Then I get busy with other things."

"Parties?"

"Charity stuff. I'm really like an old maid in that respect:

soup kitchens, hospital visits. There's a lot of work with children at that time of year. And I have to keep hustling—sorry—looking for paid work, too. I know I've been profligate, keeping the hotel all these weeks—probably given you the idea that I'm astoundingly rich, but I'm not. Comfortably well-off, independent, but not rich."

I was glad I was leaving her money.

"Men?"

"Have you really been worrying about that? No. There are no men. I've been celibate for years."

"But . . ."

"But what?"

"You like it so much. Sex."

"I like it with you." She expected me to smile then, to be happy at my specialness, but I wasn't. What would she do without me? She saw my worried expression. "C'mon, Aidan. It isn't so bad. There's sex and there's sex."

"What do you mean?"

"This will sound a little kinky, but I know that when I write well the words can touch people—not just their minds, not just their emotions, but their bodies, too. If I get a poignant scene just right, the person who reads it might cry—real tears; if the scene is gruesome, they might feel a little sick to their stomachs; if it's an erotic scene, and it works, they may blush or get aroused. It's as if I am reaching out through time and space and making the bodies of strangers respond to me. And I never have to touch them."

I looked across the room at her, my eyes filling with tears at her words.

I felt guilty about living.

I felt guilty about dying.

Three days later, in the midst of a quiet morning, Mira's fist banged down on the table as she shot to her feet. She stood, staring straight ahead, her right hand clenching and un-clenching while her left hand rested casually, unmoving, on the stack of paper that was her novel.

"It's done." She looked at me, martyred with the feelings of her accomplishment, flames of glee and gloom licking up her throat and face.

I decided to respond to the glee.

"Congratulations! Will you let me read it now?"

"Almost. I want to read it through once myself, from beginning to end—to say good-bye. Then I'll be able to let it go. You can read it tonight in bed. Will you promise to be gentle?"

"You know me in bed."

The conflict in her face resolved into vulnerability. "Then into thy hands I commend my spirit."

"At least tell me the title."

"It's called *The Name of the Father.*"

My mind ran through her life, her exploding fathers, myself, our lost son, the many men that came after me, Robert Myers, God, myself again. "It's a good title." She smiled and then turned back to the papers to consider her work again. She did not see my grimace of pain, and I was glad, for it would have marred her moment of accomplishment.

I was living with the pain all the time now, but had so far managed to keep it from her. Once or twice, when it was especially torturous, she had questioned me—and I fretted convincingly about my writing, still caught as I was in the midst of my troubling creation, though I had glimmers of a finale. And Wally's extended absence provided me with another appropriate excuse for my distressed appearance.

"You worry too much," she chided. "He's an adolescent boy now. He'll be going off in search of adventure and romance, just as we once did, and you and I, his adoptive parents, will just have to bear it."

"He's never been gone this long," I grumbled.

"He'll be back. He's attached to you, in his fashion."

"He likes you better than me."

"Listen to you, listen to us." And we laughed at ourselves, which always eased the angina.

I sat watching her now as she began to reread her novel. She was wearing a plain black dress that I had never seen her wear before. Ebony, against her translucent skin, was startling. It made her appear far more fragile than I knew her to be. Mourning would suit her. Now, unmarked by grief, she looked like a serious little schoolgirl, a teacher's pet poring over her math assignment, bent on the best mark in the class. I was happy for her—happy that she had found her way to the completion of her book. But I worried, too. I expected that she would now be eager to return with the manuscript tucked safely under her arm—back to the States—to a life I knew I would never share with her.

"We'll cross that bridge when we come to it."

"What did you say?"

I didn't know I had spoken aloud.

"Let's go to the Accademia Bridge tonight."

"Why?"

"The newspaper says there is to be an eclipse of the moon. It would be an ideal place from which to view it."

"It's a celestial idea."

"And let's celebrate your success. Let's go to dinner at Harry's Dolci, which wouldn't even exist if Hemingway hadn't made Harry's Bar famous, and afterward ride in a gondola past Mozart's house—and Byron's and Goethe's."

"In the moonlight."

"Before the eclipse."

The evening was memorable. Although memorable was a word that holds little meaning for me now, with, as I imagine, only hours left to live. We walked at a leisurely pace to San Marco. I couldn't have marched briskly along as I did such a short time ago. I took her first to Florian's.

"There, my novelist, you have a right to sit here now." And she glowed at the idea. "You have dreamed of this all your life, haven't you? To take your place among the novelists of the world, among the spinners of fantasy, who catch us up in their designs and somehow make our real lives seem more meaningful in the face of the lives they imagine."

"I'm afraid it won't be good enough . . ."

"Have you drawn the thing as you see it for the God of Things as They Are?"

"Kipling?"

"Kipling."

"Yes. With all the artistry that I possess."

"Then it will be good enough. It will be very good."

At my request, she had worn the white dress in which I had first glimpsed her, and she seemed to me even more beautiful than she had on that not-long-ago morning, as though the fruition of our love had inspired the Creator to a few light brush strokes, a few final touches, on his Botticelli.

I had hoped to enter the Basilica this night of all nights, and to finally light a candle in the midst of the glassy magnificence. But we were too late and the huge, wooden doors were firmly closed against us. This task, like so many others, would remain unaccomplished.

"Who would you light the candle for?" she asked me as we walked down the Piazzetta.

"For remembrance."

"But for *whom*? Who do you wish to remember?"

"You. As you were at fifteen."

We took a gondola across the basin, all the way to Harry's Dolci, an unheard of extravagance, and then topped ourselves by asking the gondolier to have a drink at the bar and wait for us, which he did with only a slight shaking of his head, offset by an endearing grin.

The meal served out by the water's edge was all that I had hoped it would be, rich and exotic and gracefully presented. After the peach-sweet Bellini's we had oysters with a good Prosecco, and after *osso bucco e rissoto* we had *zabaione* cake and homemade vanilla gelato and cappuccino with extra cream for dessert. Mira, who was almost always in a good mood, was in a better one than usual throughout the dinner. She seemed to find everything we ate and everything I said delectable. Her coppery hair, caught by a whisper of breeze blowing off the water, danced about her merry eyes.

"Oh, Aidan, we've won, haven't we?"

"Won what, my darling?"

"We've won at life."

"Yes, I believe we have."

"Look!"

The moon, full and great, had come up above the skyline of Venice, promising a night of ancient mysteries.

We sailed back across the black body of water, under the spell of the moon, in the gently rolling boat, and then stood close together on the arching Accademia Bridge, tightly holding hands, as the majestic shadow of the earth slowly wiped away the orb of light, taking the Grand Canal and all the glories of the city into an opacity more awesome than night.

"I love you, Mira."

"I love you, Aidan."

And we walked to the apartment on now familiar streets,

our footsteps echoing in the night-abandoned campos, listening to the sound of tidal waters, confused by the wayward moon, murmuring plaintively in the nearby canyons of stone. At home we made love, for what I believe was the last time, with the elemental forces of the universe pulsing through our flesh.

We slept away most of this morning.

An hour or so ago Mira left to check out of the Pausania. At the first mention of her intention, I was frightened, thinking a confrontation about our return to the States had come at last, and at a most inauspicious time, but, with a charming seriousness, she announced she wanted to live with me—that her years of carefully defended independence were at an end. I had not the heart to disillusion her. She left me with a promise to be back by nightfall. She left me with her novel for company.

I stand here now, in the garden of my arrival, alone, in love, with gardenias at my feet. A shiny black butterfly, speckled with iridescent blue, darts among the blooms. Wally has come home and sits, as usual, high and untouchable on the wall, with a new and gallant pride, for a little marmalade cat sits at his side, and she is clearly smitten with his roguish appearance.

I look beyond the cats, directly into the setting sun. It glows like the fierce red eye of a mortal enemy. The world has grown very hot. Fortunately, the San Michele wind is blowing.

The anguish in my chest is so intense that I can no longer work at my typewriter, and I can barely hold a pencil, but I want to keep on writing until the very end if I can. I have taken the writing to heart, but I will not finish my story. The rend in my relationship with Michael will remain unrepaired, unless Mira can effect a miraculous, posthumous healing. Perhaps she can.

I will die here, an exile. I will die in Venice, like stodgy old Aschenbach, after all. But I will not die alone, and that is a comfort to me. When Death comes, I will look up into the cool green eyes of the woman I love, and then I will go with him into the cool green waters of the lagoon, unafraid.

I wonder what her novel is like. I wonder what will become of her . . . and Michael, and . . .

Epilogue

The sunset that evening was unsurpassed in the history of Venice. Some think the strange, ethereal effect was a result of the lunar eclipse of the previous night. Others think that it was, simply, the hand of God.

I was hurrying back from the Pausania, dragging along two heavy suitcases. I was eager to settle into the apartment—into my life with Aidan—finally, completely.

The sky had turned from blue-white to pale rose in a casual, usual way when, quite suddenly, it reddened and then seemed to explode with color: lemon yellows, lush purples, iridescent blues, scarlet and olive and silver and gold. The evening air was luminescent, infused with unearthly light. Tourists stopped dead in their tracks; shopkeepers came out to gaze in amazement, and for a few dazzling minutes all of Venice stood still, looked up, and marveled in pleasure or fear at the once familiar heavens, now pulsing from horizon to horizon with glowing rainbow colors—like living stained glass.

Aidan!

I ran. I dropped my luggage and I ran.

But I was too late.

I found him in the garden where he had collapsed. The Christ of the Butterflies. He looked very peaceful, and for the briefest of moments, as I knelt and slipped my hand beneath his head, I thought he was still alive. He seemed to look up into my eyes with an expression of calm acceptance. He had died surrounded by the flowers he so dearly loved. His notebook and his pencil were nearby. And nestled in the crook of his arm, a tiny sentinel against the dark of loneliness, was Wally.

THE DEVIL'S HOME ON LEAVE, a mystery by Derek Raymond*
THE BALLAD OF THE FALSE MESSIAH, a novel by Moacyr Scliar
little pictures, short stories by Andrew Ramer
THE IMMIGRANT: A Hamilton County Album, a play by Mark Harelik
HOW THE DEAD LIVE, a mystery by Derek Raymond*
BOSS, a novel by David Handler*
THE TUNNEL, a novel by Ernesto Sabato
FOR FOREIGN STUDENT, a novel by Phillippe Labro, translated by William R. Byron*
ARLISS, a novel by Llyla Allen
THE CHINESE WESTERN: Short Fiction from Today's China, translated by Zhu Hong
THE VOLUNTEERS, a novel by Moacyr Scliar
LOST SOULS, a novel by Anthony Schmitz
SEESAW MILLIONS, a novel by Janwillem van de Wetering
SWEET DIAMOND DUST, a novel by Rosario Ferré
SMOKEHOUSE JAM, a novel by Lloyd Little
THE ENGIMATIC EYE, short stories by Moacyr Scliar
THE WAY IT HAPPENS IN NOVELS, a novel by Kathleen O'Connor
THE FLAME FOREST, a novel by Michael Upchurch
FAMOUS QUESTIONS, a novel by Fanny Howe
SON OF TWO WORLDS, a novel by Haydn Middleton
WITHOUT A FARMHOUSE NEAR, a nonfiction by Deborah Rawson
THE RATTLESNAKE MASTER, a novel by Beaufort Cranford
BENEATH THE WATERS, a novel by Oswaldo França, Júnior
AN AVAILABLE MAN, a novel by Patric Kuh
THE HOLLOW DOLL (A Little Box of Japanese Shocks), by William Bohnaker
MAX AND THE CATS, a novel by Moacyr Scliar
FLIEGELMAN'S DESIRE, a novel by Lewis Buzbee
SLOW BURN, a novel by Sabina Murray
THE CARNAL PRAYER MAT, by Li Yu, translated by Patrick Hanon
THE MAN WHO WASN'T THERE, by Pat Barker
I WAS DORA SUAREZ, a mystery by Derek Raymond
LIVE FROM EARTH, a novel by Lance Olsen
THE CUTTER, a novel by Virgil Suarez
ONE SUMMER OUT WEST, a novel by Philippe Labro, translated by William R. Byron

*Available in a Ballantine Mass Market Edition.